Mauwee Nibi – Crying Water

Rejean Giguere

Second Print edition Edition
Revised 2020
Copyright 2015 - Rejean Giguere
ISBN 978-1-927047-27-9
Ontario, Canada
rejeangiguere.com

I0556082

Other Books
by Rejean Giguere

MAUWEE NIBI

This book is dedicated to increasing awareness of Canada's missing Indigenous Women through fiction. I hope that in some way it can shine a bit of light on this serious issue.

— Rejean

PROLOGUE

Streaks of wind-blown cloud careened across the sky, grey against black on the moonless night. Waves lifted the ship high in the air, metal groaned as it twisted under load, then sinking downwards the vessel rode out the rolling swell. Rain pelted the deck, sheets of water blowing sideways made the super-structure barely visible.

The figure struggled along a drenched gangway, wrestling with a dark object. There might have been screams and howls in the air, but no one heard anything over the roaring storm. Mid-way along the deserted walkway the figure stopped, grabbing hold with one hand, his other arm struck downwards once, and then twice. Bending over, he lifted the weight onto his shoulder. Now he made progress, using his free hand to hold the railing, he walked around the massive corner of the structure, following the small ledge at the back of the ship.

The storm rocked the boat violently, his arm wrenched in its socket as he damned near went over the railing.

He couldn't turn back. He couldn't put this off any longer, they would be docking in three days and he might not get another chance.

Once he was around the corner, facing the boat's churning wake, he flipped the bundle on his shoulder up into the air, thrusting with his arms to push the weight away as it fell.

The figure leaned against the railing, watching the bundle until he lost sight of it in the darkness. Then a small splash as it hit the water. Fascinated, as always, he gripped the railing, watching for any sign of movement. Trying to keep his eyes on the spot where it landed was impossible as the boat pitched and rolled with another set of waves.

It was over in seconds. There were no more screams lost to the wind.

CHAPTER 1

Saskatchewan, Canada

Billy Simon kept his eyes on the road as he headed east out of Regina. He was having trouble keeping his mind in one place as he began the trip to Ontario. Glancing out the driver's window at the passing scenery, scanning the endless flatlands of Canada's prairie, his thoughts seemed to be going in all directions.

Running a hand through the crew cut that all the cadets had been forced to wear, his pride kicked in. Although there had been others before him, he knew it was rare for a native to graduate from the RCMP training depot in Regina. He was the only one in the 2014 class. When he walked forward to take his oath and accept his badge, he stood tall, his back rigid, his cap straight above his eyes. It felt like he stepped forward for his entire family, even his tribe.

Throughout his time at the training centre the only thing that ate at him was the intermittent prejudice. It still bothered him. It'd hovered over him from the very first day he arrived, right to the end. As usual, it was only a few assholes, but they had made their opinions obvious, turning their backs and ignoring him throughout the entire course.

When a few of the other students stood up beside him, showing their support, he decided to let it go. Billy had been taught early to live with it, to accept it, and it wouldn't deter him now, because it never had. But still – a small ember of anger flared at the memory.

Checking the rearview mirror, he passed another in a long line of semi-trailers.

It was easy to let the pride he was feeling soar a little higher at the thought of his mother, she would be proudest of all. A smile spread across his face. He owed her a lot for keeping him out of trouble and putting him on the right track. He knew her pride in his accomplishment would be her reward. It would mean everything to her.

The act of smiling pulled at the fresh scar he had acquired on his cheek during final field exams, the anger he was dealing with resurfaced. Absentmindedly, he ran two fingers along his cheek, tracing the jagged edge of the mark. He'd been on a timed five-mile run needed to graduate. The cross-country run finished at a series of buildings that required running up and down flights of stairs, some in near darkness.

There wasn't much sense in thinking about it, he'd never know which of them had done it. But one thing was sure, it had been planned ahead of time.

Billy'd run the course before, they all had, many times. That day he was laying down a good time, running on memory. Rounding a corner at full speed, a piece of two-by-four thrust out from the shadows, catching his foot, tripping him headfirst towards the wall. Reflex took over, he jerked his head sideways

4

to protect his face. His cheek slammed the wall, taking most of the impact. The skin split open while his face briefly slid along the concrete.

He must've been knocked unconscious, because he came to suddenly, quickly realizing where he was and what was happening. Pulling himself to his feet, he sprinted to the finish line, way too close to the deadline for comfort. It shocked him they took it that far, doing something that sabotaged his future.

The wheat fields and grain elevators flew by the window, the towering silos the only markers breaking the line of the flat horizon.

Billy squeezed the steering wheel so tightly his forearms started to shake. His career had been that close to ending before it even started. Deliberately, he pulled his mind away from the shit that dragged people down, forcing himself to focus on the future. As a new Mountie he could be assigned anywhere in the country, to any number of jobs.

After spending almost his entire life on the Big Grassy reserve in the Lake of the Woods northwest of Thunder Bay, he was hoping a big city was his destination. He'd always wanted to explore more of the world than the wilderness of Northern Ontario and its Native reserves.

The only city he had seen before Regina was Thunder Bay. And that wasn't what he would call "big city lights". The old working town was dirty, rundown, and too many natives were struggling to survive there. So many, that he didn't feel the separation from the reserve that he was looking for. It was a city that could never satisfy his need for something new.

At twenty-six and a lanky six-foot four, Billy was not the normal sized native, but his high cheekbones and flattened nose clearly marked him as Indian. The new scar on his right cheek joined a long jagged scar above his left eyebrow that faded out as it curled down around the outside of his eye, the remnants of a hockey fight where neither combatant had dropped their sticks.

He guessed he was lucky that his mother had kept him from running with the rough kids, pushing him towards sports instead. While he had played them all, his favorite had been hockey. He'd played up to Junior B with a reserve team in the isolated rinks across the north of the province. There were fights on the ice, and usually some sort of bullshit in the stands, but she continued to push him to participate. He would never forget one day asking her about the violence in sports.

"You want me off the streets because of the crazies, but there's just as much fighting here at the rink."

"Young men have to learn about physical contact Billy, it's a part of life. But you don't go to jail when it happens in a hockey rink." She didn't condone fighting and expected that he play fair, but she also expected him to stand up for himself and others less able.

Smiling again, he remembered it was his teammates who had him fighting most of the time. He was usually last man in if someone started something, but once he got involved, once he was mad, he was usually the last one standing. This determination, the fierce will of heart, came from his father. A hunter and man of the woods, his father carried on the old traditions that had been in place for centuries.

A sudden unease settled over Billy as he thought of their conversations, his dad hadn't understood his son wanting to work like a white man. He had sensed a disappointment from the old man whom he had not seen much of as he grew up. His father was always away somewhere in the north, on hunting trips, fishing trips, or working the timber on the Indian lands.

It was hard to measure up to a man who was recognized by the elders as a descendant of warriors, considered a true native in their eyes. It was said that the elders questioned those who left the land to work in the cities. They thought that once you left you lost your heritage. It was something that Billy wrestled with.

He glanced at the clock on the Chrysler's weather-beaten dash. The curled, peeling vinyl imitated the paint peeling off the hood. Fourteen hours to go. Billy looked out over the never-ending landscape, the sun was starting to set and the wheat fields were shifting from yellow to pink.

Rolling down the window, he let the wind clear the stale air out of the car. It was time to start thinking about where to stop for the night.

*****

Lac Des Mille Reserve

The mature buck tentatively moved again, just one hesitant step, nose in the air, scenting the unknown. The early spring weather had it foraging in search of easy food, looking for fresh shoots and leaves on the early shrubs.

Shanya Marin watched patiently. She sat in the tree stand, still as a rock, eyes locked on the animal, she wouldn't even

7

allow herself to blink. This was the moment: she watched the deer as it found her scent, saw the ears go straight up as the animal leaned forward in full alert, it's nose twitching in earnest. The thrill of the chase, the moment of contact, had arrived. Now she waited for the animal to find her location.

The stag reached a hoof forward, then pulled it back. It looked backwards, as if contemplating retreat. Then it slowly turned its head from side to side. Finally, it turned her way again, this time lifting its eyes upwards, expanding the search.

"Bingo. Gotcha."

The two of them stared at each other. Shanya wasn't sure what the deer thought at that moment, but she was spellbound. The buck snorted aggressively once, then twice. She watched the deer's head move left and right as it tried to look at her from different angles. Then she almost laughed out loud as the animal stamped its hoof twice in front of her. She watched intently, she knew what was coming next.

The deer couldn't stand there much longer, the need to take flight would be too much. Suddenly the buck sprang sideways, lunging into the air off his hind legs, sprinting in random bounces, zigzagging across the field.

Letting out the breath she'd been holding, Shanya smiled. It never got boring. She loved the wild animals. Slipping her packsack over her shoulder, she climbed down the twelve feet from where the hunter's blind was attached to the tree. She wasn't there to shoot. The chase and close encounters were enough.

Seventeen years old, the athletic girl explored the forests, canyons and anywhere she could reach on foot from her home on the isolated south end of the Lac Des Mille Reserve. Her father wanted privacy and space for the wooden art he made, so the isolation was always part of her life. Being shy, it worked in her favour, and although she didn't see many friends except at school, she loved the wilderness and ran with nature.

Friends at school said that her parents protected her too much, that her life was too sheltered. *That wasn't true was it?* She just chose to spend her time with nature instead of her friends. Besides, all they ever wanted to do was listen to loud music that didn't make sense to her. She liked the rhythm of simple drums, like those her father and the elders played. The rhythm was life to her, beating in the heart, beating in the animals that were running through the forest. When she hummed along with the drums, it was like her body came alive, she could feel her spirit.

Returning to the house, she paused at the top of the path. It always reminded her of an art piece itself, her father had built archways along the walkway leading to the front door. The long sweeping angles reminded her of Chinese-style ridgepoles, right out of her schoolbooks, extending up and crossing each other at the peak of the house.

Slowly, she looked around the clearing they'd carved out of the woods, the house, her father's art barn, her mother's garden, they all seemed to fit as a natural part of the forest.

As she wandered under the arches, she could see her mother bent over, working in the spring garden.

"Mom," she waved.

"Come Shanya, help with these seeds."

The two of them worked in silence, digging and placing, shuffling over and beginning again, working up and down the rows. Finally, Shanya started to relive her day.

"I found a new canyon today and followed it north until I had to come back. It was getting late."

Her mother listened patiently.

"I saw another deer when I stopped at Uncle Erwin's tree stand by the river."

Her mother stopped working and turned towards her daughter, intrigued. Carefully, she put her trowel and gloves on the ground in front of her knees. "What did you observe?"

"It was a mature buck and very alert. I had to sit quietly for half an hour just waiting for him to move around to the front of the tree." Shanya paused. "Then it challenged me, or something. It stamped its hoof on the ground."

Her mother seemed pleased with her answer. "And why would it do that?"

Shanya scratched at the soil with a fingernail and thought for a moment, there really wasn't a reason she could think of. A hunter would have just shot it. She hadn't been scared by the buck, but then she'd been up in a tree. This started her thinking again. What if she had been face-to-face with it and the buck stamped the ground like that, what would she have done?

Sitting in the tree, she'd almost laughed at the uselessness of the tactic, but now she realized it would have been different if they had been closer.

"The deer was hoping I would run away?" Shanya looked sideways.

"Did you run away?"

"No. But I might have if I was on the ground."

"So what you have learned Shanya, is that you should try to scare a threat away, just in case it will run. It may not work, but it can never hurt."

She nodded, the deer had to try anything, even aggression when it's life was in danger. She thought of the bigger animals trying to run wild in the forest. She didn't say anything to her mother, but it was hard to imagine trying to intimidate a large moose or a bear. What courage would that require?

As she carried the tools back to the shed, she started thinking about dinner, and about her mother's last words.

"Remember Shanya, every situation is an opportunity to learn something. And everything you learn, may help you some day."

*****

S.S. Slate, Lake Superior

The big lake freighter rocked gently in the rolling waves. Alone, it moved slowly over the waters of Lake Superior. The moon cast a white light on a figure leaning against the railing at the bow of the ship.

Jared Stone stared out at the night, thick hands gripping the rail to hold him stable. It wasn't a conscious act, just his body's natural reaction to the waves below and the years at sea. He stretched his shoulders back and forward before rolling then in circles, his neck cracking as he leaned his head from side to side, another unconscious ritual.

You couldn't see the gap of two missing teeth, or smell the liquor-laden breath as the bosun did a scheduled check of the deck covers and security hatches. Staring out ahead of the ship, the veteran seaman let the cool wind wash the haziness out of his head. It was years ago he'd settled into the habit of doing the last couple of scheduled walk-arounds himself.

The nightly drinking was just another old habit, one that took its toll. He found he slept better after some air.

They weren't far from Thunder Bay, just another day or two. He felt a twitch of excitement at the prospect. Some habits were hard to kick, especially when you made so much money from them. Tilting his head up, Jared drew in a long breath of fresh air, then headed for the stuffy confines of the living quarters.

The crew was split between licensed and unlicensed employees. The captain, chief mate, second mate and third mate along with the engine and systems engineers were all officially trained and certified. Their quarters were two levels above deck, just below the bridge.

The crew that assisted these men, that performed all the labour required to load, unload, and keep the ship functioning were called the ratings employees. At thirty-six, Jared was the senior rating on the ship, the bosun, most experienced and longest in service. The ratings crew quartered one level above deck, just below the officers.

He poked his head through the open hatchway. The small labourer's lounge was almost claustrophobic, a few couches and chairs crammed together with an old TV chained to a wall to keep it stable in rough water. The small table in the middle of the room was more of an obstacle than any useful piece of furniture. It was stepped on more than stepped around.

Grabbing a beer from the tall thin fridge in the corner, Jared sat down as a couple of the guys made room on a couch. His eyes scanned all the faces, it was like putting your back to the wall in a bar, a precaution. As usual there was no defiance or attitude staring back. Music blared from a ghetto blaster tied down to the top of the fridge.

"What the fuck is that shit?" Jared was sure that while he was gone deck-side the rookie had talked the guys into this new techno crap that was screeching out of the speakers. "You put that on rookie?"

The kid, who called himself Ronnie, said he was twenty-years old, but looked sixteen. He still had pimples, and looked like it was his first time away from home. Right now the kid stared back, unsure what to say.

"You got no mouth kid? You put that crap on?" Jared stared the skinny kid down, almost hoping he'd stand up.

"Yes, I did. Though everyone might like a change." He said the last part slowly, like it was a question.

"Oh, we did need that change. Jesus, are we ever lucky you made this trip." The room was silent until one of the men burst out laughing. The kid wasn't sure what the bosun meant now, he couldn't read the narrowed eyes that bore his way.

"Okay rookie, turn that garbage off and put on some real music. Any of the other ones will do."

Ronnie ejected the CD and stuck in a random disk, unsure what would be correct. The electric guitars of ZZ Top's *Sharp Dressed Man* started reverberating through the room. Leaning back, Jared tipped a beer up as the boredom kicked in, he knew it was better than previous venues where he'd spent time. Here he had a level of control, one he'd carved out himself. Endless nights stuck on ship took their toll, the monotony had to be broken somehow.

"All right boys, what you say we break in the rookie tonight?"

Cheers went up as everyone immediately sat up straighter in their seats. Everyone that is, except the rookie. Ronnie wasn't sure what was going on, and didn't seem to like the idea at all. His eyes darted from man to man, searching for answers.

"Get out the whiskey." Jared locked eyes with the kid as he reached back and grabbed a shot glass from a shelf. Someone produced a bottle and he pushed it and the glass across the table towards the kid.

"Pour rookie."

Clapping his hands in rhythm, he started the others chanting, putting pressure on the kid. "One, two, three."

A shaky hand reached out and grabbed the bottle, the kid topped up the small glass, spilling some of the liquor in his haste. Jared watched the boy's Adam's apple bob up and down a couple times, there was the fear. The kid's eyes scanned the room, now he was looking for help. Finally, eyes rose to meet the bosun's. There – that was what Jared was waiting for.

"Down the hatch, four, five, six."

Beads of sweat ringed the young kid's forehead as Ronnie lifted the glass up and took the liquor in one go.

"Again. One, two, three." Jared stopped chanting for no more than a second, then clapped his hands harder the more riveted he became by the game. "Let's go kid. Four, five, six."

Twenty minutes later the initiation was well under way, the crew were laughing at the night's entertainment. The kid struggled to stay sitting upright, leaning left, almost going over before jerking himself upright and then tilting in another direction moments later. He was drunk and the men were taking bets on when he was going to pass out and fall over, but he kept up the fight.

Jared never let up.

"One, two, three." He watched the kid spill the liquor over either side of the shot glass. "Four, five six."

This time as Ronnie raised his arm, his hand never found his mouth. Instead, he went over backwards, pouring the shot on his face as he fell, hitting his head hard against the wall.

Jared stopped laughing long enough to end the night's festivities. "All right guys. We got to work in the morning. Time to call it a night."

The bosun waited while everyone stacked their empty beer bottles and headed towards their sleeping areas. Then he moved on the passed-out rookie.

Rifling through the kid's pockets, he stripped the leather wallet clean, pocketing the cash. *Dumb fuck*, Jared couldn't believe the kid had three hundred bucks on him. Well, he just paid for that lesson. He wouldn't carry that kind of cash around again. Or he wouldn't pass out with that much money in his pocket.

Jared smiled as he left the rookie collapsed in the corner. The kid would be sore in more places than his wallet after lying twisted in that position all night.

He started thinking about Thunder Bay as he headed to bed. The money would be put to good use. And that brought another smile.

CHAPTER 2

Lac Des Mille Reserve, Ontario

Visitors during the week were a surprise. Shanya and her neighbor had become friends, mostly due to the closeness of their houses. The Pontasons lived on the same road, just a little closer to the reserve offices and general store. Erin had walked the mile between houses just after supper and the two girls now followed a path through the forest that Shanya knew well.

They found a large log at the edge of a clearing where they could sit and watch the sun set. "What are you doing this weekend?" Erin wanted to know.

Shanya's face lit up, "It's my birthday. My mom will make me a special dinner."

"You should come out and party with us." Erin had been trying to get the shy girl out for a few years.

Shanya tried hard not to be judgmental, her mother had taught her to see the best in everyone. Looking her friend over, she could see the differences between them. Erin's long dark hair had blue highlights, kind of matching the tattoos curling around the side of her neck. Her face piercings, the small diamond in the nose, and a silver ring in the left side of her bottom lip, were things Shanya would never wear. Her friend was a little overweight and always wore black.

Shanya couldn't know that Erin was silently staring her way, envious of her looks. If Erin was Shanya, then she could get all the attention from the guys at the parties, especially Derek.

"Party with who?" Shanya didn't even know what their parties were like. She assumed there would be lots of booze and loud music, stuff the kid's talked about at school. Her mother had always preached against that type of thing. She said people on alcohol were not themselves. They became invincible in their heads and then trouble came.

"Everyone will be out somewhere; we always have someplace to go." Erin started naming boys and girls from school who would be going out for sure.

"I don't know," Shanya had never needed the social setting and was comfortable in the quiet, studying or learning. "It's really not my thing."

"You're eighteen. You're a woman now, with a life to live. You know your mother can't do that for you." Erin's words were a rebuff to all the lessons that Shanya had said she'd learned from her mother.

Then Erin asked, "You aren't going to live here at the house forever, are you?

Shanya paused, that was a valid question and the answer seemed different as she turned eighteen. Really, she hadn't thought much about her life after high school. How would she meet someone? She did want to settle down and have a family like her mother didn't she? The brief thought, that maybe she was living too sheltered of a life, struck her. Erin had said it before, and suddenly Shanya wasn't so sure her friend was wrong.

"Thanks for the offer. You're a great friend to encourage me." Shanya studied the other girl as they headed back home along the trail. Erin had run away from home and gotten in trouble a few times and come back. She looked like a tough girl with black leather jacket and boots, but Shanya remembered her mother's words. *Everyone should be judged by what is inside, not what we see with our eyes.*

"Well, let me know if you change your mind."

*****

RCMP Detachment, Thunder Bay

Billy had been slightly disappointed when he was given orders to report to the detachment in Thunder Bay. He'd hoped to be given a posting in Toronto, Montreal or Vancouver. As he sat in the waiting room, straightening his new uniform for the tenth time like it was never going to fit him right. He hoped that this meeting so close to where he lived was purely convenience, and not an indication of where he would be working.

It was more than just wanting to travel or see new places that had him eager to get away from reserves for his career. He'd thought about it many times and today was no different. He kept feeling like his own people would look at him like he had gone over to the other side. The elders wouldn't answer any questions from the white man in authority, didn't believe they had to. Nor would most Indians. In the end it would be better if he worked away from the reserves.

MAUWEE NIBI

Becoming a cop had never been a life-long goal. He'd only written the entrance exam because a teacher had suggested it. It had been a challenge at the time. He'd been more surprised than anyone when he'd passed and been accepted. Going to the training depot didn't scare him, but had required a second level of commitment that he hadn't been sure he was ready for. He glanced towards the door. *Was he really in the right place?*

"Constable Simon, Superintendent Kelly is ready to see you. Can you come this way?"

Billy smiled in response, it was the first time he'd been addressed as a constable, he liked it. "Yes, of course."

The walk took them past a number of closed doors before he was directed into the last office. Standing at attention in the center of the room, he realized it was the most important office he'd ever been in. The smell of leather and faint cigar smoke held an aura of business, secrets, and judgments.

The frames on the walls were all business, their contents meant to remind you of where the authority came from, the Queen, and current and past commissioners. The biggest object in the room was a dark, imposing desk larger than the pool table he'd played on as a youngster.

"Simon, have a seat."

The senior officer's hair was red, his freckled skin almost pink. The collar on the man's dress shirt was so tight it seemed to pinch at the neck. He was smiling and seemed nice enough.

"Thank you sir."

The jovial manner was obviously intended to put Billy as ease.

"So it seems congratulations are in order." The superintendent smiled genuinely. "Well done graduating the academy."

Billy nodded his appreciation at being recognized, then waited patiently as the man recited his own experiences as a recruit years ago.

"I assume you're curious about what your new assignment will be? Most new recruits are." The superintendent seemed to be enjoying the job of delivering what he assumed was good news.

Billy hesitated before answering, this was it. He mentally crossed his fingers, knowing it was a white man's superstition. Then he reached in his pocket and gripped the braided leather strap wrapped with beads given to him by his grandfather to bring good thoughts. "Yes sir. I would like to know."

"You've been chosen for a special assignment. You'll be working out of Thunder Bay..."

He never heard the last words out of the superintendent's mouth. His heart had jumped at the words special assignment, but dropped just as fast at the mention of Thunder Bay.

Damn, that wasn't what he wanted. He pictured some task on a reserve somewhere. Finally, he zoned back into the sound of the superintendent's voice.

"Not what you wanted to hear?" The senior man's face said that Billy wasn't doing a good job hiding his disappointment.

"Honestly, I was hoping for a city assignment. Getting away from the north." Billy figured he'd lay it out straight.

"You don't understand this opportunity. You could have been sent to a detachment as a regular member. You would have been stuck doing paperwork, cleaning vehicles, taking bicycle patrol and handing out traffic tickets. Everyone has to pay their dues." He seemed to stall while the new officer contemplated that picture.

"We're offering you undercover work right out of depot. It's almost unheard of. Most members never get this kind of big opportunity in their whole career son." The superintendent's eyebrows rose as he finished speaking, emphasizing the situation.

Billy assumed what had been said was true. Every job he'd ever had he'd started at the bottom, and everyone he'd ever worked with had taken advantage, or reminded him of his position. Did he expect he'd be doing high-stakes surveillance and major cases right away? Well yes, that was what he wanted, and now he realized that the cities might not be where that was going to happen. This assignment had him curious.

"So what is this job?"

"You know that there aren't many natives signing up and that makes you a rarity. That gives you an opportunity to tackle something that is a growing concern."

Billy still hadn't heard exactly what the assignment was, but stayed patient even as his curiosity grew. He stared at the senior man's uniform, recognizing the long-service ribbon, the one bronze star signifying twenty-five years in. There was also the service and good conduct medal attached to a ribbon and clasp.

"Your name is changing to Billy Blackwood, and you're going undercover on the freighters working the Great Lakes." The superintendent beamed with satisfaction. It was obvious he thought it was a special opportunity.

Billy couldn't see why. From the city lights to the confines of a freighter, suddenly he thought everything was falling apart. This couldn't be true.

"Why would you assign me there?" His face must have registered what he was thinking.

"I thought you would have put it together," Kelly leaned his elbows on the desk. "You personally, being a native, must be aware of the missing aboriginal women who have disappeared from local reserves."

Billy stepped back to absorb the mental blow. He would be working on a native issue. Missing women. He had heard. He did know. But criminal involvement would have only been an assumption on his part. There were many stories, but very few of the women ever returned and therefore it was never clear if they'd moved on, were still alive, or anything about why they were even gone.

Shocked, he leaned forward, could it be that organized? "And you think they're going out on ships?"

"Yes. We do."

*****

Lac Des Mille Reserve, Ontario

Shanya's parents stared at her, the direction the conversation was going was alarming. The wrinkles around her mother's eyes failed to hide the intensity of her worry that matched the disbelief on her father's face as he leaned back, wide eyed. The news hadn't gone over well.

"You want to go out to celebrate your birthday?"

MAUWEE NIBI

It was the second time her mother had asked the same question. Shanya realized she needed to answer.

"It's just some people getting together to hang out and listen to music." They hadn't said she could or couldn't go yet, but Shanya felt a resentment building towards them that had never been there before.

"What kind of people are you talking about?" Her mother took a deep breath, but her fear was slipping out.

"Does it really matter now that I'm turning eighteen?" Shanya shrugged, questioning. She couldn't help but use Erin's words. "You don't expect me to stay here forever do you?"

That set her parents back on their seats. Finally, her father, a man comfortable in his methods, shook his head. "Of course not, we expect you will do as you wish. We've given you the tools to make your own decisions."

Her mother, leaned forward, unable to leave it that simple, that it was up to her. "Shanya, we have always tried to be involved, to give you our wisdom and insight. It was always to help guide you, never to rule you."

"I know that," she nodded. "I've listened and followed that advice. Now I need to learn about other things, things about being a grown-up and where my life will go."

Shanya headed to her bedroom, they hadn't had any answers to that. She loved them, and appreciated all the care she had been given, but this week she'd started to question things. Erin had her realizing that she would need to get out on her own sooner or later, even if it was just to have some fun or see how other Indians were living away from their families. The idea of meeting boys wasn't new, but the thought of becoming a woman made the idea more real. Besides, it could only grow her spirit.

*****

Thunder Bay, Ontario

Derek Jacobs stared out from the fifth floor of the remodeled condo project. He wasn't in the penthouse – yet – but he was one floor below and had the same view out over the waters of Lake Superior.

Standing there in his briefs he looked out over the lake, the glass wall facing the water could produce a fear-inducing queasiness as you stood there with nothing but air in front of you. From here he could see the freighters anchored out in the bay waiting to enter port. Who would've thought the dumb-assed Indian kid from the reserve would end up leading a double life. He smiled at the knowledge he was pulling it off.

Turning to look at the bed, blankets were scattered about, a long slim figure was wrapped up in the sheets. Yes, he was pulling it off.

The cell phone buzzing on the night table broke his train of thought. Derek grabbed the phone instead of the woman and walked back towards the window. The caller ID showed a nickname. "Well if it isn't the Clipper, good to hear from you."

"Putting in in a day or so. You around this weekend?"

"Sure, what's up?"

"I'm looking for merchandise."

Derek looked over his shoulder, the sheets were still a mess, the woman still sleeping. "How many?" There was no more humor in his voice.

MAUWEE NIBI

"Three. Is that a problem?"

"Not at all, I'll call Saturday." Derek stood there looking at the floating freighters, there hadn't been any boats out there just a few months ago when the bay was frozen over, but since spring the ships had been stacking up to get the summer runs started.

Quickly, Derek dialed another number. It rang at his other house on the Fort William reserve. This condo was a secret, somewhere he looked successful, somewhere he brought well-to-do women, white women. And finally, somewhere he felt distant from his past.

He'd done everything wrong as a young guy, stealing, fighting, being someone else's lackey, dropping out of school, and eventually running into the law. How he'd stayed out of juvie, or the jailhouse was luck he still didn't fully understand. At twenty-two his brain had kicked in and he'd stopped telling others what he was doing. That was when he went solo.

Derek started out with a few bucks for seeds, growing pot for sale. Slowly, the money from the drug deals between reserves north and west of Thunder Bay added up. Now he had a crew that did the growing, all he did was collect a cut when moving it. Now, he was the one with the money.

"Yeah?" Someone had answered the phone.

"Hey Daren, how's it going over there?"

"Everything's cool, you back?"

"Will be Friday. I want you to get a big party set up for Saturday at the house. Let's have some fun. Lots of girls."

"Sure boss, I'll have the place rockin'."

Derek hung up and moved to the edge of the bed. He was starting a new life on the side. These days he slipped into the condo like he belonged there and moved among the occupants like he was a successful businessman. Not even his buddies knew about the second location, but then he had become good over the years at keeping things secret.

The honey blond hair that drew him down to the bed belonged to the sexy bank executive that lived one floor below. She'd taken a day off work to play. He pulled the sheets off her, exposing the show. Climbing between her legs, he spread them with his knees. *Let's play then.*

*****

SS Slate, Lake Superior

Activity was picking up on the freighter. Docking was a day away. Officers finished logs and finalized their paperwork, engineers were giving out maintenance schedules. Everyone had responsibilities.

The captain watched over everything, usually from the bridge. The first mate had all the deck duties; docking, anchors, loading and unloading. The bosun reported to the captain and first mate, and led the ratings crew. The second mate handled navigation. The third mate was a backup, earning his certificates.

Jared walked across the rolling deck supervising a pair of newbies. The wind snapped at his black t-shirt, cut-off sleeves exposed his arms, tattooed wrist to shoulder. Reaching the bow, he turned and watched the crew. He didn't do much of the lifting anymore, the bosun was a go-between, the man who kept the muscle working for the officers above.

He noticed the captain walking along the deck. Hans Schultz, the German, had a slight limp from a chain accident on a logging boat years ago. His blond hair ruffled in the wind as the captain carried his hat in one hand. Watching the older man approach, Jared wanted to knock on wood and count his lucky stars. Things wouldn't have worked out as easily if it hadn't been for the old bugger's help.

"Afternoon Captain. Nice day on the water."

The stone-faced German was tall, didn't carry much of a smile. As always, he got right to the point. "We dock tomorrow seven am. The crew is ready?"

"Yes sir. Everything is top notch."

The veteran seaman walked past Jared and laid his hand on the railing as he stared across the water. This would be their third trip into Thunder Bay this year. The old man ran his hand along a patch of rusty steel, "Another coat of paint this summer." The captain wasn't much for putting orders in writing, he liked to talk to his men and get things done because they were needed, not because a piece of paper said to.

"Probably just the front, where it takes a beating," Jared offered. He wasn't looking to minimize the work, just offer his opinion. There was a cost to everything, and it took a lot of paint to cover a ship.

"You will be getting supplies this trip?" The captain's eyes stayed fixed out over the water. He never looked at his bosun.

"Yes sir. Fresh stock. Would you like the usual?" Their relationship was a strange one, but Jared took full advantage.

"Yes bosun, let me know when things are ready." The captain turned on his heel and walked away. To anyone watching, it didn't look like they even had a conversation.

The sudden thought that the old man was close to retirement sent a shiver up his spine. Jared hoped it was years away.

CHAPTER 3

Duluth, Minnesota

Billy stared at the ship. The SS Forester was about the ugliest thing he could imagine. Large patches of peeling paint revealed the lines where the boat was welded together. Even the rust seemed to have rust. The different ways he'd talked himself into and out of this assignment were giving him a headache. It was time to stop deliberating and get at it.

After a crash course in Thunder Bay on ship functions and then a basic test, he was a qualified rating ready for work. His application had been floated around, and here he was staring at a dark blue hull fading to bare rust. Finally, someone noticed him hanging around on the dock and he was waved aboard.

"Captain's up in the wheel house." A seaman in grease stained coveralls pointed towards the bridge, three floors up.

Billy followed the man's finger up to a large glass window revealing figures staring his way. He nodded at the grease monkey. Boots echoed in the steel enclosure as he walked up the flights of grated metal stairs.

As he entered the bridge, the instruments stood out, big navigation screens were laid flat on consoles, Billy could picture someone walking back and forth between the two stations. Large panels with rows of dials and meters lined a back wall, with an empty chair in front of them. It looked like there were hundreds of things to monitor.

Billy's eyes settled on the captain. The middle-aged man's eyes were alert and appeared to be staring right through him. The boss waved the new-hire over with a casual motion as he turned back to the window. At his side, Billy turned to look at the view. It was a lot higher up here than on deck.

"So, you don't have much experience on the lakes?"

"No sir. Just starting out."

"Not much good then, are you?"

It felt like he had just volunteered for the garbage work.

"Well, I run a tight ship here son. You'll figure out your duties shortly. Make sure you carry them out." There was a neutral tone to the man's voice as the captain turned to add, "I'm not much for giving second chances, there's lots of rope on this boat kid. Don't hang yourself with it."

"No sir." What else did you say to something like that?

Billy liked the honesty though. Usually there was someone complaining after the fact that they would have done something better if they knew the consequences. Others made sure they did their best the first time 'round, in case there was more opportunity to be had. He realized the captain was done with him and started for the door.

"Fucking Indian."

The words almost knocked Billy over. He took another step and then stopped, his face at the door. Did he just hear right? That didn't just happen, did it? Billy turned towards the person he knew had said the words. The Captain.

"Did you just say what I thought you did?" His voice rose more than he wanted.

The captain turned his way, seeming confused, "What was that son?"

Billy's first thought was, *I'm not your son.* His second thought he spoke out loud, "What did you just say as I walked away?"

The captain didn't bat an eye. He pointed to the engineer, "I complained to John here about the fucking engine."

Billy wasn't sure what to do. Had he heard wrong?

He turned back to the door and walked out. Five minutes aboard and it was already a friggin' nightmare.

He didn't see the captain and first mate share a nod or the captain's grin as he made notes in his logbook.

*****

SS Slate, Thunder Bay, Ontario

The procedure of docking a big laker was kind of like an elephant ballet, machinery moving in concert. Jared orchestrated it like a precise operation. Everyone knew their tasks and the deck was a hive of activity.

The captain above directed the boat as it sidled up to the concrete docks that ran for hundreds of meters alongside the storage factories. Spotters watched over the sides and yelled distances. The ropes were prepared to throw ashore, they would guide the chains as they were mechanically spun out and attached to cleats on the dock.

Jared watched the deck hands begin the tedious job of un-securing the hatches and releasing the chains. Six hatches with hundreds of bolts that had to be released before they could be opened with the on-board crane. The job would take hours.

As the day wore on the tasks changed to refueling and loading the cargo, replacing what had been unloaded. This is where Jared worked his magic. The docks were busy and supplies were arriving from every direction at the same time. Food, fuel and maintenance supplies. It was in the mix of this chaos that Jared had vehicles stop by and restock some of the more essential items required for the long nights at sea.

He didn't get on-shore and into the bars as much as he used to, but then he'd been an idiot in those days and now he had so much to do. So much fun to prepare for. Getting drunk was fun for a night when they were docked, but getting set up for fun every night on the water was much more rewarding.

*****

Fort William, Ontario

The party was in full swing, thirty or forty teens were drinking and lounging throughout the house, mostly natives but some white kids and a few black. Shanya had come a little reluctantly, she hung close to Erin as they mingled and slowly worked their way into the crowd.

Erin said something to a tall blonde guy on the way past, and suddenly there were beer bottles thrust into their hands. Shanya studied the crowd, recognizing some of her fellow students who had also made the hour and half drive to the party. A few called out to her, others waved a beer in the air. She sipped at the liquid, when it didn't burn like she expected, she took a bigger mouthful.

MAUWEE NIBI

A lot of people were checking her out and she assumed it was because she was new. The boys weren't shy with their stares, and she found herself blushing as she took another swallow from the bottle. For the first time she felt self-conscious, like her body was on show. Was that what she'd come here for? Quickly, she turned and followed Erin.

She was on her second bottle when she realized that there was more to the beer than taste. Sitting with Erin on the couch she felt herself wobble slightly, even sitting, her balance was off. Strangely, she felt good at the same time, enjoying the music she hadn't appreciated before pounding in the background. The beat's deep bass was so loud she felt the couch vibrate.

It was obvious the sudden cheering was for a new person who came into the house. Shanya watched as everyone welcomed the new arrival. She was surprised that they all seemed to be trying to get his attention. He was definitely Indian, and well dressed. She noticed the long ponytail held back by a shiny silver clip where there should have been beads instead. It didn't go unnoticed that he looked well off, like he had money, which wasn't what she was used to seeing. But then money didn't mean much to her.

Suddenly, Erin jumped up and left her alone to go and meet the new guy. As quickly as her friend left, a chunky native dropped down onto the couch beside her. Shanya was immediately disgusted, he stunk of liquor, she looked around for Erin but didn't see her, then the guy moved and their thighs were touching.

"Hey, you look good. We should have a few drinks." The guy's smile didn't improve the picture. This wasn't the type of boy she intended to meet. When his hand landed on her lap and squeezed while he tried to move even closer, she bounced off the couch in one motion and started walking away. Any direction would do.

The first three steps she was moving on adrenaline, one, two, three, then the alcohol kicked in and she almost toppled over face-first. Her head spun a few times before she managed to regain her stability and her focus settled. Not knowing where to go, she closed her eyes a second to centre herself and take a breath. Then she heard the drums. Opening her eyes, she followed the sound away from the living room.

Stopping at the door to a small bedroom, she watched three guys playing hand drums in the centre of the room, while five or six others sat around watching. Shanya felt better, she could listen to this over the stereo all night.

"Come in and join us."

Looking up, one of the guys had stopped playing, he was inviting her in. She didn't need a second invitation. Sitting on the ground with the others, she refused the marijuana joint that was being passed. It was something her culture accepted more than alcohol, it sure did them a lot less harm. Shanya took a second glance at the guy who had invited her in, she noticed he was looking back.

*****

Derek stood outside the party house. His name had never been on the deed, it hadn't been hard to find someone willing to put their name there instead of his. You wouldn't find his name associated with the harbor-front condo either. It was just something you did when you finally got your shit together.

MAUWEE NIBI

The music pounded inside the house, the walls were shaking. He used to get so charged up over these parties. There was a time when this was his reward. A week in the trenches making money, taking risks and moving loads would get him more money than most people had ever seen, and he'd always throw the party. Then he'd have the pick of the women. In a way, it had been great times.

Derek chuckled to himself. Beer, drugs, and easy Indians used to satisfy his needs. Now the finer things had become his vices, fancy dinners and expensive bottles of wine. He'd come to envy the attitude of the rich, able to float above society's issues and not have to worry about daily life. He wasn't there yet, but he was moving faster than ever towards his goal.

The party house was a tool, a meeting place, a stash house, and recruitment center all rolled into one. As he pushed open the door, he asked himself when it would be time to be done with this place.

Entering, the partier's cheers jacked up his ego. He liked knowing that he was the life of the party. Someone passed him a beer and he waved it in salute to some of the boys he recognized.

Settling against the kitchen counter, sipping the beer, he pretended to listen to a conversation that was fighting to be heard over the music. He really only had one thing on his mind, and his eyes started to roam over the partiers. There was a good collection of girls dancing and sitting around. He spent a couple seconds checking each one of them out. In the back of his mind he cataloged who they were with, and what they looked like.

These days he had the process nailed down, but it had been an evolution. The first time he offered a drunken woman to someone else he'd been twenty-years old and just joking around. They had been drinking in a house on an isolated reserve and the girl passed out. The other Indian who was visiting had no idea who she was but kept showing an interest. "Twenty-five bucks, you can have her," Derek kidded.

"You sure?"

Derek, seeing the desire, and the opportunity, had nodded and pocketed the twenty-five bucks. The next weekend he got two girls drunk and took them to a hang out where a bunch of guys were partying. The next couple years he made money off the women that he kept fed, clothed and on a short leash. It was three years ago that he stumbled onto the next stage in his career. It had been timely, he'd needed to transition to making money with white men instead of with only Indians with the limited number of reserves. Since then he'd taken his scheme to a whole new level.

A girl he'd known for years pushed her way through the crowd. Erin something-or-another, she was an ugly thing. Jesus, he couldn't believe he'd banged her once. He shook his head at the memory of it being more than once. She'd been hanging, always available, and he'd been drinking and taking advantage of everything in those days. Now she wouldn't leave him alone. She'd been young and clean at one time, but now she looked like the wear and tear of a rough life was starting to catch up with her. She was too young to have those kinds of lines on her face.

Derek swore under his breath for letting her pull him through the crowd looking for someone she wanted to introduce. Then they were standing at the door of one of the bedrooms where some pot smokers were playing drums.

Erin called out, "Shanya!"

Derek felt his heart jump, his wide smile must have split his face. This was what he was looking for. She was perfect, and she was native. The girl glanced up at them without a clue.

*****

Erin was on a high, Derek was really interested in her. Well, Shanya to be exact, but that had been whole point hadn't it? He'd been asking questions about her all night.

"Does any of her family sit on the council?"

"No, her father is an artist."

"Does she come from a large family?"

"No, I don't think so."

Later, as the party was winding down, Derek asked her to join him in the bathroom. Her heart was doing double-time as he closed the door, shutting them in together.

When he fondled her, she became excited and offered no resistance, she closed her eyes, accepting his touch.

"You want to have some fun later when everyone is gone?" He squeezed her tightly around the waist

"You know I do, of course." She leaned in against his body.

"Will you do me a favour?"

"I'll do anything for you Derek."

He let her go and grabbed a full beer from beside the sink, then reached into his pocket and brought out a small pill. She knew what he was going to do with it, as it dropped into the beer. She was shocked when he said, "Get your new friend, the Shanya girl, to drink this."

She took the beer she'd been handed and stood there a second. Before she could really think about what he was asking her to do, he turned her around, caressed her ass and pushed her out of the washroom. "Make sure she drinks it all, then come and see me."

*****

The forest whizzed by, Shanya attempted to focus her blurry vision. She had to be dreaming, because her body wouldn't move no matter how hard she tried. Her head tilted to the side, and she realized she was looking through glass. This couldn't be the forest.

Shanya strained to sort out the colours mixing with the images. She felt herself slow down and the images became buildings and storefronts with streaks of bright lights above the entrances. Then she was moving again, and it was all a blur. How could she be moving if her body was still?

It took time to realize she was in a car, there was a moment where adrenaline cleared the boozy haze from her brain and she was suddenly scared. She welcomed the fear, recognizing it was a real feeling, as she fought to clear the fog. Closing her eyes, she breathed slowly, in and out, regaining some control of herself. With considerable effort her head lifted slightly, enough to look around. She was slumped in the back seat of a vehicle with her body bent at an odd angle. Why couldn't she move? Shanya was sure it wasn't a dream.

Falling back against the seat, she struggled to see into the front of the car. There was no way to see the passenger, but the driver was there. Something silver seemed to be swinging in front of her, then a ponytail came into focus, a head kept looking back at her. She recognized the face, it was the guy that everyone liked at the party.

One part of Shanya was trying to get a grip on what was happening, the other part was screaming inside her. *Get out, get out of here!* She leaned her head forward and with effort looked to the side. A second rush of fear surged through her and she started to panic. Two other Indian girls were passed out and dumped like her, twisted on the backseat.

She had to get out of the car. *Where was she going?* The vehicle started to slow down and Shanya let her eyes stare out the window. She couldn't make out what she was seeing until they were almost stopped.

Screaming once, then twice, no sound left her lips. *Why couldn't she speak?*

She recognized a large ship. What was going on? Why was she at the harbor? She wanted to go home. Then the car door opened on her side.

Shanya heard the words echoing in her brain. *Mother, what have I done?*

An arm went back, a fist smashed into her face, and everything went black.

CHAPTER 4

S.S. Slate

A figure stirred in the darkness. Shanya couldn't see, but the rough surface of the cold floor hurt her face, small bits of dirt and grit stuck to her skin. She blinked once, then memories raced in front of her eyes. Her body clenched in response. Where was she?

Careful not to make a noise, quiet as if she was in the forest, she rolled to a sitting position. The floor moved one way and then the other. Confused at first, quickly she pictured the car stopped alongside the large ship at the dock. She had to be out on the water.

A tear forced itself to the corner of her eye. She was in trouble, certain that she was far from the simple place she called home. Picturing her mother worried and sick with fear, tears left lines down both sides of her cheeks.

Why was this happing to her? What had she done to bring this about? Her eyes scanned the darkness trying to recognize anything, to get herself oriented. *Think, Shanya, think.*

Stories flooded through her mind, quick snips of legends and lessons she'd learned from her mother. Had she gone too far? Her mother always told her the stories would help her when she couldn't decide what to do. The story of how the birch tree got its burns came to mind.

In the winter, spirit Nanabozho, who was sent by the creator Gitchi Manitou to teach the Ojibwe, was sent to find fire that was with Thunderbird in the west. Disguised as a rabbit, he asked the Thunderbird to allow him inside to warm himself for just a short period of time.

Then when Thunderbird turned away, Nanabozho rolled in the flaming coals and ran for home with his back on fire. Thunderbird chased him, shooting lightning bolts his way. Nanabozho yelled for help as he ran, and a birch tree spoke, "Come hide with me brother, I will offer protection."

Thunderbird flashed and thundered, even though Nanabozho was protected, dark burn marks scarred the white bark of the tree.

Shanya pictured the black marks on the birch. She wondered if she had tempted the spirits. Where could she hide?

Her stomach was still uneasy from the liquor at the party. There was anger suddenly mixing with her fear, but she wasn't sure why. Was it because she went to the party? She wasn't even sure why she went. Was it to meet a boy? To take hold of her independence? Or to prove she wasn't a sheltered little girl anymore?

As tears trickled out of her eyes again, she knew her emotions were all over the place. *Mother what story or lesson should I use here? Mother, where are you?*

Shanya's sheet of long dark hair closed in front of her face as she hung her head, closed her eyes and took a breath. The slight sound to her left snapped her eyes open again, and she felt movement in the dark. An image of the back seat of the car flashed in her head and she thought of the other girls that were taken with her. Was this one of them?

"Aaniin." *Hello.*

The answer sent a chill up her spine, all the focusing Shanya had done to compose herself vanished into thin air.

"Ningotaaj." *Afraid.*

The girl had responded with one word but Shanya knew the feeling.

"Niin Shanya nindizhinikaaz," *My name is Shanya.*

The whispered conversation took time to get started, but eventually she knew their names. Sixteen-year old Abby was the youngest. Chakwanina was eighteen, like Shanya. Both girls came from reserves near hers.

They were as devastated as she was. The young one was the worst, she kept mumbling to herself, ningoitaaj – *afraid,* nimbakade – *hungry.*

The mention of food brought Shanya around to the subject and she wondered how long they had been in this place. How long had she been knocked out?

Her hand came up to feel her forehead, the bump sticking out felt the size of a plum, fitting into her palm. She kept trying to shake it off, the mounting dread, but the soft groans that murmured through the ship as the steel twisted, and the darkness and cold of the rough floor kept reminding her she was in a cage. No longer free, no longer running with nature.

*****

MAUWEE NIBI

The long ropes were cast from the shore and wound back into the freighter. The S.S. Slate was almost ready to push away from the dock. Jared stood watching over the side, his eyes skimming back and forth along the dock almost expecting trouble.

There was a certain amount of vulnerability while they were still docked, and the sooner they moved out onto Superior the better. He welcomed the adrenalin pumping through his system, it had him fully alert. While continuing to scan, there was no movement along the deserted dock. Thunder Bay at midnight was a pretty quiet place. Still, he squinted an eye and ground his teeth – old hallmarks of an earlier career.

Over the noise of the winches pulling the rope up into the ship he pictured that first robbery like it was yesterday. In the middle of the night he'd walked calmly up the deserted main street, stopped in front of the jewelry store and looked both ways. Reaching up, he'd pulled down his balaclava.

Jared understood now that he'd been someone else's tool at the time, used by them to make money at his expense. How much did he make off the job? Two hundred bucks?

He broke the store's front window with a roofing hammer and performed his first smash and grab. Within the hour the jewels were in a vehicle driven by someone else, on their way to Toronto just a few hours away.

Ten minutes work for a few bills had been a windfall at the time, but really it was the gateway to bigger and better things. Jared laughed at his stupidity, it took years to figure out that he was doing it all wrong.

Steel slammed against the steel hull as the chain at the end of the rope ran up the side of the ship. His thoughts broken, Jared scanned the docks again, another half-hour, he thought, and we'll be out of the harbor.

Then shaking his head, at the memory of standing in a Becker's grocery store, eight-inch hunting knife held out in front, him threatening the clerk. It was the first time he saw real fear in someone's eyes and understood what power was. For that brief moment, he had complete control of the situation.

Of course, the four-year sentence in Kingston for armed robbery changed the amount of control he had significantly. As happened whenever he thought about the past, his fingers played across the three-inch scar he had under his chin. Then anger rushed in, mixing with the sudden adrenaline.

Memories of the penitentiary did that, he just had to deal with it.

A full moon lit the way as the freighter headed out into the bay. Easing past stacked-up freighter's waiting their turn in dock, the S.S. Slate headed south.

Jared felt the tension release as the land drifted from sight, how many times had he done it? Too many to count, yet he still expected something to go wrong. Just a thought of the girls below forced a smile across his face. The deep breath was one of satisfaction. Another score, another scheme on the go. And so much easier than when he was younger.

Two more visits to the pen, too many fights latter, his manner was hardened and he was always on edge, ready to go. He remembered trying to live out in society, following all the rules and listening to people's shit. After his time, he couldn't put up with it. A finger from another driver, some asshole cheering for another team in a bar, even just a look from someone who looked tough required a response from him.

Looking out over the slow rolling water Jared knew it was more than that, he couldn't look at those innocents around him without wanting to take advantage. That was it in a nutshell, after his time, you were either predator or prey, and there wasn't much in between.

Living on a freighter most of the year had come by accident. He'd tried it on a whim, and realized it was easier to deal with a crew than all the people that would fill a town. There were no cops, and life aboard a ship was a consistent routine. Routine was something he had become used to as a convict.

Once he gained some experience on the job, and applied his muscle and intimidation to the other workers, he could see making it work for himself, just like they did in the pen. Life on a freighter was isolated, and there was no place for anyone to go once they left land.

Becoming the bosun, in charge of all the workers, had been the final nail. He'd organized everything after that, the booze and the drugs. Sorting which officers would and wouldn't partake fell to his ability to read people, another skill that came quickly while doing time.

He smiled again, thinking of the girls hidden in a storage room near the kitchens. The freighter would turn east soon, heading towards the locks in Sault Saint Marie. Patience, he told himself. As usual he would wait until they were out of Canadian waters. Jared knew his adrenaline would be up again as they approached the locks, he wouldn't feel they were out of danger until they were off Superior, it was the last chance for Canadian authorities to stop them if some alarm had gone off.

Then, he thought to himself, then the fun can begin.

*****

S.S. Forester

Son of a bitch. Billy swore under his breath, his sweat-soaked shirt stuck to his back. He'd been scrubbing the deck most of the day. Any paint it ever had was long gone, and all he was cleaning was rust. Who let a ship get this bad?

"Blackwood! Get your muscle into it, we ain't pushing dust mops here."

No, we sure aren't. Not doing much undercover either. What a mess this was going to be. He pressed down harder on the thick-bristled broom, moving the broken pieces of rust around with the soapy detergent.

"Jesus Christ! You ain't even half-done yet rookie. We don't have all day."

"Sure boss."

"You'll call me bosun."

He knew it was bullshit, meant to show him the ropes, and who was boss. But this guy was starting to irritate him. He didn't like the whole dammed idea of the word bosun, and if this kept up he'd be calling him a bonehead instead. Billy looked around the deck, he could see the stares. In fact, he'd expected them, it was nothing new.

His mother had taken him off the reserve to shop at times when he was a youngster, and he'd noticed the stares in the malls and fast food joints. The white people would step away as they gave you a forced smile.

Whenever he went to athletic events with school the same thing would happen. Of course, it didn't seem strange there, as he was doing the same thing, checking out the white people.

It was only as he became older and began going places on his own that he realized it bothered him. In stores they would follow him around like he might steal something. And people feared him it seemed, turning their faces to avoid eye contact.

So, the other men staring at him was expected, especially as the boss shit on him. He kept fighting with staying undercover, which meant embellishing the dumb Indian routine, or speaking up for his rights. He was already working like a dog, and the guy wanted more. Billy kept scrubbing the deck, he was pissed enough that he wanted to scrub a hole right through the steel plate.

The freighter rolled slightly in the calm waters and Billy felt his stomach move again. No one had warned him about the motion sickness. He'd been in canoes endless times, he never expected this.

It was mild so far, but it wouldn't take much to get his stomach heaving. Day one and he was sweating and ready to puke. Could it get much worse?

Someone walked up beside him, and Billy straightened to see who it was.

"You look pale son. You want a cigarette?" The other man blew smoke his way, and Billy coughed. His stomach churned over once more as he stood back and shook his head.

Bastard. He realized he must look as bad as his stomach felt. Billy didn't raise his head a second time as he heard laughter. He forced his food back down, gripping the broom harder as he pushed it back and forth.

*****

S.S. Slate

Hans eased himself into his favourite chair in the captain's quarters. He'd stood the bridge while the freighter secured and left dock. He's been nervous the whole time, he couldn't get used to it. As he sat there, his body slowly stopped vibrating and the fear soaked away.

He'd searched the docks constantly, and knew Jared was out there doing the same. Hans hated this part, the regret and fear he had as they left the dock. It was like he was holding his breath the whole time, and only now was he able to breathe normally.

Once the ship was clear of the harbor and churning south he'd left the bridge to his first officer. Hans needed to get somewhere quiet, somewhere to control his anxiety. Here in his quarters he let his thoughts shift from guilt to the girls that would be below deck somewhere.

It dawned on him that he didn't know where they were hidden – didn't want to know for that matter. The arrangement was better this way, not seeing anything. Hours would have to go by before the fear would settle completely, but he was getting used to the process and knew that his time would be soon.

MAUWEE NIBI

Calmer now, he reached for a bottle anchored in a desk drawer. Pouring the bourbon into a shot glass he prepared the night's first drink. Anyone who noticed the puffy face and bloated red skin would know it was a regular ritual.

Hans paused with the glass in mid-air, he noticed the hand was shaking. It was nothing new, but he wondered if it was the alcohol, or the fear of getting caught with the girls below that caused it.

Two quick shots later he leaned back in his chair and imagined what she would look like. A few more shots and he could picture what was coming, looking at his bed, picturing a naked body waiting for him.

The thought of his wife was brief. Long overweight, and bound by religion, the thought of her brought no excitement. He was no winner himself, but believed that power and rank should have some reward.

Hans smiled as he tipped up the glass again. He was getting over his fear much quicker with each trip.

CHAPTER 5

S.S. Slate

Shanya bent her legs up close to her chest, her arms wrapped tight around them as she buried her face in her knees. She was tired, scared and frustrated, and she was fighting the urge to sleep.

Finally, unable to sit still any longer, she stood. Then the floor moved under her feet, causing her to reach out and grab the wall. It took her a few seconds to feel the whole motion of the wave as it rolled under the ship, lifting them and twisting at the same time. A few minutes later she had the rhythm figured out enough to start moving cautiously along the wall.

Everything was pitch black, so the slight lines left by the welds established distance as her hand slid along the cold steel. Running into a wall of boxes, she worked around them until she was feeling the wall again, continuing to work her way around the exterior of the room. She had to know how big this place was.

Another pile of boxes and then she was in a corner. Shanya retraced her steps and went the other direction until she found another corner. The room wasn't very big, no more than twelve feet. As she turned back towards her sitting place, she noticed a change in the light and looked up. It was only a small round window, but for some reason it offered hope.

Rummaging in the dark, she pushed a few boxes towards the window, which allowed her to climb up. At first she felt her spirit jump, she could just barely make out the moon, obscured by moving clouds, its outline barely visible.

Her mood immediately took a shot upward. Just seeing the world outside buoyed her courage, but as her eyes dropped lower and she saw nothing but water spread to the horizon the dread slammed back into her, almost knocking her off the boxes. She really had been taken. Most concerning, where was she going?

Crawling down off her improvised ladder, she staggered back to the place she started from, but couldn't sit down. Instead, she moved towards where the other girl's voices had come from, closer to the door.

"Can I join you?" She didn't care who answered she just wanted company.

"Please." Shanya recognized the timid response of young Abby's voice.

As she sat down she heard Chakwania scuffling as she moved over to sit with them. As they cuddled in the dark it felt worse, Shanya could feel her own fear mirrored as the other two girls shivered and shook.

"Gigikenimaa ina?" *Do you know him?* When no one answered she asked again. "The guy that was at the party. The one with the big silver clasp in his hair." Shanya couldn't get him out of her mind. She kept seeing him turned around in the front seat of the car, looking back at her.

The conversation was forced and filled with emotion, sentences breaking into tears at intervals. Neither of the other girls knew the guy who was so popular. They were like her, new to the party scene. They had no idea what had happened to them. Like her, they had been having a good time and then they were waking up in the dark. The situation sat heavy on their shoulders, Shanya found comfort in their presence, and thought hard for a way out.

She thought about the porcupine, and how he got his quills. When the earth was young, the porcupine had no quills and bear almost ate him. But he escaped to the top of a tree. The next day he was under a hawthorn tree and noticed how the thorns pricked him. It gave him an idea. He broke off the thorns and put them on his back. Next time he met bear he curled up in a ball, then bear had to go away because the thorns pricked him too much.

Nanabozho saw what happened and peeled the bark from some thorn trees and used clay to attach them to the porcupines back. Thus the porcupine could stand up to wolf and bear.

Shanya looked around in the dark, could she find something to use? To help her adapt? To keep her safe?

*****

At two a.m. the freighter was like a ghost, silent as it pushed through Superior. Anyone not on shift was long sleeping, the lounge area deserted except for one man. Jared sipped at the beer, his fourth. He was winding down still, it took time.

52

MAUWEE NIBI

It had always been the same. Just as much energy after the job as before. He'd been enough of a pro to keep off the juice before a job, it required too much attention when quick reactions were needed. But once he was safely out of the danger his blood still surged with adrenaline and he vibrated with tension. Tonight he wanted to add a little liquor to a shot glass to go with the beer, but held off, there were other priorities, like merchandise to sell.

He dialed the numbers from memory, the conversations all went the same, "Yo, Clipper here, I'm coming to town."

"Good man. Call when you get in."

Jared had always made money on the side, illegal money. That's what his kind did, looked for opportunity, no different than any businessman. The simple drops he made as he went around the lakes were easy cash. Pick it up in Thunder Bay and move it south. It hadn't been hard to find others willing to buy, at least not if you knew where to look. A few nights in the bars were all he ever needed, he could spot the hard cases with ease. His people, the guys sitting with their backs against the wall pretending they didn't notice who came and went, unlike the rest, who turned to look before he was ten feet inside the door.

Another task taken care of. Another swig of beer. Jared unconsciously tapped the bottle on the table. Winding down was never easy, but the potential time he was looking at for this kind of offense was too serious to ignore. He shrugged, no risk, no reward. He let out a half-nervous laugh, an old habit.

The girls kept creeping into his head, they were hard to ignore. The rest of the crew – at least those in the know – had done their best to look normal, but earlier, smiles and winks were flying around the dining table. They were looking forward to the party.

It was a hassle to manage, keeping everyone engaged and satisfied. But once you learned the power of spreading around the chaos, you realized the importance of inclusion. The more people involved, the less chance of anyone rocking the boat.

Jared had taken a while to get his gig set up, but now it was running like a machine. As long as he strong-armed it, took care of the business, there should be no interruptions.

The details had all been worked out long ago and the plan was in process. Three was one more than usual, but he had done it before. It seemed this time there was an opportunity to do things differently. The lip on one side of his face curled slightly, he might be able to have one of them to himself. There was no doubt which one.

There was something different about her. He hadn't put his finger on it yet, but she didn't look like she'd been around the block like they usually did. She'd felt so firm when carrying her downstairs. She'd been in shape, had muscle and flex in all the right places, revealing that she worked out.

He could relate to that. In the pen he worked out daily, partly killing time, and partly keeping ready. Jared knew he needed to call it a night. Even if he was thinking hard about taking a walk down to see the girls, he put it off. The empty beer bottle slid across the table as he stood up.

The time was coming, he told himself. As usual man, just wait for it.

*****

MAUWEE NIBI

S.S. Forester

Two men stood near the bow of the freighter, one smoking a cigar, the other a cigarette. Much time slipped away between words. Finally, the one who seemed superior in rank nodded, "Okay, test him."

The other man flicked the cigarette over the rail, and turned towards the superstructure at the rear.

*****

The first night on board, Billy kept it simple, a quick dinner with the others, some fresh air out on the deck, a late shower, and now all he wanted to do was lie down. The sleeping quarters were no hotel, bunks on either side of the hall made for little privacy. The little sliding curtain sure didn't offer any peace and quiet. It was too bad he hadn't gotten one of those new boats with private quarters.

Around nine he made his way towards the end of the hall where he was bunked. Halfway down the narrow corridor he ran into a couple workers headed the other direction. The short one in front was looking back at his companion as he talked. He slammed right into Billy's chest.

The guy bounced backwards as his head swung around to see what he'd hit. Then his face registered shock. "What are you doing, you fucking shithead?"

Billy was taken back by the immediate aggression. The guy went off so quickly, it was like he wasn't even considering that it had been an accident.

"You as dumb as you look? Get the fuck out of my way."
The guy stepped forward right into Billy's space, like he was
asking for a confrontation.

Billy only had a second to decide, but being undercover
didn't mean being a wimp, and years of standing up for himself
kicked in. "You ought to keep your head straight, watch where
you're walking there buddy."

The guy was standing so close Billy could smell the booze.
He sensed rather than saw when the guy started to move his
right fist. The forward motion of the shoulder came first, then
the weight-shift as the arm came up.

Billy was already moving.

He twisted sideways to avoid the blow as the fist swung up
and went past his head. When he straightened back up, he
shifted his own weight and drove in with an elbow. At the last
second the guy got an arm up in front of his face to take the
blow.

Billy moved his weight back, and then forward again, as he
drove another elbow at the head. This time the guy ducked
instead of blocking the shot. His mistake, Billy had hoped for it
and now he brought a knee upwards, putting everything into
the motion. Feeling it connect, his knee slid off something, the
head, then he felt the body sag slightly.

Now engaged, Billy was ready to strike again when he
heard the others behind him yelling, he backed off and left the
guy alone while the asshole's buddy held him on his feet.

Billy's heart was pounding against his ribs like a two-stroke
engine. Standing with his feet spread for balance, his arms held
at the ready, he breathed in and out, trying to calm down, but
he felt cornered. Turning, he shoved past the men huddled in

the hallway and headed topside, he needed air for the second time that night.

What had just happened? The more he thought about it, the more he felt pushed into the fight, another thing that wasn't new.

Hockey fights were mostly spur of the moment, or retaliation for rough play. But the brawls he'd had in bars or at school had all felt forced. Someone would start egging someone else on; fight the Indian, let's see what he's got. As long as he could remember he'd never started one, but had been forced to fight back in quite a few.

Some people reacted strangely when seeing an Indian. Billy had seen it too often, he'd had to quit a job doing newspaper delivery because people complained when he came to the door. That some people wanted to fight just because of what he looked like was just another reaction he couldn't understand. Not many of them took time to talk to him or get to know him, it was his race that was the beginning and end for most. Maybe it was just the booze that had the crewman fired up.

Later, as he lay in his bunk Billy wondered where the guy he'd fought was. He realized he'd be resting lightly, one eye on the curtain on a night when he'd wanted to really get a decent sleep. The work on deck had taken its toll.

Closer to midnight, Billy rolled restlessly in his bed. One eye closed, trying to sleep, the other watching the shadows in the hallway that he could see through the gap along the edges of the closed curtain.

He was sure he must be the only one still awake, the only one stupid enough to be wasting recuperation time. He was about to roll over when he heard something that made him freeze.

Eyes closed, barely breathing, he listened intently. There it was again, quiet sounds of something moving out in the hall. Nothing was moving outside his bunk, but he lay motionless and waited. Another few minutes passed, maybe twenty. Time seemed to be standing still in the dark. Then he heard something else, similar but different at the same time. He was sure it was someone walking softly, making as little noise as possible.

For the first time in his new career, the new constable, the rookie undercover, had his instincts kick in. Everything told him these guys were up to something. Was something being hidden? Or was he over-reacting?

That was enough for day one. But Billy knew he was on a case now, he had information to find. Information he would get.

*****

Writing in his journal the captain made the first surprising entry. He hadn't expected the kid to come off as hard-assed as he had. It didn't matter at this point, there was a long way to go. Still a seaman would have a helluva black eye.

He finished up the entry with positive remarks, he had to, the kid passed the test with flying colors.

CHAPTER 6

S.S. Slate

Shanya didn't know why she kept thinking of the room as a cage, but the visual had settled into her mind. She sat alone against the outer wall, taking a break from consoling the others. Dealing with their despair made it hard to think, she needed to focus and keep her own self together.

Hours had gone by and no one had come to save her. She wondered if anyone would. How could her mother or father know where she was? Or the cops for that matter? For the first time, since this whole mess had begun, she thought of Erin. What had happened to her? Surely Erin would tell the authorities where they had been.

The more she considered Erin sending help to search for her, she couldn't help wonder why Erin had let her be taken in the first place. This was frustrating, no matter how many times she went over it, she couldn't remember the end of the party, what had happened to her.

It didn't seem like a mistake at the time, going out with Erin. Not like her mother had clearly warned, but now she was thinking it might be the worst decision she would ever make.

Just thinking of the future brought doubt and fear again. Did she even have one?

During the day, the room had lightened up, from sunlight through the little round window and a small bit of light leaking under the door. Shanya finally saw Abby and Chakwania up close, and the three of them talked and felt better. Then the sun had gone down, and with it the mood inside their cage.

Shanya didn't want to lose hope, but the night coming again signified one day gone and that hung heavy, the weight of it dropping her shoulders even closer to the floor. It seemed to her that any rescue was slipping farther and further away.

Sounds at the locked door shocked her. Every muscle tensed, her body jerked and she jumped to her feet. An overhead light flashed on, blinding her for a second. The door swung open and heavy boots walked in. The person took a few steps into the room, swinging the door closed.

Shanya watched carefully, but he was still in the shadow by the door and the light caught just his pants up to the knees. As he stepped forward into the centre, she watched the light rising up his body. When he finally stopped under the overhead bulb she could see everything, and her body shook once.

Everything about this man scared her. A sneer crossed his pockmarked face, menacing tattoos crawled up arms and gripped his neck, but it was the dead stare of his colourless eyes that showed no mercy. She felt his presence in the room like an evil Windigo spirit.

Her mother had told countless stories about the spirits. Were they meant to help her now?

Only one story of a Windigo being defeated came to mind. The legend told how no one was willing to face the coming spirit, so a little girl asked for two sticks of peeled sumac as long as her arms. That night it was cold, and she asked her grandmother to use the kettle to melt tallow. Now the river froze as a Windigo as large as a tree came over the hill. The little girl walked towards the spirit and grew in size as she walked. Now she was the same size as the Windigo, she beat it over the head with her sumac sticks that had turned to copper. With the spirit dead, she drank the hot tallow and returned to her normal size.

Shanya looked up at the man again, he looked mean and strong. She couldn't imagine trying to hit him over the head. He stared at her again and her body shivered once more in disgust or fear, she knew it didn't matter which.

Trying to breath, to center herself, her heart beat hard against her ribs and fear was taking over. His first words came out loud and clear. As he pointed to the floor Shanya started to shake.

"All right bitches, get your asses up here."

*****

Jared stood outside the door for a second, just enjoying the anticipation. He loved this part, getting the ball rolling, putting them in their places. Mostly it was the control he liked, and it didn't get better than this; anything, anything he wanted.

Patience had got him this far. Nineteen hours had put them through the locks in the Soo, now they were off of Superior. He'd been alert the whole time through the narrow passage. It was an easy place for anyone to intercept the ship. No one had bothered them, and now here he was, about to begin the introductions.

Reminded himself that there was a purpose to this first visit, there was reason for how he handled the relationship from the beginning. Grinding his teeth back and forth, he stowed the smile and pushed open the door. With the door clicking shut behind him, he stepped to the center of the room.

"All right bitches, get your asses up here."

One sucked in air while another whimpered. Forcing down his smile, pointing at his feet, he lowered his voice to a more menacing tone.

"Don't piss me off ladies."

He loved the moment of confusion as they contemplated first their courage, and then his offer of violence. Their shuffling noise as they rushed to kneel at his feet was music to the ears.

"That's right girls, do as you're told and you won't be hurt."

"Look at me."

Once he had their complete attention he laid it out for them, "You squaws belong to me now. There is no one coming for you. Shit, no one even cares that you're gone."

The young one was close to tears, but the older two were holding it together, showing no emotion. Jared didn't care either way.

"You're going to do as your told, and take care of the men. Then you will be fed and rewarded." It was bullshit, but he had learned long ago that shaping situations allowed you to lead people's expectations, to get them thinking what you wanted. And he wanted then thinking they had a chance.

MAUWEE NIBI

"You can make this hard on yourself, or easy. It's your choice. But I guarantee you that I will hurt you if you piss me off. So you should be thinking of just doing your part and getting back home in the end."

There it was, the carrot. The thing that allowed people to justify their actions, whatever they were, so they could attain something that made it worth it. Jared had used the system many times.

Tell a wannabe that if he eliminates some guy, he can take over the guy's action, whatever it be – drugs, stolen merchandise, vehicles, whatever the racket. It always got more interest than just a cash payment.

Another time it could be; Do this job for us, it's a small one, but we have some bigger jobs if you do this one right. It not only made them want to do well to get further work, but they also took a low pay for the first job, expecting more later.

He offered the gift of home to them as something to focus on and try to attain. It would make it easier for them, but in some corner of his head he really didn't care, some had fought in the past and he'd always dealt with it.

Jared clapped his hands together, hard and loud. All three girls froze in place at the sudden noise. "Now which one of you wants to get on my good side?" He paused a second, "I might have a surprise for you."

At first no one moved, he waited. Then the youngest one started to fidget, she looked sideways at the others who didn't return the look. He could tell those two weren't giving in easily. This one though was close, "What's your name?"

"Abby"

"Why don't you come with me and we'll have a talk?" He reached his hand out to her, waiting. It was obvious that she was still hesitant, but wanted an end to the fear. Finally, she reached out and he pulled her to her feet.

Jared walked her to the outer wall away from the other girls. Everything had a purpose.

"Now get down on your knees." He started to undo his belt, then the button of the jeans. When she didn't move he reached out and grabbed a handful of hair.

"Do as you're told bitch, be a good girl." He pushed her down with his hand.

"No!" she squealed out in protest.

His other hand was about to pull at his zipper, but he used it to slap her once on the side of the head. He made sure to use an open hand or she'd be out cold, which defeated the purpose. Then he finished opening his pants.

Complete control, fuck it never got old. His hand guided her forward.

*****

Shanya shook in anger, Abby had given in. She hoped by not showing any support the girl would have gotten the message, but damn her, she caved instead.

She knew there was no good to come from this man, no surprise worth giving in for, no promise worth believing.

When Abby cried out Shanya went from anger to fear in the blink of an eye. She knew something was going to happen. When the smacking noise circled the room her shoulders hunched and her palms covered her face.

MAUWEE NIBI

It sounded like Abby was gagging, then the man moaned. Shanya closed her eyes and shook her head, she didn't want to be here in this place. In some ways it felt like she had been assaulted too.

Now her hands covered her ears as the anger rose up again. It flowed through her body, heating her up, making the hairs on her arms stand up. It was that, or allow herself to imagine that her time was coming.

*****

Hours were slipping by. Billy laid on the hard mattress, listening for more noises out in the hallway. Other than the earlier shuffling sounds he hadn't heard anything. He had to settle his thoughts before he could sleep. Too many issues raced around in his head. Well that, and the bunk was too damned small for his long frame and he kept flopping around trying to find a comfortable spot.

He figured if the drunk from the fight was coming back for a second brawl, he'd have done it by now. The alcohol fire in his gut would wane as he slept it off. It could probably be assumed that whoever had been moving around earlier was finished whatever they were doing. He doubted they were still out there, but he still wondered what had been going on.

Billy was beginning to fully understand the meaning of working undercover now. There was no back-up coming if he needed it. Out here you were on your own. He'd worked hard to get through training, it didn't seem right to be pretending to be a deck hand, especially if it was for nothing. He knew he might not find anything useful on this damned boat. How could he? One person on a huge ship, it seemed a hopeless task.

Billy found himself thinking about the missing women, native women. How many times had one of them vanished over the years? No one ever knew where they were, or if they went willingly.

Often there seemed to be some sort of assumption they were visiting relatives or friends on another reserve. At least until they didn't come back.

For the first time as he thought about it, he realized it seemed strange. White people noticed as soon as someone was missing, there were missing persons posters, photos on milk cartons, searches that kicked in quickly. Yet natives didn't have the same results when dealing with someone missing. He wondered if that gap was created by the lack of trust on the native side when dealing with the white establishment, or if was how the police perceived the situation as just another drunken or irresponsible native that would show up in a few days.

It made him think that people being unsure where others are, or where they had gone, must be more accepted in native culture. There was always constant movement between the settlements, even to other provinces. The fact that over half of young native women moved every year only amplified the migration issue.

He remembered a girl in his class at school who didn't show up one Monday morning. She'd been there for months and suddenly she wasn't. Another native dropping out of school was all he'd thought. It happened all the time. Then some fishermen found the body of the girl near the edge of a lake. He'd heard she'd met a hard end.

MAUWEE NIBI

Billy thought of the cousin who went to visit relatives in Alberta. She never did get there. He wondered if his own family had gone to the police at the time. It was something he knew natives didn't always do. Eventually it seemed that with her absence came acceptance, he realized he hadn't asked about her in years.

Realizing he was answering his own earlier question about how white people dealt with their missing, he knew it wasn't as simple as that. Whites did call the police the moment someone was missing.

The band councils didn't have the time, money, or resources for the natives to launch into a search and rescue. Yet many issues were still handled by the elders instead of the police. It was just the way it was.

Billy's eyes were closing and he knew he was just scratching the surface of a problem too big for him to solve. He told himself to focus on what he could do, get to know and search the ship, and work on learning what he could from the other guys.

Before falling asleep, fleeting images drifted through his consciousness. He saw Manitoba's Red River, where too many native bodies end up floating. His eyes were long closed, his breathing slowed, but some part of his brain was still trying to process the concept.

How many bodies could a Great Lake hold?

CHAPTER 7

S.S. Slate

The low groaning sound of the steel hull twisting against itself was ignored by those used to the big freighters. In the dead of night it was unnerving Shanya. No two sounds were alike, some were short, some long. The groans could be close or far, it all added up to fear. The long wail sounded like the boat was an injured animal.

It was taking all her control to keep her mind settled. She went through periods alternating between sweating and chills. She cried uncontrollably, got mad, then really angry. Angry that she was in this place, angry that this had happened to her, angry that she knew what was coming. She could go on, there was more. She was angry because she'd went to the party, angry because she'd wanted to show Erin she wasn't coddled. There were too many reasons, all of them pissing her off.

Her heart took off a few times, pounding against her chest. She closed her eyes and breathed slowly, purposefully slowing it back down. If she could just get settled, she could start thinking.

"Mother what am I going to do?" The words spoken out loud without her noticing.

MAUWEE NIBI

A vision of her mother's garden came to mind. She considered her mother's question about the deer stamping his hoof.

In her head she rolled around the notion of showing aggression to a threat. What would a deer do if his bluff failed as a wolf or bear approached? Run as fast and far as he could, she supposed. She didn't have that option, there was nowhere for her to go.

She wondered what happened when a deer was threatened by another deer. She assumed that he would have to follow through on his bluff and attack the intruder.

Mulling that over, it was obvious there was no chance she could follow through on any bluff. There was no way she could attack that man. He was dangerous looking in every way. Evil seemed to radiate from his very being. Shanya's mouth went dry, she tried to swallow and had to force down the bitter taste at the back of her throat.

Abby was crying again, Shanya could hear Chakwania whispering, consoling the scared girl. It hadn't been any consolation that she'd been correct about the surprise that the man had hinted at. If it wasn't enough that he'd abused Abby, the chocolate bar he dropped on the floor as he'd left her collapsed against the far wall had been nothing but an insult.

Unexpectedly, Shanya's anger flared up again. This was a monster, a crazy man. It was like she was living in a bad dream that was going to turn into a nightmare at any second.

The clanging at the door, as someone worked the lock from the other side, flushed away the anger as fast as it came. Fear and desperation took over. She grimaced, froze, and stared wide-eyed at the opening. Immediately defensive, she pulled her legs up wrapping her arms around them, turning herself into a little ball.

The door swung open at the same time the light switched on. The brightness caught Shanya off guard again, forcing her to squint. She didn't want to look at him, but her sense of self-preservation was strong and she peeked up to see what he was doing.

Standing in the center of the room he stared directly at her. Her heart pounded hard, once, twice, three times, and then he turned to look at Chakwania. Shanya almost gulped loudly enough for all of them to hear.

"How are you honey?" He was talking to Chakwania, a smile on his face.

Shanya cheered on the inside. There was no answer to his question coming.

"Don't want to talk tonight? Don't worry you'll get your chance soon enough." He smiled.

She could tell he enjoyed scaring them. Unfortunately, he was good at it.

The beast walked over to Abby curled on the floor, weeping. He told her to get up, then didn't wait a second before reaching down and grabbing a handful of her hair to lift her by. Abby started to scream.

He repeated his order to get up, starting to drag her towards the door. Abby fumbled to her feet and scramble after him with her body bent forward awkwardly at the waist, the man's hand twisted in her hair holding her head down. Just when it seemed she was going to scream again, he hit her hard on the top of the head and stifled any further noise.

Shanya didn't realize until the door slammed shut that her mouth was hanging open. Opening and closing it a few times, she cringed. Every bone in her body told her this wasn't good for Abby.

As she shook her head the tears rolled down her cheeks, it wasn't good for her either.

*****

Jared shoved the teen ahead of himself, she stumbled past the food storage rooms. He passed one of his men who was guarding the hallway, and nodded to another watching the stairwell.

Before taking her up the stairs, he pushed her out the steel hatch onto the wind-blown deck of the freighter. The sobbing girl sobered in an instant, her back went stiff as she refused to move. He knew she realized the danger, the waves had picked up, a cool wind blew, and water was spraying across the steel structure.

Reaching out and catching a fistful of hair again, he pulled her backwards, bending her neck until her head touched his chest. "You do as you're told from now on bitch. You hear me?"

He snapped her head back and forth before bringing her face close to his. "You cause just one problem," He pushed her hard towards the edge of the ship, never letting go, just showing the motion to her, "And you're never going home."

When he shoved her back through the hatch to the stairwell she gasped in relief, sucking in mouthfuls of air.

"Up the stairs!" Jared smiled at his temporary guard as he followed her, she was fully compliant now.

Knowing the Captain was expecting him, he knocked softly on the door. Pushing the native girl ahead, he stepped in quickly. Sparing a moment to look around, Jared never managed to get over his jealousy of the Captain's room.

The officer's bed wasn't a simple bunk like the rest of them had, instead the Captain had a double mattress up against the wall, with a small carpet in front to stand on during those cold mornings. There was a bar fridge under one corner of the desk near the door, a double locker, and a private bathroom. After opening the door to let them in, the Captain had returned to his chair pulled up to the table in the corner. A small lamp fixed to the wall above the table lit the area.

Jared walked the girl to the bed and told her to sit. Joining the Captain at the table, the old man already looked drunk, his eyes were red, a grin was pasted on his face and the half-empty bottle was in the center of the table. There was anticipation in those bleary eyes.

Jared could relate; he kept thinking of the two girls still in the storage room. Actually it was just the one who had his attention. Tonight he reasoned that it didn't matter, this was just about getting the process started, and taking care of the Captain.

"How are you sir?" Jared gave him his due respect. It wasn't always easy, but a worthwhile sacrifice. It wasn't that the guy didn't deserve it, Jared just didn't give anyone respect.

The Captain set a shot glass on the table, knowing he didn't need to ask, Jared would drink. Pushing the bottle across the table was the extent of the old man's hospitality. Jared nodded as the captain turned his chair to get a better view of the new girl on the bed.

"How old is this one?"

What had he been told at the party? He couldn't remember, he was sure it was younger than the other two. He understood the importance of putting spin on something, and this called for a positive answer. "I didn't find out. Thought you'd get that information."

He watched the captain licking his lips. A bead of sweat showed on the man's face as he became more interested in the girl. "Yes, we'll talk." He nodded.

When the man put his hand on his thigh, close to his own junk, Jared knew it was time to leave.

He tipped his head back and downed a third shot. As he headed towards the door he caught the girl's eyes, speaking loud enough for the Captain to hear. "You call me if she gives you any trouble."

Pulling the door closed he looked back into the room. He didn't need the mental image of the captain playing with himself, but Jared nodded his head in satisfaction. Step one was complete, just a little more patience he told himself. *You'll get yours soon enough.*

*****

S.S. Forester

With the weather change, Billy was going through hell. He was laid up in his bunk, holding on for dear life, trying to settle his guts. The wind was making the ship roll higher with each wave and he was sure he was going to puke.

He'd tried walking around, and tried getting out in the fresh air, but he kept being slammed against the walls as the ship shifted one way or the other. The idea of being outside was crazy, he didn't want to be washed overboard.

Mentally he sifted through the conversations he'd had throughout the day while chatting up the crew. He'd open up the talk with whoever he ran into. Most of the men on board took a second and responded.

If he could, he tried to ask their names and a few innocent questions about their families. His aim was to keep it casual. What they did on the freighter? How long they'd been working on the water? Just some simple questions to see their reactions.

Interpreting facial expressions and the body language of people was a skill he was supposed to have now that the he was trained. Of course, when you run into some people you don't need any skill at all. One conversation was all one-sided.

"Hey how you doing?" He'd walked up to a maintenance guy working on the seal of a window at deck level.

The guy stopped what he was doing, but kept his eyes staring straight ahead for a second. Then he turned slowly, like he wasn't amused with the interruption. He stared Billy in the eye for a second. Then he spit on the steel plating at his feet before turning back to his work.

"Alright well you have a great day." Billy hadn't let it show, but as he walked away he was pissed. The guy could have spit over the railing, but he spit on the deck, knowing Billy would be the one cleaning it.

The ship heaved and fell like a roller coaster then slammed sideways. His stomach churned again, it felt like it was pushing up into his mouth. *Damn it*, it wasn't often, but each time the big ship was banged around there was nothing he could do but hope his dinner stayed down.

After reviewing the day's conversations he had to admit that he didn't find anyone who was really suspicious. They all seemed guarded and selective of their words, even if being polite, but Billy put that down to his being new, or a native. It could be either.

Were a few rude? Sure, and he'd expected that, his experience dictated that it was always the same. For some reason or another, there was always someone who looked down on natives. There always had been. The dreadful residential schools could only have existed if someone had wanted change. That original need to change the Indian set the precedent that they were not equal.

Billy felt he'd bided his time long enough, it was going on ten-thirty. The ship was still rolling with the larger waves as he slipped quietly out of the bunk. Being close to one end, he stepped along the hallway to the door and out of the sleeping quarters. With only more quarters above him, he headed for a walkway down to the lower decks.

His heart was pumping, which was strange, because he shouldn't be in any real danger. He had a story ready, he'd say his stomach and head were turning with the waves and he wanted to get lower in the ship.

It was a gamble for sure. First, he wasn't sure if going lower helped with the seasickness or not. Second, it was going to be hard explaining seasickness when this was his job. He smiled to himself, it was all he had, and he realized the improvisation they talked about in training was hard to apply in the tight confines of a freighter.

Tucked in between a couple crates that had been stashed under the stairway, he waited out a better part of three hours. No one had come his way, or been down in this area of the ship. He felt that was long enough and edged out of his hiding place.

As carefully as he had worked his way there, he headed back, moving in the shadows, keeping up against the walls to stay out of sight until he was finally in the stairwell to the sleeping quarters. He thought he was home free when he slipped back into the bunk.

Before falling asleep he lay there thinking about what part of the ship he would search the next night.

*****

The figure stepped away from the stairway railing when he heard the door open below. He peeked out to watch down the center of the staircase, seeing the new native deck hand as he headed to his floor and quietly opened the door to the bunkroom.

Rubbing his beard he leaned on the railing, deep in thought. Finally, he smiled and shook his head. Just to be sure, he looked down to the floors below once again ensuring the kid was done for the night before turning to the door to his own hallway and sleeping quarters.

*****

MAUWEE NIBI

S.S. Slate

The door to the captain's quarters closed and the room went silent.

Hans watched the girl look around the room, concerned now that she was left with a stranger. His hand groped the growing bulge between his legs.

He'd been through it before, had rushed the first few girls, attacked them in raging lust, fought them to submission and taken his due. Now he knew better. This was a dance better enjoyed fully, and it went better if she cooperated.

He let her look around and get comfortable. Her eyes kept coming back to his face, and he drank in her youth. She had to be the youngest yet, the bulge twitched between his legs and his smile spread even wider. He'd waited a day; what were a few more hours? Instead, he spent his time picturing her naked in different positions. Not just her, but him as well, thrusting and having his way. Hans slammed the brief thought of his daughter into the back of his head, chasing it away with a shot.

Reaching up to his collar, he undid a few buttons on the tight shirt, it was time to begin the dance.

"My god, are you ever beautiful." The slight German accent emphasized the last word.

She smiled just briefly before looking down at the floor.

"My name is Eric. What is yours?" Hans never used his own name even

though he knew she would never tell anyone. He watched her trying to decide what to do. That was a good sign. Give him time and she would let him help her with those decisions.

He reached into a drawer of the desk, pulling out the cigarettes. "Would you like a smoke?"

That's it, he thought to himself, she wanted it. He could see the quick looks, *anything to get her comfortable*. He opened the pack and walked over to the bed. After she took one out of the pack he casually returned to his chair. He was hard as a rock now, he'd stood in front of her and saw the moment when her eyes went to his bulge. The eyes had quickly shifted elsewhere, but he knew she'd seen it and it excited him.

He put another shot glass beside his and poured two measures out. When she was half done the cancer stick he asked if she wanted a drink. Again, he could see the hesitation, but his experience said she would join him. He was never sure why, was it to try and please him? Keep him from being angry? Or was it to forget the circumstances? Numb the senses even?

Hans tilted his head sideways a touch, looking at her body from different angles, He'd had plain missionary sex his whole life, until the bosun had presented these opportunities. Now he was exploring and experimenting, doing as he pleased.

In the end she really was just a squaw, and there was no respect for them, a whore was no different. He'd felt guilty taking the first few, it was against everything he'd been raised to believe. A woman was special and delicate, deserving of care and courtship.

Of course, you knew the woman's family and everyone was accountable to each other in white society. But who was this native? Who cared? Hans had come to realize that there were no consequences, and the only limitations were his imagination and desire.

Shyly the girl took the shot glass back to the bed. When she was done the drink he waved the bottle at her, offering her another. As she came to the table he asked her again, "What is your name beautiful?"

This time he got a sweet-sounding voice, more importantly the first wall had come down. He knew she could see his hand stroking his member through his pants because he watched her eyes looking there. Then she looked up at him while he poured the shot. "My name is Abby"

"Neither of us want that guy coming back." He waved his shot glass in the direction Jared had left, alluding to the fear she had of him. "Why don't you sit here and join me for a drink where it's quiet and safe."

He pulled the chair close to his and patted it with his hand. When the girl sat down beside him they both knew she had relented, and he placed his hand on her leg. The electricity as he gave her a gentle squeeze was exhilarating. Unconsciously, Hans licked his lips again.

"For a young girl you sure look like a real woman." Hans leaned back, everything was progressing well, a few more drinks, a few more compliments, he'd have her there. He tamped down the urge to just grab her, flip her over and rip down her jeans. But there were days of enjoyment ahead and he'd have her soon enough.

He thought of his wife again, and almost lost the buzz he had working. His hand went from the girl's leg to the bottle sitting on the table to pour another shot. The other hand pulled open his belt and released the buckle, then he flipped the top button open and reached for the zipper.

REJEAN GIGUERE

CHAPTER 8

S.S. Slate

Three days had passed. Shanya was sinking deeper. Her spirit was waning. Dark, everything was dark. The fear had become like a rock in her stomach. Her body curled sideways against the wall unable to find warmth anywhere. What else could she do? All the positive thoughts that had come earlier, the idea that she'd be rescued, that she'd find a way out, were all slipping away.

Her stomach groaned in unison with the ship, she hadn't thought of food until her body complained. It was the least of her worries, and she ignored the pains. Water would be nice, but really didn't mean any more than food right now. Living was all that she was focused on, her needs had narrowed until nothing else mattered.

The full degradation had sunk in when she had to use the small bucket in the corner for the washroom. Worse than embarrassed, it made her feel dirty.

Abby hadn't come back after being taken during the night. Chakwania hadn't taken it well. She kept bringing it up, wondering out loud what had happened to the other girl.

Shanya didn't want to think about it. She wondered how many men were on a ship like this. How could they all be monsters?

The only way to go forward was with the hope that someone was going to help her. It was the only way she'd get out of here. That begged the question – who on this ship even knew she was locked in this room? It could be hardly anyone, and that sank her mood deeper into desperation.

All she had to rely on were the lessons she'd been taught. It all seemed meaningful at the time, but why weren't they meaning anything now? Closing her eyes Shanya sorted through the stories she'd been told again and again, trying to find one that would fit the situation.

She thought of the natives who had laughed at the lessons. She knew some didn't believe anymore. They said the lessons were for a time long gone, that they didn't translate into today's world. Her mother had said the lessons were for all time, they were our heritage and therefore part of our future.

Different natives believed whichever lessons they wanted to, and discarded those that didn't fit, or made them uncomfortable. Shanya could see why those who left the reserves could eventually lose the lessons over time. It was becoming clear in the darkness of this steel cage that native lessons were meant for those living on the land.

The stories always referenced the land or animals, flowers and sea. There was no way to connect with the lessons in a city, or locked in a cage on a ship.

Anger flared up again, her eyes narrowed, she hadn't wasted her time, had she? She straightened slightly. Did she spend all those years listening for nothing? Some said the lessons held back the natives, kept them stuck in the past.

MAUWEE NIBI

Shanya knew this would be a bad place and time to learn that truth. She hoped it wasn't the case, but her body slumped even further as she slipped a few more inches down the cold wall.

*****

The second part of the process took some getting used to, but Jared knew how to adapt. He'd needed more than one officer in on the gig, it was the only way he could control everything. Having the captain was critical, but getting another higher-up on side had been the only way to make it work.

He'd worked each of them just like he'd worked the captain, laying out hints and waiting for them to take the bait. The captain had been shocked at the prospect, but a few days of alcohol fueled imagination had changed that. The old man had become eager. Yes, the Captain's morality had been easy to sway.

The officers had been harder, they were younger, mostly still in the throes of new marriages. Still in love. Jared had no idea what that was. He'd fucked girls in school, but the partying had been more important, and then the late-night jobs took over.

Then jail, and eventually the Pen, had come. And there sure as hell weren't any females there. A few of the young boys he'd preyed on came to mind, but that was just taking what could be taken.

It had been everything to not lay his hands on the few women he tried to date after finishing his time. They'd expected him to cater to their needs and emotions, or they dumped him after a few good nights of sex. Fucking women today. No, he couldn't see the attraction of the love these officers kept talking about.

Not being one to quit easily, he'd kept at a few who looked like good prospects. The officers often showed up below to drink with the workers, to escape the captain's scrutiny for a few hours. So Jared would sit with whoever had come down and drop hints. That it was the tall nerdy one with big round glasses who finally took the bait was a shock, but Jared knew you couldn't tell from looks. Maybe the hardness, but not the morals.

The Second Officer was strange, Jared would give him that, but years later they had settled into a routine, just like he had with the Captain. Having sent a text earlier, he was waiting for the officer to show up.

Looking around the new room he smiled, the native had fought him from the second he grabbed her off the floor and that was the spirit they were looking for, he almost wished that he was the one playing with her. But as he'd left the room he knew it was the other one who had his attention. He'd dragged this one down the hall to the next storage room. It was mostly filled with cardboard boxes, but enough clear space existed to have some fun. A simple arrangement with the chef who ruled this part of the freighter ensured that he had full access to the storerooms.

The towel he'd tied around the girl's mouth was helping to keep her quiet. The equipment he needed had been stashed there earlier, and he'd dragged the girl over to a crate about three feet high. Roughly, Jared pushed her over at the waist until her chest was lying across the top of the crate.

Before she could stand back up, he took hold of a wrist. Grabbing the end of the rope that ran under the crate he quickly wrapped one arm, then the next. The girl jerked and struggled, but there wasn't any place she could go now that she was tied down on the crate. Finally, he walked behind her, doing the same with her feet. Now he was able to do as he pleased without being kicked.

Jared reached around and undid her jeans, pulling them down along with her panties, she started to pull and twist in place. He reached down pushing the pants as low as they would get. Then he stood back to admire his work. It was a nice sight.

"Save it bitch. Save it for later."

Long ago the officer had made it clear he didn't want to handle anything, or touch anything. The guy wanted a plug and play scenario, Jared chuckled at his own twist on the computer slang.

Banging at the door raised the stakes. The atmosphere heightened as the girl looked over her shoulder, jerking and pulling at the ropes. Jared let the man in and stood to the side.

The officer nodded his way, his bulging eyes blinking hard. It was obvious he was up for it, Jared had seen eyes like that in jail, and he knew this guy was capable of doing something crazy and always kept an eye on him whenever he was around.

Now he watched the senior seaman walk towards the girl, his hands fumbling at his waist. Jared realized the man was undoing his pants and quickly turned to the door, leaving the two of them alone.

Stage two complete.

Now the fun could begin. The crew would be in on the action and he was going to finally get to that little honey he had waiting.

Jared stopped dead in his tracks. For a moment he thought he heard something, sure it came from the room he just left. Then a scream floated out from under the door.

Cracking his neck from side to side, Jared got rid of his sudden unease. He picked up his pace as he headed towards the stairs. He didn't want to imagine what was going on in there, but he really didn't care either.

*****

S.S. Forester

Another day done, the winds had died down and the ship was sailing quietly across the glassy lake. Billy had worked all day scraping old paint off one of the deck hatches, new paint would be next. He talked with whoever he could get to stop and visit on their way past.

One guy was an ex-hockey player, like he was, they'd even played in the same junior league at different times. So that conversation went on for a bit, and Billy took a chance, "What you guys do for fun around here?"

The guy had clammed up at that point, and next thing he knew, Billy was by himself. He assumed that had been one question too many. Later, over dinner, he just listened to the others talk. He'd learned a lot over the years and in training about being quiet. First, it made others feel you weren't judging them, then that you didn't really care much. It sometimes loosened lips.

MAUWEE NIBI

After darkness fell, Billy lay there in the bunk passing time. No one had said anything significant at dinner, but he didn't expect much to happen in a group setting. He was killing time before venturing out around the ship again. There were living quarters at the back of the ship as well as the front, the engineer's bunks were there to be close to their machinery. Since he'd checked the forward end of the ship last night, tonight would be the rear.

A while later Billy jolted awake. Damn, he'd passed out. He shook his head and then listened for sounds in the hallway. With no noise, and his watch saying eleven-thirty he slipped out of bed and moved quietly to the hatch at his end of the corridor.

No one was out walking about, but still the adrenaline pumped through his system, and he heard every moan from the freighter as he slipped from one hiding spot to another. Slowly, he worked his way across the deck towards the rear of the vessel. He knew that anyone watching from the bridge would have to see him. *Wouldn't they?*

Eventually he was inside looking down a set of stairs, nothing stood out or set off warning bells, so he continued. At the bottom nothing stood out, and he started to walk down the hallway.

"Where the fuck you going boy?"

Billy stopped in his tracks, he didn't have the upset stomach excuse tonight. He hadn't even thought of a reason to be here and that was a mistake. He hadn't expected any trouble and thought he was going through the motions. *Now what?*

The word *boy* didn't go unnoticed either. As he turned to face the voice, a body slammed him back against the wall, then moved closer, cutting him off, pinning him in place.

"I asked you a question."

"I'm taking a walk" Billy's answer seemed out of place, so he added, "I couldn't sleep."

"You're full of shit. You always slip around so quietly? Looks like you're snooping to me."

The idiot didn't just say that did he? Billy couldn't believe his ears, what was there to be snooping around about. The guy must be stupid, he sure let the cat out of the bag. But Billy knew he wouldn't get any further that night, at least not with this asshole watching.

"I don't know what you're talking about man. If you don't want me here, then I'm gone, simple as that." Billy stepped to the left to go around the guy towards the stairway.

The guy reached out, grabbing an arm. Billy forcefully pulled back surprised at the strength of the man's grip. But the guy held on, digging his fingers in. "That's right boy, you don't want to fuck with me. Now get your ass out of here."

Billy jerked his arm free. He wanted to settle it right there, but what end would that serve? Nursing his wounded pride, was part of being undercover. Besides, he was now sure that something was up.

With observers lurking around the ship, it would be hard to find out exactly what was going on. As he walked back to his bunk he realized that the only way he was getting any answers was to take out the observers. That meant the guy back there, or another like him.

Things seeming to be accelerating and he knew the case was going to come to a head shortly.

*****

S.S. Slate

Shanya cringed with each scream. Chakwania had been ripped out of the room, it was the only way to describe it. The beast had dragged her away without words, slamming the door as he left.

She's heard a door opening somewhere else in the hallway, the hinges squealing. It was a while before the door squealed again. She had assumed it was the beast leaving, but then the screaming had begun. Even covering her ears, she could hear Chakwania.

Shanya felt her strength waver, she struggled to stay focused. Holding her hands over her ears, she closed her eyes and started to sing softly. The words were from an old song about a beaver. She pictured a pond that had been dammed up at one end, then the beaver's house at the other.

The slight screams that still invaded her defenses must have been a bird in the forest or a chipmunk high in the tree.

It was what worked best at the moment, and Shanya clung to her vision.

CHAPTER 9

S.S. Slate

The night seemed to stretch forever. The door squealed open in the hallway and Shanya hoped that Chakwania was finally alone. That the other girl hadn't been brought back was concerning. Shanya didn't like being by herself. The whole situation seemed worse that way.

First Abby and then Chakwania, it could only be a matter of time before her turn came. It was going on three days without food, and Shanya was getting weak. Thinking of the deer again she knew he was full of energy and adrenaline when he stamped his hoof, how much did she have left?

Desperation was like a sack of potatoes on her shoulders, it kept pushing her will and spirit lower to the ground when she needed it to soar. Shanya had started wondering what she'd done to deserve the horror that she was certain was coming. Her head slumped forward, resting on her knees. Had she had it too easy and now there was a consequence?

She knew that Gitchee Manitou made things so that it was easy for the people. However one day Nanabozho decided to go see how the Anishinaabe were doing. To his surprise he didn't find them in the village hoeing their land, gathering berries, or fishing the streams.

Nanabozho found them in a grove of maple trees just lying on their backs with their mouths open, letting the maple syrup drip into their mouths. This was not right. Nanabozho took a bucket to the river and returned many times, pouring water over the maple trees, thinning the syrup. Now the syrup wasn't thick, but watery, and just barely sweet to the taste. Nanabozho was happy with his work, now the Indian would have to work to get the prize, gathering wood and building fires. The last thing he did was make sure the syrup would only flow at a certain time of year so as not to stop the fieldwork, fishing and hunting.

Shanya tried to tell herself if it was Nanabozho making her life harder, it had to be for a purpose. But she couldn't find it. The lessons were failing her, none of them were easing the constant dread she lived with.

Her nose was running from the cold and dampness of the steel room, she rubbed her shirt across it to clear it. It wasn't the only thing running, Shanya shivered violently, so hard it hurt. Time was running out.

*****

The crowded workers lounge vibrated with Steppenwolf banging off the walls, heavy smoke hung from the ceiling. The drinking crew all knew what was coming. All of them except the young kid. Jared always made sure to get them together. If they wanted fun it was going to be as a group. He knew that just one of them uninvolved left a loose thread. Everyone's participation ensured silence. No one wanted to incriminate themselves.

The others on the ship, working or clearly not interested, had settled into a not-seeing and not-believing mentality. Jared was okay with that, as long as they stayed away. The fact he'd influenced the hiring, and more importantly the firing, of workers, had helped him build an agreeable crew, one he knew and could predict.

It was Jared who got out the whiskey bottle, pouring shots for everyone. There was no room for hesitation or second-guessing. He knew after years with this crew that the booze wasn't necessary, they were used to the process and liked it as much as the captain and officer. Still, he wanted them laughing and ready to party. The memory was better that way, with less chance of regret tomorrow.

"What you guys think, time to have some fun?"

The cheers echoed around the room, anticipation had been building since they left port, and the crew shouted their approval.

"Bring your drinks. Let's go."

He led them down the stairs, waving the whiskey bottle like a drunken pied piper. Turning down the corridor into the storage areas, he opened the door to let them in. Once the door closed, the party heated up. Everyone had become used to this, and no one rushed anymore. Upstairs, the boys had drawn sticks and everyone knew their number.

First, the crew went quiet. The sight of a naked women tied over a crate never got old, it still carried the possibility of danger, and they knew what they were doing was a crime. Finally a whistle emerged from one of the men as he walked over to check out the goods.

MAUWEE NIBI

Someone lifted her head up by the hair to see her face, another reached underneath to grab a breast. Hands ran over her bent body, running from shoulder to ass.

"Okay boys, that's enough, I got first dibs," the lucky holder of number one pushed to the front. "Give me some room." The worker was laying down his claim on the girl, he had the low number. The others were reluctant to let go once they were that close, but managed to peel themselves away and retreat back near the door, giving their companion some room.

The conversation became excited, rising in pitch as some stared up at the ceiling or into the corners, while others less shy just watched.

Jared kept his eye on the rookie. He didn't do the hiring, but he sure made the decision of whether they stayed or not. The kid didn't know it, but it was how he performed here that was determining how long he lasted on his job, not how he did on deck. Deckhands that worked hard were a dime a dozen, those that kept their mouths shut were a lot more valuable.

When one of them was done with her he would stand over by the door zipping up his pants. Whoever had the next number made their way over to where the girl was tied to the stack of boxes, taking their turn.

The girl wasn't saying a word, she had no fight left. Jared wondered what had happened between her and the officer, but brushed the thought from his mind just as quick. Focus on what mattered.

Some of the men left as soon as they were done, others stood around to watch. As it got down to the kid's turn, Jared could see the confusion on the boy's face. He hadn't known what the hell they were doing when they'd started drawing numbers in the lounge.

When someone said it was to see what order they got laid in, Ronnie froze, looking around questioningly. Jared had kept the stick with the highest number in his own hand.

"Don't worry kid, I got the last number here for you, you get to go last." It hadn't helped Ronnie sort out his thoughts. As the count got to his number, the kid began to shift his weight from foot to foot, Jared grinned as he noticed the sweat making the kid's face shine.

"All right guys, clear out. Let the rookie have his turn. I think he may be a virgin."

The guys laughed out loud, whistling it up, "Go get her rookie."

Jared slammed the hatch door behind the last crewman and stood in front of it with his arms folded. Smiling, he waited while Ronnie stared at the girl. "All right kid, go have some fun."

The kid turned towards Jared, "I don't think I want to." His face was turning a pale color.

"You don't got a choice kid. Not if you want to stay on this crew." He let the consequences sink in. He didn't normally force this decision on people, but this kid was so young he could be forced to comply and become a part of it, willing or not. Jared knew when you could manipulate, you did.

"Get over there, rub your hands on her, squeeze a tit or something, you'll figure it out." Jared laughed to himself, the kid had no fucking clue. This was a bad time for his mama's morals to kick in.

Jared had to give the rookie credit, in the end the kid walked over and stared, then he started to touch and caress the girl. Once Jared was sure the kid was involved, he left the room. Unlike some others, he had no interest in watching.

A few minutes later the kid slipped through the slightly open door. He was fumbling with his belt buckle as he looked up awkwardly at Jared, forcing a smile.

"Alright kid. Keep this to yourself. You know what loose lips do to ships." Jared raised a finger in warning, waving it back and forth. The kid watched the finger and then saw the real warning, making note of the darkness in Jared's eyes.

As the boy walked away, Jared re-entered the room. If there was any remorse or sympathy he would have been gentle, but Jared didn't know those feelings. He undid the Indian and dragged her towards the door.

She tried to reach down and pull her pants up so her feet could move, but he never gave her the time. He jerked her down the hall, holding her up by the arm. Opening the storeroom hatch he pushed her in and let her fall just inside the door, shutting it behind her.

He didn't want to go in himself because he had to wait until the next night for his turn, and he'd noticed he was becoming obsessed with the one girl. Seeing her now after watching all the boys have fun might tip him over the edge, he might lose the hold he had on his control.

As he headed back towards his bunk he couldn't help the excitement he was feeling. *Tomorrow baby, and you're mine.*

*****

S.S. Forester

Billy woke to the ship bell sounding so early that the sky outside his window was barely grey. A quick look at the wristwatch lying on top of his jeans showed that it was four-thirty. With no idea what was going on, he headed to the deck looking for someone to ask what was happening.

The deckhand pointed. "Docking in Green Bay."

Billy walked back to the bunk and lay down. He was in Wisconsin on the American side. Lake Michigan was new to him, all he'd ever seen was the big Superior. He was too tired to get up, and too awake to get back to sleep.

He knew he should get some more shut-eye, he'd be busy in the next few hours as the cargo was unloaded. Billy pulled the blanket over his head. Now his feet stuck out the bottom. Curling up was the only solution, eventually he was covered, but his knees were mashed against the wall.

With his eyes closed, he hoped for sleep. Something he hadn't been getting enough of.

His mind racing, he calculated the outcomes, he would work all day, but tonight would be the night. All hell was about to break loose.

*****

S. S. Slate

The door opened suddenly and Chakwania was dumped inside before the steel hatch slammed closed again. Shanya stayed where she was, waiting to see what the young woman did.

MAUWEE NIBI

A minute went by then another. Shanya realized the girl wasn't going to move. Then the thought hit her that maybe she couldn't move. Perhaps she was in pain or had been hurt. Shanya stood on wobbly legs stepping closer to Chakwania who was lying in a heap, her body twisted onto itself, legs tangled up in what? Shanya leaned closer in the dark and realized in was the girl's jeans around her ankles.

Horror filled her every pore as she understood the girl was naked. Shanya sat down next to the other girl and started to straighten her legs and pull up on her pants. To accomplish the task Chakwania was forced to sit up and straighten out, Shanya looked her in the face and the other girl started to cry soundlessly, tears slowly trickling down her cheeks.

With no idea what to say, she had no lessons for this situation. She didn't have time to think about it, but she was starting to have an annoyance with the lessons at this point. They were useless.

Chakwania was the most important thing right now, and Shanya reached out to hold her. She pulled the wounded girl in tight and offered the care she'd want herself after what must have happened.

She tried to offer comfort as her own mind screamed in fear. Now she had an idea what to expect and it scared her to the core.

CHAPTER 10

S.S. Slate

Shanya wanted to keep track of time. Not because it mattered, but because she needed something to hold on to. Four days now. It was long enough for everyone to know she was missing. Long enough for her to lose hope.

It happened a lot to natives, everyone knew someone who had disappeared. She thought of her mother, and quickly pushed the image aside. It hurt too much to think about her, to imagine what she would be thinking. Her parents would blame themselves for letting her go, even though Shanya had the right. That she'd pushed them into accepting her decision was the hard part to deal with at this point.

It seemed that with each day, she not only got farther from home but further from her beliefs. Her spirit was dimming in the confines of the steel cage. She'd finally been fed earlier in the day, it had tasted bland, wooden, and hadn't helped her feel any better.

Chakwania had been taken out again a couple hours ago by the beast, and she knew they had just gone next door as the door squealed open again down the hallway. Why hadn't she been taken yet? She stopped that thought as quickly as it started. Don't ask for trouble, she told herself. Be happy it hasn't happened.

It was hard to stay detached. They had been taken together, and right or wrong, Shanya felt a connection to the other girls. And she kept wondering about Abby. The young one had been gone for two days at that point. Where was she? Shaking her head in denial, Shanya shivered with all the unwanted images that were stuck in her mind. She was losing perspective, her world was becoming smaller with each day.

The tears were warm sliding down her cheeks, she heard her voice and hadn't realized she was talking, "I'm sorry mother."

*****

The workers lounge was full, the crew piled in together. Liquor flowed as the men invented toasts and reasons to knock back another one. Jared noted that the boys were a lot happier once they'd been serviced.

The blaring tunes bounced off the walls in the confines of the small room. Everything was shaking. Jared always made sure the first night was a group thing, he wanted everyone committed to the project. This trip would be no different than any other, except this time he wasn't sharing with them. He tipped up the beer, taking a long slow swallow.

The last day had been hectic, the freighter had come through the St. Clair river system at the bottom of Lake Huron. The small Lake St. Clair was followed by the Detroit River.

They'd docked in Cleveland last night, which was their first stop on Lake Erie.

Tonight it was Buffalo, New York. Now they would turn around and start the return run.

Lakers plied the Great Lakes from spring break-up until ice stopped them each winter.

A new tune started. Aerosmith broke through his thoughts for a moment.

The Great Lakes were no joke to anyone who knew them. Especially the weather. Wave height on a lake was figured out by wind speed and fetch. Fetch being how long of a water surface you had without obstructions like islands to break up the wind.

The second worst lake, Michigan, has a potential for thirty-foot waves. Superior has the incredible potential for eighty-foot waves. Everyone knew the story of the Edmunds Fitzgerald and many seamen believed it must have been hit by one of the big waves.

His beer empty, Jared called for another. As he listened to a pair of deckhands talking about the Indian downstairs his mind did a quick switch to his own girl in the storeroom. Someone tapped him on the shoulder with a cold beer and he reached back for it. It would be a quick one, a smile played across his face, but his eyes narrowed as he unconsciously ground his teeth.

*****

Hans grabbed on to Abby as she tried to skirt around him, heading for the door. He laughed out loud, "Come here you bitch."

100

The honeymoon was over. Experiment might be a better word. He squeezed her wrist and twisted her towards the table in the corner. It was a game he liked to play, plying them with booze and cigarettes, seeing how far he could get them to go without using force. But after a while that became boring, and he just imposed his own will.

Two nights ago the booze and cigarettes along with some conversation and attention had been the start. After a few hours of nursing her along, he'd told her he didn't want to cause trouble with anyone, but he'd really like a blowjob. Watching her decide to do it on her own was priceless. He'd spread his legs and she'd crawled right up.

The next night, after she'd had a good night's sleep in his bed, he'd explained to her she was better off with him in the comfort of the Captain's stateroom. "You could stay here," he offered it up as an invitation, "or you can end up with the other men. I'm not sure how nice they are."

When he asked her later if she wanted to leave or stay with him, she'd been quick to ask to stay. Later that night in bed he'd started to caress her, before lifting his overweight body on top of hers. He took as long as he felt like, using the opportunity to enjoy himself. She excited the hell out of him.

That's where it always went downhill. Hans knew he wanted more than she was most likely willing to give. The game was usually over when he started getting rough, or making demands that she didn't like.

As much as he liked the role of making her want to please him in the beginning, he liked the stage that was coming right now. Hans turned her body towards his and lifted her by the waist onto the table. They were both naked. When he set her ass on the wooden surface she started to struggle again, trying to get to her feet.

Hans pushed her and she ended up on her back. When she tried to kick out, he moved between her legs, spreading them wide. She kept attempting to lift her body off the table, trying to sit up, so Hans grabbed one wrist and then the other.

Placing them together, he used one hand to pin them to her chest. He noticed how small her wrists looked in his oversized fists, but it didn't matter, he had her where he wanted her.

*****

S.S. Forester

The rookie cop was all business. He'd spent the entire day mentally preparing for his next task. Every move he made was planned as he worked his way through the darkness. It was a funny thing about working different types of undercover, his in particular.

There was a mandate, but no set expectations. Because of that, there were no right or wrong moves. An officer had to decide when and if he came out of hiding. Something might force him to act, or he may stay under for years.

He hadn't been given much direction in Thunder Bay, but Billy didn't expect they wanted him riding the lakes on the same boat forever. He figured they hadn't given him direction because the situation had to be played out as it came, by Billy's rules and timetable, no one else was there.

Forcing his breathing to even out, he got closer to the stairway. Listening from his bunk all night he'd heard at least three different sets of sounds as people came and went from the sleeping quarters. Tonight he was finding out where they had gone.

At the entrance to the stairwell he made shuffling noises with his feet, then moved to the side of the door. He wasn't walking into another trap. It was better if he was the one doing the hunting.

Sure enough the rustling noise enticed someone to come up the stairs. It was a mistake to be staked out in the same place as the night before, and the guy would pay. Billy waited until the man was halfway up the stairs, then he tossed a small bag he'd made of cloth wrapped around a water bottle.

It landed with a bounce, then another before settling, the cloth slowing the spring of the plastic bottle. He'd wanted the diversion to stop bouncing quickly, to sound like a person moving a few steps. The sentry came out the door, already turning towards the sound, which was his second mistake.

As the guy stopped in mid-stride, realizing there was nobody there and beginning to turn around, Billy hit him for the first time. The shot ended up just a little high, catching the man with a glancing blow on the side of his head above the ear.

There was shock on the sentry's face as he started to react, but Billy's second punch was already on the way. It slammed into the guy's forehead as he managed to drop an inch or two, just enough to save his nose and hurt Billy's hand.

The seaman stumbled back and fell against the wall. Wanting to take advantage, Billy rushed in to hit him again. The guy came back off the wall using it for leverage, he was mounting his own charge at Billy. He was fighting back.

The two men swung as their bodies collided, both of them finding skin. Billy rocked as another shot hit his shoulder. Swinging from in close, he connected with the seaman's jaw. It was strange, but it seemed the guy had left his face open and stepped forward at the last second, either way, down he went.

The noise had to have alerted others and the cop looked around, expecting someone else to come through the door. When no one did, he took a long breath to slow his heart down. *'Keep moving'* echoed in his head.

Billy took the stairs two at a time, landing in the hallway below. He stood for a moment and just listened. There were music and voices at the end of the hall that pulled him in that direction. Around the corner he found a door to a storage area. Sound escaped under the door where a crack of light leaked into the hallway. *This was it.*

There was no turning back now. Billy sucked in a long stream of air through his nose. His chest pumped in and out. Ready for anything, he reached out and pulled the door open, stepping quickly inside.

"Hey guys! What's up?" He had the words out before his eyes caught up to the scene in front of him.

Everyone looked up in shock. Six men sat around a large table in the middle of the room, playing cards. His first guess was poker. Money heaped in front of the players and beer bottles lined up around the table were a dead giveaway.

"Shit." The seaman holding the deck of cards looked pissed.

Billy couldn't believe it. *Just a card game. What the hell?* Why all the security and why the goons in the hall? Before he could contemplate any more, he got his answer.

"Hey rookie. The captain don't like gambling on his boat. You don't got a big mouth do you?"

Billy didn't know what to say. "Hey I'm just checking the ship out. I could care less about cards." Shrugging his shoulders, he walked back out the door.

There was an expectation that someone might jump his back, but it didn't happen and no one waited for him at the top of the stairs. He wondered where the guard had gone, but had more important things on his mind.

Billy climbed into his bunk and pulled out his cell phone for the first time since he'd left Thunder Bay. The text was simple and direct.

Blackwood. Nothing here. Need to change ships.

Leaning back on the bunk, there was a sense of satisfaction. He had rooted out the situation, realized the waste of time, and was going to move forward somehow.

That answer came in a return text.

Disembark Milwaukee.

He didn't know what was waiting in Milwaukee, or how head office knew he would end up there, but it didn't matter.

What mattered was that they agreed. He had to find another freighter.

*****

The figure leaned over his desk, tapping his pen against the wooden surface. He was done writing up his report and he stared at the last line.

Individual seemed angered at the discovery of a cash card game.

A smile played across the face, the individual had been disappointed. He wondered what it would take for the individual to be satisfied. He nodded to himself. It was looking good.

*****

Jared slammed the door shut before turning to the native. Watching the fear explode in the girl's face, he started towards her. It made his own adrenaline surge in anticipation. His pupils dilated as he focused on her.

There was so much to enjoy at this moment. He marveled at the rush he got just before the violence began. In the pen you could sense when something was going to happen and everyone became tense. Jared excelled in the confusion, ruling during the chaos, and this was no different.

The girl was off the floor and running. There was no place to go and he angled her back towards the corner where eventually she was trapped.

"You want to make this easy bitch. It'll be better for you."

He watched her look side-to-side like an injured animal. Jared jumped forward at the same moment she sprang away from the corner. He caught her in midflight and spun her back towards the wall as she screamed, reefing on her tiny arm in the process.

"Come here you fucking squaw."

*****

Shanya jumped when the door opened, there was no one else left but her. The beast was starting her way. Fear took over, shear panic hit her, and she started to run.

Ten steps to the closest wall and ten back to the other. Behind a crate and back out, there was nowhere to go, and he kept getting closer. She didn't dare get close enough that he could grab her, and now she was stuck in the corner.

She couldn't stamp her foot, but she was going to bolt. Looking both ways offered no options and she made a split-second decision, suddenly charging left. The beast reacted at the same time and grabbed her.

She realized that the screams were her own as he slammed her back against the wall. He had her wrist, and she yanked at it trying to get it free. Out of nowhere she suddenly swung out with her other hand and hit her attacker in the face. With fear propelling her actions she swung her arm as many times as she could, hitting him around the head as he laughed, moving left and right to avoid her blows.

Shanya let all the anger out as her feet joined in, kicking at the man's legs. She heard the next words he said, "You crazy bitch." But she never saw his fist. There was a second where she was still there, then the room was tilted and blurred, and she was sure she was falling.

CHAPTER 11

S.S. Slate

The darkness was welcomed now. The pain was all she could feel. Shanya cuddled herself, rubbing her hands up and down her legs, creating friction and heat. Her sobbing came in sporadic bursts that she had no control over.

Her head was sore from the punch to the forehead. She had touched the spot once and the bump shocked her, she wouldn't touch it again.

The desperation was becoming overwhelming. Shanya had been struggling to keep her mind from sinking for days, now she was just free falling.

Not allowing herself to think of home, she buried her face in her knees. There was no facing her parents now after what had happened. The violation to the core of her soul made her feel dirty and worthless. Everyone would look down at her.

Everything had changed in an instant. Beliefs that had been a part of her for years suddenly became irrelevant. If this was the real world, how would she cope? Horribly, was the answer.

Flashes of the attack kept surfacing. If there was any pride in her someplace, it was smothered by sorrow. She had fought the beast with all her might, never giving in. It provided the only positive feelings she'd had in days.

The pain that came with it was another thing. How many times could she go through that? Her legs were so bruised she could hardly move them. The bump on her forehead ached constantly, and both the actions of getting up or sitting down made her wince.

She knew there was no escaping it. Her time had come, and now the nightmare would play out to whatever conclusion it was destined.

The panic that kept overtaking her was hard to control. The breaths came quick, faster than normal. She felt trapped, and her chest felt like it was collapsing. Shanya closed her eyes to focus on her breathing. In and out. Slower. Calmer.

She thought she was going to lose her sanity and with it her last chance to stay alert and aware of her surroundings. Once more she slowed herself down and tried to pull herself together.

Trying to keep the lessons out of her head, she realized they hadn't helped her, and now they only had the effect of making her angry. She wondered what use were the lessons if they didn't help.

The thought hit her like a tree falling on her head. Had she been fooled, or seen everything from the wrong light? Then she saw Nanabozho and the cranberries.

Nanabozho was walking beside the lake when he saw cranberries in the shallow water. Sticking his hand in the water he couldn't reach the berries. After endless attempts, Nanabozho gave up using his hands and stuck his face in the water. When this also failed, he stood and dove into the lake.

To his surprise the rocks in the shallow water hurt his face. Nanabozho gave up and lay on the shore to rest. When he opened his eyes, there were the berries hanging on a branch above the water. Realizing he was only seeing the reflection in the water Nanabozho stomped away in anger, not even taking the berries.

Shanya asked herself if she was looking in the wrong place. Was she looking at it from the best angle? What possible way was there to be positive?

No matter how hard she tried, conversations she'd had with her mother kept surfacing in her thoughts. It angered her at this point, because they brought no comfort. Shanya pictured the garden, her mother's words in her ears.

"You can learn from anything Shanya. You might not use it right away, but you may use it sometime later in your life."

Shanya's head swung side-to-side unconsciously, realizing how stupid that sounded, just how out of touch with her reality it was. There was no hope left now, no good ending to this nightmare. Her life had taken a turn for the worse and she knew her concern about it all was leaving fast.

The words "later in life" stuck with her. From this point on Shanya didn't think there'd be one.

Worse, she didn't care.

*****

The kid was pissed, but he wasn't going to complain or put up a fight, so Jared continued to harass him.

"You sure you put it in her Ronnie?" The rest of the guys were laughing themselves silly. "Or were you just pretending?"

"I know what to do with a woman." The kid wasn't rolling over completely.

"A woman? Jesus Christ boys, he thinks he could handle a woman. He couldn't even make a girl squeal. How's he going to handle a woman?"

Ronnie's face went beet red, he visibly vibrated with anger.

Jared didn't let up, it was another thing you learned in the house of barbed wire. Once you had the upper hand, you used it and reminded those under you where they stood. This kid would be fish bait in prison.

"Hey boys, I think we might have a queer in our crew. This one might be a little on the girly side." The room was loud with hoots and hollers.

Jared watched the kid flex his fists once. He was sure the boy didn't know he'd even done it, it was involuntary. To Jared it was close to a threat. *Don't do something you can't recover from son.* Don't push the wrong button.

"Don't hold it against the kid boys. He was born that way." The kid shook his head and charged out of the room. *Good choice kid.* That would have been a mistake. Jared's shoulders relaxed. He'd flexed up in response to the kid's actions, and relaxed just as quickly when he left.

A little later Jared slapped the shot glass down on the table, they were celebrating tonight. He joined in the conversation as they finished off another night on the lake. At this time most were in their bunks, but the hard-core drinkers were still pouring down the last of their beers.

Jared was still high on the fun he'd had with the native girl earlier. Multiple thoughts were circling at the same time. Having his own woman to play with was an improvement. He should have done it a lot earlier, years ago. With this one he didn't feel the need to get everything over with as quickly as he could before the others got at her. No, this one he could take his time with.

Chuckling to himself, he realized there hadn't been much taking his time earlier. Feisty was the word that came to mind, that – and sexy as hell. The body on her was perfect, firmest shape he'd ever seen. The twitch between his legs spread the smile on his face wider. The feeling of ownership felt good. He tipped back the beer and reached for the liquor bottle at the same time. He owned her, so now he would enjoy her.

With a finger on his forehead, he traced the slice caused by her fingernail as she'd fought back. Jared loved the action, he could see it happening over and over. He'd ripped at her clothes, encouraged and spurred forward by glimpses of her warm skin. It had drawn him in like a bear to honey. She'd lashed out, and he hit her open-handed across the face.

The kicking had caused him a moment of annoyance, and he'd almost hit her hard. Instead he gave her a short straight punch in the forehead. It had knocked her out, allowing him to lay her back onto the pile of boxes. He was already between her legs when she woke up and started to kick out again.

The phrase 'wild thing' came to mind as Jared held each leg tightly while he continued to use her. He was hard again now, the liquor, the booze, the vivid memories still so fresh.

He couldn't stop thinking about the native. She was different that the rest he'd had, but he still couldn't put a finger on what it was about her. His pants bulged as he realized the night might not be done yet.

*****

The captain's room was almost dark, the light in the corner was turned down low. Hans sat in his leather chair, feet propped up on the table, watching the young girl curled up in his bed. He nursed his fourth shot since arriving from the bridge half an hour ago.

He couldn't get much more bothered than he'd been the last few days. Horny as hell was more like it. The girl was so young it was a sin. That's what his wife would call it.

Hans cringed at the thought. The wife of his kids and that was about it these days. They lived two separate lives anyway. He was lucky to get laid when he was in port because she was always laying down rules and expectations.

He remembered back in the beginning, coming home and they would party his whole leave away. Nights out in clubs and restaurants, sex late into the night, even if it was always missionary. It was odd to actually have any work to do around the place.

Now there was a list as long as his arm the moment he walked in the door. This needs fixing or that needs painting. The list didn't leave any time to unwind or enjoy his limited time off. The wife was busy with this group or another, usually with plans already set long before he got home.

Shit, all he wanted was a beer, some ass and a big screen for a few weeks – but that was too much to ask. If the bitch smelled booze there was no sex at all. No booze and it was boring as hell with her. Hans lifted his head, he'd been staring at the floor instead of the gorgeous piece he had in the room.

He was going to take her again, wouldn't even bother waking her first, just climb on. And he was going to drink first. Hans poured another shot. His leaves had become a chore, and this had become his break to look forward to. There was no doubt he looked forward to this more than going home.

Here anticipation ruled his thoughts. One more shot – maybe two. Hans stared at the bed, he'd be there soon.

*****

S.S. Forester

The freighter left Green Bay during the night. Billy worked his shift on Michigan as they plowed south along the west side of the lake, heading towards Milwaukee, which was a coincidence, cause that was where he'd been told to disembark. Something was off, but he couldn't put his finger on it.

He went about his business, keeping his head down, expecting trouble at any time for his actions the night before. The guard he'd dropped had to be pissed, and retaliation could be around the corner. Instead, he seemed to get along with everyone better.

A couple of guys nodded his way when he walked past, and another said hello out on the deck. He wasn't sure, but he thought he caught others looking at him when he wasn't looking. It was like they were talking about him.

In the end it didn't matter, Billy was sure the ship was clean. He had a job to do and he had to stick with it. He waited until near the end of the day to make his move. As the shift ended, he climbed up the stairs towards the bridge instead of heading below for a shower.

Hesitating before opening the door to the bridge, and getting his face straight, he reviewed his answers. On entering he was relieved to see the captain was by himself, another crewman was present but he was in the back, bent over some instruments.

Billy didn't waste time, he wanted the conversation to be private.

"You have a minute Captain?"

The older man turned his gray beard towards the newcomer, folding his bushy eyebrows together. "Who are you?"

"Blackwood, sir. I need just a moment of your time."

The man seemed to think about it a second, then he nodded, "Hurry it up son, I don't have all day."

The man was in a rush. It didn't bother Billy at all, he wanted it over quick as well. "I'm leaving at the next port sir."

The captain registered the news, eyebrows rising, then they folding together again. "What the fuck you talking about? You're quitting?"

Billy hated the sound of the words. He wasn't a quitter, but he knew there was no other way to get off the freighter. He wasn't going to argue about it. "Yes, sir."

He watched the captain stare out the window for a few minutes, "You want to tell me why?"

It was going to be a lie, but then so would any answer he gave. What was one lie over another? Who cared which one was better?

"It's just not a good fit sir. I need to try a different crew."

He wasn't ready for the captain's reply, but in the end he got the result he wanted.

"You useless piece of shit, don't ask me for a reference. You won't like it. You get your ass off this ship as soon as we dock in Milwaukee." The Captain paused a second, "Or I'll throw you off."

Billy knew when a conversation was over, and this one was clearly there. "Thank you sir." He headed out the door relieved to be over with it. Now he could look forward.

Forward to what? He wasn't sure, more of the same he assumed, but only time would tell. It registered as he walked away that headquarters had been right, the ship was headed to Milwaukee. For some reason that detail was important, but he shook the strangeness off.

*****

Captain Flynn watched the young native leave the bridge. He smiled to himself, knowing that he'd played his part well. The kid would be sure to think the captain was pissed. Flynn would've preferred more time together, but sometimes the time tables had a life of their own. It wouldn't be the first time, nor would it be the last if his experience meant anything.

Opening up the logbook, he made a daily entry. This one would be his last he figured. A summary was more to the point. He had to admit there wasn't much to pick at.

Finally, he closed the book and smiled, something he was doing more and more often when it came to that young man. The observed individual would do all right, and that was what he put in the logbook.

MAUWEE NIBI

He looked out across the lake, knowing it could be a lonely place at the best of times. Reaching up, he reset his hat in the right place, a long-time habit. A hand groomed the bushy beard as he watched the sun begin to set. Flynn spoke out loud to no one in particular. "You're on your own now."

CHAPTER 12

S.S. Slate

Rattling at the door for the second time that evening jerked Shanya from her sorrow. Her heart jumped once as the fear gripped her. Her eyes searched the darkness, but there was nowhere to hide.

The boots walked into the light, it was him again. Shanya screamed inside her head, it was too soon. She wasn't ready to fight again, there was still too much pain.

Trying to get to her feet, she fell back in place. Looking up, he was almost on her. Quickly she jumped up to her feet, forcing her legs to work.

"You ready for some more?" The words hit her like bricks. There would be no rest with this monster.

She pushed away from the crate she'd been leaning against and headed for the back of the room, even though there was only a corner there.

He jumped forward, faster than she thought he could, stopping her movement, and pinning her to the wall. The alcohol he reeked of was disgusting.

This close, she couldn't avoid seeing him. The front half of his head was bald, rough curly hair tangling in the back. Shanya could see old scars among the pockmarks along with the fresh one she'd put there.

She wondered if all the others were from women like her. The guy was muscled – but not overly big. He looked like a criminal, and guys like that were in fights a lot.

"You still got some fight left honey?" He pressed against her as she tried to turn her face away.

When his hands landed on her shoulders and started to push her down to the floor, Shanya resisted. Her feet spread out for stability and she forced her knees to lock in place.

"Okay bitch. Let's do it your way."

The punch to the stomach knocked the wind right out of her. All her effort went to sucking in air, to staying conscious. She realized as she wheezed in air – she was sliding down the wall.

Shanya fought the stars that floated through her vision, she sank to the ground then felt herself jerked up onto her knees. She heard a sound that was familiar and it forced her to focus. She watched through a daze at the zipper sliding down. The words echoed in her head.

"Now you listen squaw."

*****

"Now you listen squaw, this is your last chance." He moved closer, putting it in her face, rubbing against her.

Grabbing her hair hard, he twisted until he felt her reacting to the pain. Smiling, his excitement grew. "Do it, or I'm really going to hurt you."

Jared was sure she was scared shitless, that made it all the more rewarding. He pinned her head against the wall and continued to move against her. She started to struggle, and when she moved her head to the side he slapped her hard moving her face back in place. Four more times she tried, and his response was the same each time.

She needed to learn her place, because he wasn't going to fight her every time, besides she would be worse for wear if that happened. When he was sure there was no more resistance, he stilled her head and leaned forward. With the pleasure flowing through his system, Jared took a deep breath as his head tilted back and his body started to rock.

*****

S.S. Forester

The rusty old freighter made its way into Milwaukee early in the day. Billy realized he had no idea what day of the week it was, or the date. Time was hard to keep track of on the water. Between working and sleeping at strange hours, nothing seemed normal.

He helped the crew land the freighter and unload some cargo. It wasn't much, four large skids of boxes strapped with metal bands. The skids were quickly craned over the side and set on the dock.

Billy hadn't planned to talk with anyone. He hadn't been on the Forester long enough to make any friends – enemies maybe, but that was it. But as he went to walk down the gangway, he noticed some of the crew standing along the side rail, watching. Strange.

For some reason he looked back over his shoulder up at the bridge, for a moment he was sure he saw someone step away. Who, he wasn't sure, the sun's glare made it hard to see through the reflecting glass.

Walking along the dock he was unsure what he was supposed to do next. Headquarters had said to get off in Milwaukee, but nothing more. Something wasn't quite right about all this, and Billy racked his brain trying to put a finger on what it was, but it still floated outside of reach

The S. S. Forester had been part of that weird feeling, and he looked back over his shoulder at the freighter as he walked away. The lines were being cast off, and they were preparing to head back onto the lake. With nothing else to go on, the feelings he'd been working on drifted away.

What next? Another freighter. He didn't think it would be that easy, but Billy started talking to the few workers wandering along the boats tied up at the docks as he made his way along the pier.

Most said that no one was looking. A couple had sought out their captain's to be sure. But in the end, as he'd expected, there was no one in need of a ratings crewman. How long would he be here? Should he find a computer and get his name on the list looking for work?

He was approached twice during the day, and once as he walked the docks in the dark. Security couldn't drive past without questioning him. He'd felt it before, but now he was sure what it must feel like being black in some States, right away assumed guilty of something. It was the paperwork he had in his wallet, the certificate as a licensed ratings crewman that gave him right to be there. After flashing his paperwork they'd reluctantly left him alone.

Billy walked in the dark to pass the time and found the service docks where ships were laid up for repair and upgrading. Then the storage docks where worn out ships were tied up looking decayed from years of sitting.

To his surprise, he recognized one of the freighters at the end of the dock. He carefully worked his way close enough to confirm his initial impression then left the area to stay unnoticed. For some reason the S. S. Forester was docked in the back of the shipyard.

Billy was sure they had been casting off lines to head back out on the water earlier in the day. They must have been just moving somewhere else in the yard.

By the time Billy got back to the main dock he was getting tired. He didn't want to walk into town and find a hotel, he couldn't afford to miss any freighters.

You're undercover buddy, you're getting a great opportunity. Billy could see the red haired, puffy-faced commander in Thunder Bay. Sleeping on a bench wasn't much better than a bunk.

Folding his arms across his chest, he laid his back on the bench. After closing his eyes and trying to rest, he wondered what his next ship would be like, what kind of crew it would have.

As he lay there trying to keep the heat in and the cool air out, he smiled for the first time in a week. This was his new life, a Mountie on the case. And more importantly, now that he was out there doing the job, he could see he was capable.

At that moment any doubts he'd had in himself were gone. He could do this.

CHAPTER 13

S.S. Slate

Jared smirked, relaxing back into the lumpy couch, legs propped up on the small table. It had been a long day, but after dinner and a few beers it was starting to get better. It was going to be a long night.

Toledo was their last stop on Lake Erie they would be heading up through the Detroit River and St Clair system to Lake Huron. He'd stayed on shift late, giving some of the boys a chance to grab an early meal.

By eleven o'clock most of them had bunked out for the night. One more beer and he'd head down to see her. It was addictive, and he wasn't just talking the sex.

Having learned to take advantage, he discovered that it was intoxicating to hold power over someone. Some people liked to restore old cars, or lay down miles on a motorcycle. He liked watching people submit.

People around him found out quick enough, if you didn't stand up for yourself physically, he was going to take what he could, favors, money, head or ass. His nature was to take over, his experience reinforced it. It was an easy step from dominating one, to shepherding a flock.

That first stint in juvie was a shock, learning about gangs, hierarchy, and racism. Before that he had been just a regular schoolyard bully, you learned quick that everyone in juvie had been a bully. Spending time in the big house, he fought to own a cell, then to keep it. He'd learned early and often that there was always someone ready to take what was yours, if you let them.

The second beer disappeared quickly. Pausing, he stared at the empty bottle, realizing he was wasting time. From long habit Jared dropped it in the beer case before heading out of the lounge.

Standing above her in the storeroom he could tell something was different. Leaning against a cardboard box with her eyes closed she was unnaturally still.

Suddenly, she jumped to her feet and started to run. That was more like it, he bared his teeth and took off after her. Stopping in the corner, she stood there, frozen, which again seemed odd. Jared walked up to her and put his hands around her waist.

Out of nowhere she ducked down, bending at the waist before he could do anything. As he reached to grab her, she sank further until she lay on the floor. What the hell was this?

He'd expected another fight, and then another forced submission. Jared stood there staring at the girl, "You lost your mind bitch?"

She was lying there staring up at the ceiling. Was she inviting him? He reached down and pulled at her shirt, there was no resistance, then her pant leg. Still no response.

Not sure how to take the situation, Jared felt his anger turn to excitement. Getting down on his knees, he started to take her clothes off, something that he never did, unbuttoning her shirt and pulling out a floppy arm before pulling the cotton out from under her. Jared sucked in a quick lungful of air, holding it in a second before letting it out with a whistle. Look at her, you bugger.

He undid her jeans and pulled them off as well. She was beautiful. He took the time to stare at her. Hesitating, he examined her carefully. Something didn't seem right. Was she up to something? Jared looked around the room suddenly, realizing his guard was down.

Nothing moved, there was nothing to fear. Looking back at her, he couldn't get started. He never did more than drop his zipper most times, if his pants fell down it didn't matter. Now he was thinking about taking all his clothes off.

Hesitating once more, he looked back at the door to ensure it was closed. Decision made, he discarded his clothes in a heap. Again he took a moment to stare at her figure before lowering himself down to the cold floor.

He wasn't sure what spooked him more, that she wasn't fighting back, or that he was being gentle. He chuckled. Neither mattered.

*****

If Shanya had been keeping track of time she would have known she was on her sixth day in captivity, but she no longer was. Instead, her eyes were closed and she ran free in the forest. The wind blew and the trees and branches swayed across her path. She felt alive again.

She couldn't remember why she ran, but it invigorated her. She pushed harder, running on a trail she could only see faintly, like it had been used many years ago. As her feet pounded into the soft forest floor she looked up, the sky never looked so blue. An eagle soared above, the glimpses through the treetops kept tugging at her.

Finally a clearing opened up, and Shanya slowed to a stop. Her senses were still catching up as the scent of grasses and wildflowers invaded her nose. She paused, was everything always this bright? The forest seemed special in some way, more alive than usual.

Atop a large rock on the right side of the clearing, Shanya wrapped her arms around her knees and relaxed, enjoying the peace. The eagle was off to her left, high above the birches that ringed the opening. Tilting her head back, she watched it circle in search of food.

It might be unusual on some level, but she wanted to take the time to investigate everything she could see. Her eyes settled on the lichen that was growing on the top of her rock.

The grey and green and orange colours intrigued her. How long did it take to grow? She focused in on the patterns and abstract shape of the fungus. Her mind was going deeper. What was lichen for?

Something was echoing in the wind. It sounded like a name, but it was unrecognizable. She wobbled on the rock while something unseen pulled and pushed at her, as she looked around, she didn't see anything. Then more words spoken on the wind. *Chakwania?* It meant something to her, but she didn't know why.

The sound kept repeating itself, like someone was talking to her. Looking around, she couldn't see anything but the clearing in the forest. Was someone else there?

It seemed like hours passed as she investigated this place, moving from flower to tree, butterfly to grasshopper. Everything seemed magical today.

Something made a noise and Shanya froze. A handful of small birds flew away, fluttering from tree-to-tree getting away from the area. They knew something was coming, so did she. She sprang to her feet, sprinting across the clearing, looking for a trail. Her eyes caught a faint depression leading into the underbrush, and she leaned in that direction as her feet flew across the grass.

There was nothing obvious to follow, but she surged forward anyway, one arm up shielding her face from the branches that snatched at her as she ran. She thought there might be marks on the ground. She continued racing forward. It seemed the trees were closing in as her options were getting fewer with every step.

Panting, Shanya stopped running and took stock. She could keep trying to find a trail, make a new one, or turn back to find where she got off-track in the first place. The hair on her neck stood up as she tried to catch her breath. Which way?

Desperation kicked in and she launched herself forward, determined to find the trail. It had to be there somewhere. The trees closed in at once, and she ducked to avoid a large branch, then had to go even lower to get under the next one.

Suddenly, she was on the ground, lying on her back. She couldn't believe what was happening, the tree branches were pinning her down and pulling at her at the same time. A child of the forest, she knew there was no fighting with nature and she let herself go. The branches rolled her around, pulling at her clothes.

She stared up at the sky, trying to find the eagle. Was he still soaring above?

*****

Milwaukee

It took a second for Billy to figure out where he was when he opened his eyes, then the old bench he'd slept on dug into his spine. He'd found somewhere away from the docks, but still on yard property.

Last night he had realized he was better off staying put even though it pissed him off. He knew how natives were assumed to be drunks and a potential problem in a lot of people's eyes. He didn't need any trouble in a city that was new to him.

At the back of the yard, where the maintenance sheds stood, he found the old bench, three two-by-fours to sit on, but one was broken. Luckily the seatback was there and Billy was able to lean against it for support, instead of sagging through the opening in the seat.

It wasn't long before the industrial sounds of the docks started to pick up. Billy heard the far-away sound of the cranes, lifting cargo in or out of the freighters. There was no hurry, but he still managed to get up off the bench. Then the aches that came with sleeping rough kicked in. Both his hip and neck had their own kinks that throbbed as he began to move.

Billy stretched his legs as he walked, bending and twisting at the hips trying to loosen up. His hand massaged his neck as he rolled his head in circles, first one way then the other.

The sun wasn't up yet, but it would be soon. Billy rubbed his hands together, finally generating some heat. As he scanned the docks it looked like a number of new freighters had come in during the night, and a few others had left, but there were still at least ten there.

Without any previous knowledge about freighters, he now couldn't believe how many must be sailing the lakes. Hundreds he figured, maybe thousands. The more he learned, the less it seemed he would succeed on his mission.

Walking beside a freighter he noticed how new it looked. The paint on the side of the ship reflected the yard lights and Billy thought it looked almost like wax on a nice car. Still, for steel and paint it looked good. His face cracked a smile, there was a good chance any ship he found would look better than the Forester.

The next two freighters looked in good shape as well. He remembered their names from the night before, he'd already asked them about a job.

"Hey you!"

Billy looked away from the freighter. Some guy was coming his way, waving an arm.

"You the Indian looking for work?"

Billy raised his hand in the air and waved back. It couldn't happen that quickly could it? He couldn't believe it. As they came to a stop in front of each other he offered, "Billy sir, and yes I'm looking for work."

The guy seemed to size him up, and Billy wondered what he was thinking about.

"You have your card?"

"Yes sir." Billy fished out his wallet and produced his ratings certificate.

"Captain says he wants to speak to you. It's the Philip, two slips down, red and black."

Billy realized this guy was just the messenger. To prove that theory, the guy headed off down the dock in the opposite direction. He also knew he wouldn't have been given a freighter name if he hadn't had the card. It didn't matter, and he started off to meet his new captain.

The S.S. Philip was a smaller freighter in great looking shape. It was another with fresh paint and not many years on it. There was only one superstructure on the back of this ship, compared to the two on the Forester, one up front and another at the rear.

Billy made his way up the gangway onto the low riding vessel, he could tell it was loaded down with cargo and realized he was more comfortable this time round. Really though, he wasn't any more experienced, five days wasn't a lot of time to shed his rookie label.

As he stepped onto the bridge there was little activity. The crew must be resting or on shore like the guy who delivered the message. The only one at the helm was the Captain. Billy almost smiled, the man looked like a hippie, then he counted bars on the seaman's shoulders. No doubt, he was the man.

"So you're looking for work?"

"Yes sir. Just got in yesterday." Billy wouldn't offer any more than he had to.

"I'm Captain George Brook. What experience you got?"

The dreaded question. Billy had worked through this scenario in his head the night before.

"Billy Blackwood, sir. Fresh out of training, sir. Just completed five days aboard the S.S. Forester."

The captain stuck a finger into the long scraggly hair sticking out beneath his hat and scratched. Billy changed his impression of the guy from a hippie to a heavy metal fan the more he talked with him. "Can't be any worse than Johnson was."

"Pardon me sir?" Billy was confused, and wanted to be clear about what was said.

"Talking to myself son. Johnson disappeared overnight, probably found some hot piece of ass. I just need muscle. You got any of that?"

"Yes sir. I work hard." It really was all he had to offer.

"You better, cause it's about all we need from you. No shit or problems on the water. You mess up here and you're dealing with me." The man was almost standing on his toes.

"Understood, sir."

It was comical in a way. The captain was a wiry five-foot tall and old enough that he didn't look like he could hurt anything. Did he raise up on his toes on purpose, or was it uncontrollable? Either way, it was hilarious and Billy chucked to himself as he headed down to the sleeping quarters.

The captain had instructed him to go down there and introduce himself. The boys, as he called them, would point him to Johnson's old bunk.

He stopped outside the door to his level, standing in the stairwell for a second. He did feel more comfortable than before, but still, he felt the adrenaline starting somewhere. Taking a deep breath, he exhaled.

This was no sweat, let's do it. Billy opened the door.

CHAPTER 14

S.S. Slate

With the freighter finally clear of the St. Clair system, the long run northbound up Lake Huron had begun. Since the weather was mild, they would head straight up the middle. No need for hugging the shoreline like they had on the way down.

Jared stood out on the deck catching air. Spitting over the railing, he grimaced. A cigarette hung from the corner of his mouth, the smoke whipping away in the light wind. Something was happening with this woman and he couldn't figure out what. He just knew he didn't want to treat her like the others.

The word "others" created a vision of the bodies he'd left piled on the side of his life. In all those years there hadn't been a single time he felt regret. He wanted to say remorse, but didn't even know what it meant.

When Jared pounded someone there was a reason, and that always ruled his consciousness. He was after an effect, no different than a corporate boss or a sports figure. They walked over others to get to their goals, justifying it in their heads, no matter the damage. What was it called? "Doing it for the cause?"

Sometimes he acted out of boredom, other times over money. Mostly though what he enjoyed was the thrill and power of putting others under his thumb, or taking what was theirs. Really, he thrived on it and became good at it. What was the saying? Ten thousand hours at something and you were an expert.

Once his anger kicked in though, all bets were off. Jared fought early in life; at home and then in school. They were duels without guns, meeting after class and going one-on-one if they wanted to or not.

The simplicity of that fighting went out the window in jail. In the pen there was no warning, no fair fight. If you didn't keep your head up and your eyes open, didn't see the signs and read the atmosphere, you could be jumped by a crew and shanked six times before you hit the floor. What was a cheap shot on the school ground was a smart move in that place.

Every other female he'd ever shacked up with served only one purpose, his satisfaction. Inevitably they needed be to put in their place, or his nature took over and he exercised his dominance. Jared knew it was his inability to read this girl that confused him. He didn't quite know what made her tick. Usually he could tell exactly how they thought, and how to manipulate them. He was drawn to her, like he'd been with the others. Free sex was a great motivator. But yet he hesitated.

Finally, he flicked the butt over the rail and headed towards the stairwell.

As he did every night after dinner, he moved the other girl over to the next room. The longer the boys were happy, the longer he would have time with his own piece.

Jared found her along the sidewall, behind some piled boxes. Caught off guard, he stared, she didn't have any clothes on. Had she been naked since the night before? Or had she undressed for him, knowing he was coming?

Looking down at the bulge in his pants Jared wondered if something was wrong with her, she looked cold. He thought of the night before, lying with her and how different it had been. He'd taken his time with her. It had been slow and special, she'd offered no resistance, and he moved her around with ease.

One part of him longed to hear her scream, maybe he should turn her over and take her from behind. Another part of him was thinking about her skin against his the night before. Shaking his head, he pushed the feelings away. This wasn't his nature, but still, she looked so innocent lying there asleep.

Peeling off his jeans he laid down beside her. As crazy as it was, he tried to lie close to her without waking her, wanting the situation to last, even though he didn't know why.

Jared turned and pressed against her, staring into her hair, smelling her, feeling her body move against his as she breathed in and out.

*****

Shanya opened her eyes, the steel floor stretched out in the dark and she forced her lids closed again. The night sounds of the forest took over, crickets and frogs, something bigger cracking twigs with its weight.

What had always been peaceful and inviting, the forest on a rain or sun-filled day, scared her now. She couldn't see anything. It was a cross roads, either nature was her comfort, or it wasn't.

Either she could embrace with her whole being, or she wasn't really connected to it.

Part of her brain was still aware of her reality on the freighter, but another part of her fought to forget it, to stay in the forest where she ran free. Shanya felt the cold on her skin and knew she was naked to the elements. On some level it didn't alarm her, the forest had no clothing either, nor the animals.

There was a cliff edge in her mind and she was about to fall over it. The dark of the forest ahead called her, yet she still wrestled in her head. Fear kept bringing her back to the present.

The cold of the storage room closed in on Shanya. She shook once violently and sat up. She didn't like remembering where she was on the freighter, or what had been happening to her.

She remembered those few times she had been late getting home for dinner, the dark settling into the woods. She had ended up running full tilt the last mile or so, watching the shadows chasing her through the branches. Every corner seemed to hide a potential harm.

But she knew the forest couldn't be any different at night, it was just a lack of light that had scared her. Nothing had ever happened on those occasions.

It was the unanswerable questions, and the agony of her situation that she couldn't take anymore. How could someone, or why would someone, do this to her? How could people be so harmful, disrespectful and abusive?

What had she done to bring the situation on to herself? How come the first mistake of her life had to have such horrible consequences?

Why would a lesson come to mind right now? It's wasn't as if they were going to help her. She didn't want to think about it, but she couldn't let it go.

Redfeather lived with his grandfather. Grandfather taught him how to shoot a bow and arrow. Then he taught Redfeather about the different ways of the creatures of the forest, like in springtime how the old-lady frogs would croak and sharpen their knives to butcher crawfish.

Redfeather went out every day with his bow and arrow and killed all the frogs and the crawfish too. One day a heron offered the boy his best feather if he would stop killing the food the heron needed for its babies.

Redfeather laughed, "Ha, I don't want your old dirty feathers.

The birds met together to talk about Redfeather's actions. In a tall tree set on an island in the middle of the nearby lake there lived a wise old owl. He came to Redfeather's house at night and hoo-hooed. Grandfather told the child to come in the house, owls had large ears and could stuff rabbits in them. He warned his grandson that Owl might catch him too.

Redfeather laughed again. He shot his arrow at the owl and missed, while he searched for the arrow, the owl swooped down and picked him up, stuffing him in his ear and taking him away to the island.

On the island, the owl wouldn't let Redfeather out of his nest. He told his babies that when they were big enough, they could eat Redfeather. He also told the other birds of the forest that they would all feast on him. Redfeather cried, but couldn't escape.

Grandfather asked for help getting Redfeather back. The spirits told him to offer a great feast and so he did. Redfeather was returned to his grandfather and the youngster promised not to misuse the food that Nanabozho had made for the birds.

As much as Shanya tried to find what she did wrong, or why she deserved to be here, she couldn't get anything. She hadn't abused anything like Redfeather, in fact she knew she respected nature.

The part of her head wanting to live with the trees was talking now, "So why are we still here?"

The other side answered, "Because I haven't given up."

"It's not about giving up Shanya, it's about salvation."

She knew the assaults were taking a toll. She hadn't recuperated from the first when the second had come. Had there been a third? She wasn't sure, which in some way was a good thing.

Everything pointed in one direction, and Shanya lay back down. The cold was covering her body with goose bumps, but she didn't notice. As her eyes closed again, she could already hear the night sounds as the forest swallowed her whole.

A midnight dew had started to build and all the grass and bushes were wet against her skin. The young native woman eased forward a step at a time, staring into the darkness. Her hand reaching forward until it touched the rough peeling bark of a birch tree for stability.

In the dark her senses were taking over. She felt the strips of bark hanging from the tree. Grabbing one hanging end, she peeled it around the tree and pulled it off. It was something she'd done many times before in the light, but this time was different. She held the bark in her hand and ran her fingertips back and forth against the smooth interior. Almost like paper, but strong enough for a basket.

Something moved again, deeper in the woods. It sounded like a big animal. The noises it made stepping on branches and rubbing against the bushes were too loud for anything small.

Why she turned that way, instead of away from the noise, was intriguing. Shanya was perplexed with her own choice, yet didn't stop herself as another of her feet stepped forward, set down softly in the dark to avoid noise or injury.

When Shanya heard an owl hoot in the distance she thought of Redfeather and suddenly became scared. She laid down and hid herself, the cold and wet suddenly amplified as she got closer to the ground.

Something was echoing in her head, "Shanya, Shanya." Then she could hear, "Chikwan, Chikwania, Chikwane." All meaningless noises she wouldn't respond to.

Much more time went by, but she couldn't make a noise, she was in hiding now. Something was out there in the forest, and she wasn't inviting it in. The echoes finally went away and she relaxed. Staring up at the stars she felt tired, too tired to care.

Later there was a warmth against her, she thought to turn and look, but knew not to. Whatever animal had come up beside her and laid down next to her was a blessing in the cold. She felt the heat radiating through her and thanked Nanabozho. Nature would save her if she could stay with it.

140

There was comfort for the first time in days. Shanya let herself settle into the ground and drift off, even knowing it could be wolf or bear about to eat her. Her peace of mind knew better though, she had seen the antlers, the white tail, and she felt the bristled hair.

Shanya's eyes closed as she drifted away.

*****

It didn't take long for Billy to realize life aboard one freighter was the same as the next, at least when you were on the bottom of the seniority list. He couldn't figure out why they needed to clean the freaking decks so often, but here he was again, first day on the job, sweating his ass off pushing a scrub broom.

Taking the time to watch what was going on around him, he was getting a feel for the crew. It was easy to see right off that these guys weren't as fit as the guys on the Forester. A few wiry Chinese guys worked alongside him, he couldn't tell what nationality the other guy was, but he looked round as a ball. A wet ball, constantly sweating beads down his forehead, the moisture gathering around the collar of his t-shirt, soaking the front and back until he looked like he'd jumped in the lake.

By the time he'd had lunch, worked the afternoon scrapping paint, and listened to the crew have dinner, he realized he had to rethink some things. First it had been a shock that he wasn't expecting, then an eye-opening revelation as he watched the racist name-calling fly back and forth.

From what Billy could see the two Chinese guys were laughed at all the time, not so much picked on, but definitely segregated for teasing about their nationality. What made Billy pay closer attention was watching the two men's responses. One was goaded on by the banter and clearly aggravated.

"I show you, cut off your balls." Everyone laughed.

Billy noted that the other Chinese never let it bother him. It seemed to go right over the guy's head like he hadn't heard it. He wondered if it was more because the guy expected it, like Billy did, or if he was used to it, which was the same thing.

In the end he thought perhaps it was because the guy was above the bullshit. As much as the prankster racist thought he was putting someone down, the Chinese guy just ended up smiling at the asshole like the idiot he was. Billy knew it didn't matter what his response was, those kinds of people would always see someone with different skin colour as a fucking problem that needed sorting out one way or another.

Seeing that others took a verbal beating like his own people was new. It was all about exposure, and he was beginning to discover that he hadn't had as much as he though. As if to bring him into the group someone blurted out,

"Hey redskin, no one teach you to talk yet?"

Billy's answer, short and sweet as he stood up and headed for his bunk, got the boys all laughing, and he felt it was a good start with the crew, "Fuck You."

Later, when someone grabbed his shoulder through the bunk curtain, his hand snapped out, instantly seizing the wrist as he pivoted in place to see what was happening.

"Easy there boy. Easy."

Billy stared into the eyes of an old-timer. Bloodshot eyes so red they almost glowed and the smell of liquor invaded the bunk. A second hand appeared swinging a bottle back and forth. As Billy resettled his eyes on the face, he noticed the old man's eyebrow going up and down while his head made small nods back in the direction of the door he must have come from.

It was an invitation that made Billy want to shake his head. It was another thing he'd seen a lot, people assuming natives always wanted to drink. How many times had he heard those words? *"Come on, don't you want a few?"*

He had no interest in drinking with the guy, but it was opportunity to get a little information. First, it set up his cover nicely as a drunken Indian. Second, the old man might have loose lips, and many secrets were spilled once the booze took over.

"Okay, old man. Just give me a second."

Ten minutes later he was being poured a second shot and wondered why he was wasting his time. He'd just gotten to sleep and now he was drinking what? Billy grabbed the bottle from the old man to look at the label. The stuff was like gasoline, it was that strong. Silk Tassel Scotch. Now he did shake his head. Why couldn't it be a simple couple of beer?

The old man tipped up his glass. "Salute."

Billy raised his. "To the spirits."

*****

The Captain's quarters had become a stage. Hans was directing the proceedings with increasing invention, and becoming agitated in the process. One night, maybe two, left with her. It made him feel like he was running out of time.

Of course, then the question if it really was the last time would come into play. What if this was it? Jared said it would go on, not to worry. But Hans always got to this point, and had to get it out of his system, just in case.

As usual, on the last couple of nights there was no playing games. There was no consideration given, there was only take and take some more. He didn't talk to her or engage her either, and the gag in her mouth kept her quiet.

The squaw was tied over the small table in the corner, as much as he wanted to use the bed, the table put her at the right height. He'd left her that way overnight and headed right at her for service this morning.

Hans couldn't tell if she was sleeping or awake. He'd just come in from the bridge. His one hand held a glass half-full with whiskey, while the other pulled at this belt. It didn't really matter what she was doing,

It was a strange sensation, getting pissed off because she made him degrade himself, and feeling his member rise at the same time.

The same thing hammered at him over and over as he took a long pull at his drink. She might be the last one. His pants hit the floor and he stepped forward.

CHAPTER 15

S.S. Forester

The big freighter had reached the top of Lake Huron, cut west to run the channel and was aimed to head down into Lake Michigan. Jared paced back and forth along the deck, his preoccupation with this decision had his full attention.

He was running out of time. There were no two ways about it, he had to make a call one way or the other by the time they got to Chicago. It had always been this way, and he never had a problem with it before.

Of course, his process was now a complete system. It had taken a few years searching bars, taking to people hanging around the docks, but eventually he'd found the outlet he needed. It was well worth the extra work, he'd always been thorough in planning the jobs he'd run. It always paid dividends in the long run. Especially if the result was attempting to never got caught.

He'd finally found the right guy in Chicago, and through him a gang that was interested in his product. How many years ago was that now? He lost count of the girls after the first year. Initially one girl on each trip had turned to two. Now it was up to three.

Jared quietly walked up behind the young kid Ronnie who was greasing bearings on the anchor winches by pumping a handgun attached to the grease nipples. The kid jerked in surprise when he noticed he was being watched.

It was probably the interruption, but the kid started to get up, giving Jared a chance to tie into him. "You missed some boy, what the fuck are you doing?"

He watched Ronnie look down at the winch, confusion on his face. He squatted back down and attached the gun again.

"Either you're one stupid son of a bitch, or you're scared of nipples. Which is it?"

Jared liked people uncomfortable, he did it when he was stressed. If he was off his keel, then everyone else would be too. Not getting an answer was like being ignored, the wrong thing to do when Jared was agitated.

"I asked you a question kid." He moved closer.

"I must have been distracted boss. The other ones are done right, you can check if you want." The kid seemed sure of himself.

Jared knew he was just blowing off steam, looking for someone to dump on.

He tried to refocus. Chicago was the final piece, the dumping ground. He had never intended anyone to get back to Thunder bay. The only question had been – where could he regularly make some cash.

Ten to twelve trips a year, a few girls at a time, he knew the numbers added up over the years. They weren't all dropped off in Chicago either, but still that many had left the north.

He got more money for each one down south than he paid, but that was his gain and Derek's loss. He wasn't sure what happened to the girls once they hit Chicago, but the gang never said no when he called.

That consistency was all part of the problem, because he needed to make that call soon. The gang needed notice and the ship was getting close. In fact, he usually called as he came through the channel, and now he was already past that.

For someone used to being in control of any situation, it pissed him off that he was this indecisive. What was he holding back for? What was making him look at her differently?

She wasn't fighting back anymore, a point the others had come to eventually. And when they all switched to trying to please him and keep him happy, he expected it. With her, it was like she was just accepting of him. There were no lies or fakeness, she just laid there for him and accepted him how he was.

There was no doubt this was different. Jared saw a picture in his head, the two of them back at his apartment. Could it be?

Just as quickly he dismissed the idea. Fucking broads, all of them, they always drove him to hit something. They wanted sex, but they wanted feelings and phone calls. They all wanted to move in, they wanted cash and gifts. Some of them even wanted kids. Shit, the list went on. Every damn one he got close to he ended up bashing around. It hadn't worked with the girls at school, and it sure didn't work with the women he met later.

There was always a female around willing to receive the built-up frustration of an ex-con, they were always looking for trouble. Problem was the trouble continued the next day, and forever after that.

He wanted to spend more time with this one, the hour or two he was able to take away from his work wasn't enough. She had drawn him in, and he wanted to know why. It seemed he couldn't really let it go, and he knew there was only one way to decide. More time.

Jared knocked back a few brews with the crew after dinner, but he wasn't really part of the conversation, he was busy thinking about her. As usual, there was anticipation, but now it was of a different kind. Her presence was almost enough.

He would have left by now, he wanted to get downstairs that badly, but he waited it out, trying not to look too anxious.

He had to separate the girls one last time. He had been nice enough to put them back together every night, but now he was sure that only one was getting off in Chicago. The question of the other girl remained open. Tonight he had to make it clear. To whom he wondered, as he said the words? To himself?

*****

S.S. Philip

The scotch in Billy's mouth burned, tearing at his throat all the way down. He was drinking one shot for every two the old guy slammed back. Willard claimed that drinking was his game. The weathered look of his face said the old man had won fairly often.

The two of them were the only participants in the late-night festivities, the rest of the crew long gone to bed. The little table against a wall was only two feet wide between them, and Billy carefully sipped part of the shot and then with his arm under the small table, threw the rest against the wall, letting it run down and puddle on the floor. Even though he was stealthy, the partial sips he was forced to drink were adding up.

He didn't drink much anymore, he'd had his share growing up, getting hammered on many occasions, but it never ruled his life and never really became a habit.

Billy was letting Willard lead the conversation, there would be silent periods and then the old guy would talk for ten minutes straight. The topics ranged from what booze was best, to tall tales about life on the water. The objective was to hear him out and eventually turn the subject towards women. Billy occasionally added a word here or there to keep him going.

"Now this here stuff I wouldn't feed to a dog. Burn his insides right out." The old guy shook the bottle back and forth. Then he took another shot and grimaced as if to make his point.

Billy wondered what liquor you fed to a dog.

"Need to get me some Jim Beam for the next leg. This shit was a goddamn gift. Should have thrown it out."

Billy couldn't picture that either. But he did agree with the other option, "Yes, Jim Beam would be a lot smoother."

"You're damn right." The old man poured them both a shot and changed direction.

"Got me a '67 Mustang in the garage. Thing goes like the wind."

"Cool." What else could he say?

Billy kept half of his brain on the drinker while the other half roamed over questions he asked the Chinese guy after dinner about the racism he'd encountered. The answer had been 'that it was just how it was', he gave as good as he took it. The other Chinese who was much cooler about the abuse said it didn't bother him, he didn't think two wrongs made a right, and therefore he ignored it. It was their ignorance and not his.

The deckhand from India spoke of caste systems and told of people who were forced to the bottom rungs of society just by their name and ancestors. None of it made sense to Billy, but he realized the plight of his people wasn't as simple, or isolated, as he thought.

There had been a chip on his shoulder his whole life, set there by his own people's stories and experiences. His mother had shaped his chip to be used as motivation to fight for his equality. To get fair opportunity and to be recognized for his abilities. He knew that in other natives it produced an ingrained indifference, one where no one seemed to think on a big enough or long enough scale to produce environments conducive to child and community growth, instead of garbage blowing through the yards and ditches of the reserves.

He'd looked across the table at the two Chinese and the Indian. These men had left their countries and traveled here in the hope of a better place. No one did it for them, they'd done it themselves, for their own needs and reasons. They'd landed in other countries, alone and probably confused, yet carried on to end up in a country like Canada. Now here they were working on a freighter, how many miles from home?

For the first time Billy questioned why so many natives were still stuck on reserves. For some reason their culture or community norm was to stay separate, which will inevitably create issues with future integration. He could understand how having been free wanderers forced onto reserves, then the family structures lost in the residential schools that those returning to the reserves would not want to step into the white world again. It might explain some of the lack of success for those who left the reserves. It struck him that he was in fact succeeding, but he knew he was also a rarity. His mother had instilled in him the importance of bettering himself.

With more serious things to consider, Billy started to angle around in his head on how to broach the main subject. What way to come at it? He wrestled with whether he should pretend that he already knew there were native women on freighters, or pretend he didn't know.

He feared that seeming unaware might not open the doors he needed. Showing some understanding about it might make it seem casual, and like it was obvious. Should he wait nights, weeks, to find the right moment? He hadn't done that on the Forester, and he wanted to move things along here as well.

"What we need Willard, is women on this ship."

The old guy's eye's twinkled slightly, and then he stared at the far wall for a second as if he remembered something.

Billy tilted his shot glass, knocking down the full contents of this one. The sound of the glass slapping the table harder than usual was like an exclamation point. He set one more hook in the water

"Yes, sir. Young ones."

"Some freighters do have females." The old man's voice lowered, "Young ones."

Billy waited for something more, but it wasn't coming. When would he get another chance? Probably tomorrow night, he was pretty certain this drunk would be at it again. But the subject was opened now, would it be again another day?

Billy frowned, now or later? Finally, he made a move.

"You mean the squaws?"

The old man's head snapped in his direction. There was clarity there that Billy hadn't thought possible. The subject obviously fired up the old man one way or the other. Then he realized it was fear that made the old man's lip quiver.

Go ahead, thought Billy. Spill it.

He figured the old man would eventually realize he was talking to a native. He would probably assume that Billy had to know about these things, and must have experienced it himself on another freighter.

Billy kept his face carefully neutral.

There was no audible answer, but the old man nodded his head up and down while his eyes took on that faraway look. Excitement soared as Bill realized he'd confirmed the concept, and completed part of his job. He struggled to keep himself in check, letting the silence take over. He forced himself to breathe evenly, even as he wanted to jump up and punch the air in celebration.

By the time he found a way to end the conversation for the night and head back to his bunk, he was no longer happy about his discovery. It meant that women were really being taken onto freighters, it also meant he still had a long way to go.

Laying there, wanting to sleep, and too filled with alcohol, he thought about the native women that were around as he grew up. He knew it had seemed innocent when they all played together as kids and everyone seemed equal.

Then as he got old enough to really see what was going on around him, he noticed women with bruises and black eyes. It was easy to blame it on all the drinking, and eventually you learned which families had drunks in the household and which were violent.

His mother had been well treated, Billy was sure of that. But he knew of many families that had problems, and it was usually the women who took the brunt of it.

The teenaged girls who came to the parties were never really respected. The guys would talk about getting them drunk and having their way. He didn't disrespect them, but didn't have much to do with them either. Between sports and trying to work, he really hadn't taken any of them seriously.

The more he thought about it, the more he realized that sometimes the women on the reserves weren't always treated with much respect. The statistics he'd seen in in the case file said on average an under-age native girl were eighteen times more likely to get pregnant, and by the time they were adults they were twice as likely to be living in poverty. If that wasn't bad enough, now he had a growing discomfort knowing native girls were being taken from Thunder Bay. Where were they going?

Too many things rotated to the front of his thoughts. What other boats? How many natives were out there? What to ask the old man next?

CHAPTER 16

S.S. Slate

The man moved slowly up and down in the dark confines of the storage room. He shuddered and lay there a few moments before lifting himself up and over to lie beside the girl. Tonight Jared had left the lights off deliberately.

He'd caressed her for an hour before finally climbing on top. This would be the longest he had ever stayed with her, and now he found he was in no rush at all to leave. In the dark he pictured his bedroom at home, it would be just like this, the two of them side-by-side, warm, relaxed.

Jared suddenly saw the one-bedroom apartment in his mind. The cheap couch with and old phone book replacing a missing leg, the crooked lamp on the table where he usually set his dinner plate, the fuzzy fifteen-inch T.V., the beer in the fridge. White walls and open space, nothing else except the matted green carpet that had seen a thousand feet. Did that matter? It shouldn't if there was love, right?

But then he'd never been able to figure women out. Why did it matter what it looked like, if he paid for the place wasn't that enough? He found himself fixating on the girl as he lay on his side pressed up against her.

This was what he needed, a woman who accepted him. She made no demands, no needs that required his attention. She even kept her clothes off. Was that for him? Or was she just a little odd?

Jared closed his eyes and let his arm settle across her stomach just below her breasts, slowly he let out a long breath, relaxing. He wanted to enjoy the time he had with her, but just that thought had him thinking about the decision he'd made.

For the first time he was going to keep one of the girls past Chicago. He had to give her a chance, or give himself time to figure her out. He'd made the phone call, and as usual the gang wanted whatever he had to unload. He'd told them he had one and they'd made arrangements to meet once they docked.

He didn't gain a lot with his move, another night maybe two. Then he'd have to make a final decision about her too. Still, as he lay there, feeling the heat from her body he knew two more days would be welcomed.

Tonight however was a long slow night on Michigan, just the two of them. His head tilted closer and his nose played in her hair. He would have to ask her at some point, sooner than later, but he didn't want to change the atmosphere right now.

He'd brought a blanket, knowing he would be down on the floor for a while, and the steel was cold. How she managed to lie on it stark naked amazed him, it showed her strength. When he pulled her onto the blanket, she didn't even show a sign of noticing. This upset him earlier because he thought she ought to acknowledge his thoughtfulness, but in the end she'd accepted it, which was just as important.

Jared squeezed her. A hug, something he hadn't done much in his life. His arm across her chest bent at the elbow and his hand landed in the crease between her breasts. The blood began to flow again, he couldn't believe how much she excited him.

He felt her moving in his arms, but she wasn't fighting. He let her continue while he held her loosely, it was like she was slow dancing in his arms. Almost somewhere else, her body moving to some unheard rhythm.

As with everything she did, it intrigued him. The heat said it was more than intrigue.

*****

The early morning sun had been a blessing for Shanya, it brought heat to her face as she sat up in the wet grass. Suddenly remembering the night before, she looked quickly behind her. Whatever had slept there was long gone.

Of course, she couldn't expect to be quieter than the animals, be as sharp, or up as early. Still, she felt like she was a part of the forest, a part of nature. She started to run. It was comforting, one of the things she liked best.

A sudden pang hit her as she felt the memory of running in the forest near her home. She forced the thoughts of another time away, and forged ahead into the unknown woodland.

She laughed at the rabbit as it spooked when she flew by. Same with the family of partridge that flushed in every direction, forcing her to raise a hand, deflecting the bird that almost flew up into her face. A few hours later she was still running, up hills, and across creeks.

At one point she looked up and almost missed it, but out of the corner of her eye she saw the eagle again. She couldn't be sure it was the same one, but liked the idea that it might be. Stopping, she stared up until her neck hurt, watching the bird soaring around and around.

Running again, Shanya came over the top of a knoll to see a small valley and couldn't help but venture down into it. It was wide open, with sloping hills rising protectively on each side.

The sun was getting low, and she realized it would get dark again soon.

She had told herself a few times during the day that the forest was her comfort, now she had to embrace the darkness and accept it. Really, she had to find somewhere to sleep, searching along the valley floor as she slowed to a walk.

The first spot she chose only lasted until darkness fell. The idea of sitting and leaning back against a smooth rock didn't seem right because she was out in the open. When she tried behind a group of rocks it felt good while she sat there. But when she eventually laid on the ground it was too hard to lay in any position for more than a minute. That wouldn't work either. Finally Shanya found a patch of grass and remembering it was soft sleeping the night before, it should work again. It was also a good place to hide.

Staring up at the stars, she wondered where the eagle had gone. She realized she had forgotten to keep an eye on it after arriving in the valley. It would be hunkered down for the night just like she was.

Shanya felt her mind fighting back and forth. She understood things were changing in the real world, somehow she knew there was still something going on, but wasn't the violence gone? What did it mean? Maybe she should be there? Was this the opportunity she was waiting for?

Another part of her mind, the side becoming stronger every day, dragged her back into the wet grasses of the cold forest floor. It was just in time.

The noise moved her way, another big animal, and she couldn't move or run. She felt it standing beside her. The bear reached out, pawing at her. He was slow for some reason and Shanya moved and weaved, avoiding each attempt to grab her. It went on like a fire dance until suddenly the bear was down beside her, and she felt the same warm of the night before, so comforting that she let her eyes drift closed.

*****

S.S. Philip

Billy was preoccupied most of the day mulling over the news he flushed out the night before. At one point it dawned on him it wasn't a game any longer. It wasn't the right word, game, but he knew at some level he'd always doubted the mission he was on.

How could he take seriously the idea that there were women disappearing in some systematic way? He knew girls had vanished, but into a structured process? The public really didn't know about this, but his operation would confirm it.

No, it sure wasn't a game at all. Billy alternated between anger and shock, as he went from planning what he could do, and considering the enormity of the situation. He might save lives. In concept it was part of the job. But he could see it now, wanted it even, especially if it meant native lives.

The freighter had docked in Michigan City earlier that day. Talking with the crew he discovered that they stayed on Lake Michigan, running loads back and forth along the southern end of the lake. They were headed for Gary, Indiana next.

Billy had made sure to catch old man Willard's eye at dinner often enough to notice the nod and suggestive raising of an eyebrow. Billy nodded back in agreement.

Now as the darkness settled, the two of them leaned against the rail, the calm night made it easy for them to stand on the deck without drawing much attention.

"Got me a woman at home, breasts like melons." Willard nodded like he was telling the truth, and tipped up the bottle in a salute to the melons in question.

Billy was still trying to get used to the damned whiskey again. It turned out that it wasn't only one bottle the old man had been gifted with, but three. Probably why he couldn't get himself to throw them away, there was just too much liquor there.

"Her sisters too." Willard looked at him after saying it and blinked once or twice, fast like he wasn't sure he should have mentioned it.

The silence built again and Billy waited him out. He took a small sip while tipping the bottle up high after Willard pushed the liquor in his direction.

"Too calm out here, weather's going change." Willard scanned ahead in the moonlight.

Billy grabbed the new opening. "How long you been on the water old man?"

"Forty-five years." The old seaman waved his bottle at the water. "So much easier today, you new guys have it made. Jesus Christ, we worked like dogs and had none of this navigation shit they use now."

Billy knew the old man would continue reminiscing until dawn broke, but wanted to shape the conversation, so he jumped in. "You must know all the freighters on the lakes after all these years?"

The old man smiled, like it was a badge of honor. "Been on thirty different ships. And you're right, I've seen a lot of them." Willard's mood seemed to lift a notch as he warmed to the new story.

After going back and forth for another hour Billy found the opportunity to make headway in a different direction, switching the conversation back to women.

"You plan on being out here a long time yourself?" The old guy finally quit rambling and gave Billy a chance to talk.

"I don't know Willard. If I had a woman with melons at home it would be hard to stay out here forty years."

It took a second until Willard started laughing. Billy joined him as the old guy grabbed the rail and roared until his false teeth almost fell out.

Wanting to keep the momentum going, Billy kept on. "I gotta get onto one of those ships with women. That would sure make the time go faster."

Worried he'd said too much, it took a second for Billy to hear the low-toned response, "...ston, Pelletier, Dobson & Sons, Slate, Deerburn, Roxxon, Blac..." The old man turned his head and his voice disappeared into the night, then he turned back, "…est, Playfair, Robinson, there's a few of them."

Was his face still straight? It felt like his mouth was hanging wide open. *An entire list of freighters.* Billy tried to lock them into memory as he blinked a few times and moved his tongue around his mouth to find moisture, having gone dry with surprise.

Thinking, he absorbed the news. *What to say next?* Should he say he'd been on one of them? No, he knew that would set him up for questions that he might not answer correctly.

Before he could make up his mind, Willard carried on. "You got to be on one of the ships heading north. The ones going to Superior."

Without realizing it, Billy reached out and Willard handed the bottle over. He was quickly sorting out his thoughts. This freighter stayed on Michigan, so it made sense that it was hard for a native girl to end up here, but it was possible, they could pass between ships.

The more he thought about it, the more he agreed that ships heading to Canadian ports were more likely to be the prime suspects. Willard's specific mention of Superior could only mean Sault Ste. Marie or Thunder Bay. What else was there?

His good mood, and the now welcomed booze had to be put aside. Billy had to set other things in motion. He took a couple more swigs of the liquor and left the old man to his thoughts. Willard wouldn't be done until the bottle was.

Back in his bunk, sitting up against the back wall, curtain closed, Billy typed on his phone, rereading the message before sending it.

No women here. Need freighter heading to Superior. Gary, Indiana next.

Billy hit send, and laid his head back on the pillow, suddenly feeling tired. He wasn't sure he would get the reply, but the answer came quickly. The phone vibrated in his hand.

Continue to Gary. Directions to follow.

*****

A text message arrived at another freighter, the dozing captain reached out in the dark for the pinging phone. It took a second to gain his focus, something that took longer with age. His eyes squinted and relaxed as the message became clear.

Head south. Destination unclear. Chicago? Will inform.

The captain cleared the message, dialed a number and waited for the answer, knowing they would see his name on the screen.

"Bridge. Can I help you sir?"

"John get us out on the lake heading south. No hurry, just start the process. I'll see you in the morning."

He smiled to himself. The kid must be getting somewhere.

CHAPTER 17

S.S. Slate

As the ship slammed against the water, thrown about by the swelling waves, Shanya opened her eyes. She didn't see the forest any more, instead boxes were piled up against the wall in the darkness, and the coldness of her cage hit home.

She didn't want to be in the present, but her conscious fought to stay. Eight days? Nine? She had no idea. She felt the blanket under her and pulled it up around her shoulders, where were her clothes?

Finding the waste bucket, Shanya relieved herself. For the first time she noticed the second bucket with a towel beside it. How long had that been there? On one level it frightened her that things were changing around her and she wasn't noticing, but on another level, it was a blessing to be blind to the kind of things that were probably taking place.

She'd gone out in the first place to meet boys. Now the thought of any man was appalling. She would never trust one again.

The memories would never leave. The pain and the fear would remain. Shanya let out her breath, her shoulders slumped, defeated.

Slowly a churning built in her stomach. An ache reached around her chest and squeezed. The pulse behind her eyes increased to headache level. Hatred and anger were taking root in her body, emotions she'd never felt before. What else was she supposed to feel?

"Chakwania?" Shanya shouted. The urge surprised her.

There was no answer. Was she next door?

Shanya didn't remember having talked in a while, and she had a pang of guilt for not keeping an eye on the other girl. The thought of Abby, who she hadn't seen since the first days on board, hurt even more. They had singled out the younger girl early.

Where were the others? Was she really alone now? Shanya's breath hung in her throat. She didn't want to think about what was happening.

In the middle of trying to survive it had just become her against him, there hadn't been room in her head for anything else except the beckoning forest. She could see images flashing in front of her eyes. The wall of forest hinted at darkness just inside the tree line.

Curling up in a ball, she pulled the blanket around her shoulders and welcomed the vision of escape. The sound of birds chirping and singing hit her first, carried on the strength of the wind ...

... it felt like a spring day, the kind where you wanted to get outside and go hiking. She approached the tree line and stuck her head past the first row of trees, into the shadows. She wanted to look back knowing her reality lived there, but instead, she plunged forward.

The temperature dropped a few degrees in the shade of the tall birches. She could see the green-tinted streaks of light coming through the canopy. Without moving, it was like she was hidden now, instead of exposed out in the open.

She heard the eagle cry out somewhere above. Was it in a battle of its own? She had often seen them circling high above, swooping and diving at each other. Why everyone had to fight for their territory never made sense to her. Especially when there was so much open space.

Realizing she was purposely staying close to the edge of the tree line, part of her not letting go of the real world, she pushed herself to her feet and walked deeper into the forest. This time she couldn't help looking back at whatever was out in the open outside the tree line. She watched the sunlight for a moment, she knew it was the last time she'd be there.

Further down the path she stopped at another clearing, only thirty or forty paces long and just as wide. Her eyes went up to the sky immediately, looking through the opening in the trees. She wasn't surprised to see the eagle riding high in the currents.

She liked this spot and sat down, the knee-high grasses meant she could just see over them while sitting. When she'd kept lookout long enough to feel she was alone, she lay back in the small field and let out a long breath. She felt home now, where she belonged.

The relief was enormous, a weight lifted off her shoulders as she closed her eyes. Sometime later, rested, she opened them again, staring up into the blue. It was beautiful, as she started to sit up, she noticed the eagle perched in the tallest tree on the other side of the clearing.

Shanya didn't move. Was it Nanabozho? Was she in danger? Was he there to warn her, or there to keep watch? The more she stared at the eagle, the more she thought it was with her. Maybe keeping an eye on her.

The comfort it brought allowed her to close her eyes, completely letting go of everything, the last thing she heard was a small insect buzzing near her ear.

*****

Some of the ports were nicer to visit than others. The lights of Chicago painted the seaboard as Jared and the freighter slipped past. He liked the big cities – not because he wanted to live there – but because they were like a living thing. Always changing, always moving.

After time behind walls, he'd needed open spaces. He preferred a small town, where he knew the layout, the ins and outs, and who could be a threat. Cities were too crowded, there were too many criminals and too many toes to step on. Still, the glamour of the clubs and the glass penthouses looking down from the towering buildings always got his attention.

He leaned against the railing, noticing the smell in the air the closer they got to the docks. Nothing beat the fresh air out on the lakes and no one could tell him cities didn't stink. He figured everyone must put up with it because they wanted the job or house too much. Fancy jobs for fancy folks, it made him shake his head.

When he was first out of confinement he'd got off in every one of these cities and hit the bars. There had been more than a few late-night fights. He won more than he lost before high-tailing it back to the freighter. A smile spread across his face. Crazy times.

The contrast of the skyscrapers sucking his eyes upward and then little bonfires along the banks of the water where street people and bums camped, was not lost on him. It was always about where you choose to look, he knew that.

The closer they got to the docks the less light and glass he saw. Eventually there were boarded up buildings and low-budget housing, nothing over two stories high.

The crew handled the work duties sharply that night, everyone wanted extra time in port. Getting everything done efficiently was the ticket. And when they got dock space straight away, that sealed the deal. They were lucky tonight. Some harbours at the wrong time of day could be stacked up with freights waiting their turn.

Although the docks were busy around the clock in the bigger cities, tonight looked like it was quiet.

At three in the morning the freighter rocked gently against the dock, the chains holding it stable. No one moved aboard the ship, except Jared and his inner crew. Two were in the stairwell, one a floor above, the other watching the stairs down to the storage rooms.

"I'm letting you go." When he'd first grabbed the girl by the arm and pulled her off the floor her face had lit up for a second before she started eyeing him suspiciously.

"I'm serious, it's done for you. It's over." He pulled her towards the door.

"I'm going to take you out of the shipyard and turn you lose," he shook her hard. "You make a scene anywhere along the way, and I'm bringing you right back here."

He knew how to dangle a carrot. People were more inclined to go after it if there was a fire burning under their feet.

Holding her by the arm, he pulled her up the stairs and out the door onto the deck, his fingers deliberately digging in deep enough to leave bruises. Quickly looking both ways, the last thing he needed right now was a surprise. One more of his crew guarded the bottom of the gangway, joining him as they walked along the docks towards the entrance to the shipyard.

Jared kept the pace quick. His fingers digging into her arm just above the elbow propelling her forward.

The gang he was meeting wouldn't come on the yard, there was too much security in the big ports, they didn't want the hassle. Jared strode through the wide gate and looked up and down the street. There was the van.

The phone call earlier had been brief. "How's three o'clock?"

"Good. Blue van parked on the street."

Now Jared walked directly to it, half-dragging, half-carrying the girl as she stumbled and tried to keep up. About twenty feet shy of the van someone emerging from the shadows. He was relieved it was a face he recognized, not someone else. It was twice in a week he'd let his guard down.

"Hey, sailor man. You got us another red one?"

Before he could answer, the doors on the back of the van swung open and another gangster appeared. Now the girl struggled, trying to pull away. Jared knew this guy, they had done this many times in the past. He shoved the native forward where she was grabbed and pulled into the van.

The guy stuck out his hand and said as Jared took the cash, "I thought you said two?"

"Just not this time friend. Next time for sure."

Jared wondered how much money the gang made off each one he dropped off. It was a lot more than they paid for her. To him it didn't matter, her purpose had been served and it was time to cut her loose.

No one said a word as the sailors headed back to their ship. Jared was lost in thought. He was glad he'd decided not to drop off the other girl. He had a sudden surge of electricity at the thought of lying with her again.

They would have the talk the next time they were together, and that seemed to fill him with hope.

*****

Chicago

Billy couldn't believe what was happening. What could he do? He was sure the woman he was watching was a native girl. The guy who had her by the arm seemed to be leading her forcefully away from the ship. Everything was happening too fast, and he needed to think.

He went over it again in his head. The text he'd sent, and the return text that had come in two hours later, waking him from a restless sleep.

Debark Chicago. Approach freighters. Especially the Slate.

He'd remembered the name from the list he'd coaxed from the drunk, the S.S. Slate. It had an ominous sound to it now. He knew it was his next target, and there was trouble ahead. He just hadn't expected it to come this quickly.

Now he watched the men walking away from the freighter, taking the girl with them. Billy had been hiding two freighters away, leaning up against a storage container keeping an eye on the ship.

Staying back in the shadows, walking between the stacks of containers and the fence, he kept pace with them. Again he asked, what can I do? It wasn't the right question. He could do a lot of things; rush them, call in support, follow and see where they went. The real question was – what should he do?

Billy had listened to the captain of the Philip cursing at him in his cabin, cursing as he walked down the stairs and onto the deck, and cursing even as he walked up the pier. Ships were mandated to have a certain number of crew aboard. Schedules and rotations relied on it. The Captain wasn't happy with the sudden resignation.

Billy had walked around the miles of docks and not found the S.S. Slate. He was starting to wonder what head office knew, and how they would know what freighters would be where. He also wondered how they expected him to get aboard.

It had happened pretty easily with the Philip, even if he still wasn't sure how. When he saw a freighter coming into the harbour, he'd followed it to its destination, and found his target.

He'd watched the Slate unload and slowly wind down for the night. Some freighters were gone the second they were done, others chose to wait where they were, planning to meet schedules at other stops.

Once it was clear the ship was staying put, Billy moved to a position and staked it out. A few hours later he now found himself stalking what he was sure was a native girl.

Where was she from? One of the reserves he knew? He wanted to run in and grab her, but his training was taking over. He needed to find out more if he could. This was just the first piece, the tip of the iceberg. He should rush it, but he could blow it.

He shadowed the men as they headed out the gate and paused for a moment before turning and heading up the street. Keeping away from the yard-lights, Billy eased closer to the entrance, and then held back trying to find a good viewpoint.

Scanned the road ahead of the walking men nothing stood out. Then the van caught his attention. He knew he was running out of time.

Billy stopped. He tried to fade back a bit and find a shadow. A figure had stepped out onto the street, heading on a line to intercept the small group. Now there were three against one, which changed the odds. It stung, but Billy knew that all that was left was surveillance now.

When he saw the fourth guy swing open the van's back doors, he felt hopeless. The girl was pulled inside and the two men from the freighter turned around heading back to the yard.

Billy scrambled backwards and took off running, thinking as he ran.

He watched as they approached their freighter. He had managed to sprint back past it, turned around, and was now walking back towards the oncoming men. He wanted to confront the two guys as they approached the Slate. At a minimum he would be able to see a face.

"Hey, how you guys doing?"

The first one stopped dead in his tracks and stared. Billy wasn't sure if it was the interruption, or the color of his skin. The guy looked around the yard suspiciously, like he was expecting trouble. Billy glanced down at the guy's clenched fists half-hidden by a jacket.

"What the fuck you want?" There was menace in the question.

"I'm looking for work. Wondered if this ship needs any crew?"

The guy's face went hard in a flash and his shoulders squared, and Billy saw some of what this one might be capable of doing. He wouldn't be a talker.

"You got a card?" The look on the guy's face said he thought Billy was joking.

"Yes sir, I do."

The guy continued to stare hard. Billy felt the scrutiny. There was an undercurrent of violence there. Just as quickly, the guy's face softened, he laughed, then headed to the freighter.

"Yeah, well fuck off. We don't need anyone."

Billy watched the two until they started to climb the gangway onto the ship. He would try again in the morning.

With a few hours to burn, he took a walk along the pier. Big city ports had endless docks, and he needed to sort out his feelings. He'd let her get away.

This was the hard part of undercover. He couldn't imagine what it was like for the cops who stayed under for years, watching stuff that pissed them off. Billy would never forget this girl. He knew he would always wonder what happened to her.

Now the bigger question was what would he do with the next one? The same thing? At some point they needed a witness, someone who could explain what had happened. It was the only way to learn the process.

He didn't think it would be as easy to let the next one go. As he continued his walk, he apologized to her, "I'm sorry."

The confusion of finding the girl was too much for Billy, was his guard down? Could he have done more? Should he have done more?

*****

Jared saw the man as they approached the freighter. It wasn't out of the ordinary for someone to be out getting fresh air, even at this time of night, especially in port. As he got closer, he noticed the guy seemed to be looking his way.

When they were close enough to see faces clearly under the yellow yard lights, the guy had said something. When Jared realized the guy was a native, bells started going off, but that only lasted a second.

You're in Chicago. Remember man. Get a grip. Life was full of coincidences and that was all this was. Still the native's appearance jump-started his heart for some reason, and fired up that sixth sense that had severed him well many times in the past.

When the guy said he was looking for a job it started to gnaw at his conscience. Coincidence on top of coincidence. In his world that was a sign. The knowledge he was already amped from taking the girl down the dock made him realize he was over-thinking it.

He laughed at his fear and asked himself if he was losing his metal. To get back his juice he added, "Yeah, well fuck off. We don't need anyone."

*****

The Captain started writing the report, long ones on operational nights like this were a pain. The first operation of the night had been spur of the moment, but successful. The second operation, planned, took longer and was also successful.

Pausing for a moment, the captain realized he was just one part of a bigger plan, and had no idea where it was going. On the other hand he smiled, since they were taking steps there were obviously getting somewhere.

CHAPTER 18

S.S. Slate

Another morning. Shanya opened her eyes to the fresh scent of the forest and the sound of birds chirping in her ears. There was dampness underneath her, the dew heavy and wet. She heard the claws scrapping against the bark as a raccoon came down a tree. It was the only animal around of that size who slept off the ground.

It was barely light out, the sun wasn't up over the horizon yet. The eagle still slept perched on the tall tree, his head tucked down into his chest, protected by the feathers of his thick wings curled around his body. Something crawled across her leg, a bug of some sort.

When the heat of the sun coming over the horizon hit the tips of the grasses, Shanya sat up, letting her face warm. She wanted to get up and continue to explore her surroundings, but another part of her was done.

This was as good a spot as any. She had found somewhere she liked. Why keep wandering? Instead, she took stock. The clearing was nice to look at, surrounded by thick trees, with grasses offering plenty of cover.

A brief thought of building a shelter took hold, but she knew it was pointless. She hadn't come to the forest to settle. Initially it had been to escape, but as time went on, she realized it was something more.

As Shanya lay back down, the eagle launched from its perch, squawking once as it took to the air. She wondered if he knew her mission, whether he approved or not. She kept her eyes glued to the bird as it climbed higher in search of altitude.

She couldn't help how she felt. It had taken days to get there, but once she'd found the forest it became easier to accept. She came for one purpose, and that was to shut down.

Knowing it would be the last time, Shanya closed her eyes just as the sun got high enough to shine through the tall grass, the rays hitting her face.

*****

Jared was livid. He'd woken to bad news all around. The first words he heard were that the kid Ronnie was missing. It happened all the time, a crewman found a reason to skip, it could be anywhere, any port. Especially with the younger guys.

He hadn't had enough time with the kid, and the little bastard knew too much. Pressure was starting to build just over Jared's right eye, he stuck a finger in under the eyebrow and pushed hard for a second, trying to relieve the throb.

Where was the kid? Would he open his mouth? Jared wasn't going to be able to let it go easily, and knew this was going to bother him. He'd taken a chance throwing the kid in headfirst, he should have taken more time to feel him out. But he'd been so sure he could bend and shape the kid's will with time. Now there wasn't any time, there wasn't even a kid.

176

Really, he knew it wasn't the missing kid that had his vinegar stirred up, it was the new hire brought on to replace him. There was no way he could accept the fucking Indian. For some reason it freaked him out.

He replayed the previous night's activities over and over in his head. He wished he'd been more serious, thinking big picture instead of focusing on the van outside the gate. Where had the Indian come from? Why had he been hanging around the docks so late at night?

The biggest question swirling around uncontrollable in his head was, what had the Indian seen? Anything? Everything?

It was being Indian that didn't sit well. Any white man, or even black, wouldn't have bothered him, but the Indian was too close to the situation for his liking. That he was looking for work had been a shock.

Finding out that Ronnie was missing this morning and the Captain had hired the Indian was worrying. Jared didn't ever remember working on the lakes with a native before, so the situation seemed so bizarre.

The lines were pulled aboard and the freighter cast off. Jared kept one eye on the workers and the other on the shoreline, he still wanted Ronnie to come running down the dock at the last second. It left a shadow on his day, a gloom that he didn't understand as the S.S. Slate left the early morning fog and city-fumes of Chicago.

When there had been a few minutes he'd asked around, trying to find out as much as he could about what had happened. The boys said Ronnie went into town with a few other guys. They found a bar and started drinking. They weren't really sure when they realized Ronnie wasn't there. They just assumed he went to check out another club. The guys had returned by themselves and never thought of the kid. That didn't settle anything, but he'd think more about it later.

The captain had been walking the deck, already annoyed that one of his crew was missing. When the Indian had come around asking about work, the word had been passed to the Captain. Jared couldn't blame the old man for fixing a problem. Jared was just having a hard time with the perfect timing of it all.

All his experience was screaming that it couldn't happen this way, but it just did. In the can, this type of coincidence was enough to go off on. Suspect something, don't hesitate, it's always you or them.

Two problems to start his day, not really what he was looking for. He watched the city disappear behind them, squinting as he fished between his teeth with his tongue, trying to dislodge a piece of tobacco.

What he really needed right now was to lay with her, hear her answer to his question. He wanted her to think about it, but he assumed she was going to say yes. She was sending him all the right signals.

Torn about not laying with her the night before just increased his desire today. It would be a long wait until nightfall.

It was funny, he had as much anticipation about asking her the question as he did getting new ones each time he went into Thunder Bay. It was an unknown, something he didn't deal well with. But then, no risk – no gain.

Jared's phone went off in his pocket. The message was simple and to the point, yet it increased the aggravation that stirred below the surface.

It's time Jared. She must go.

Ronnie missing, the Indian crewman, and now the Captain wanted closure. It was a good thing he had something to look forward to that evening, because the way things were going he would spend the day wondering if it all was worth it.

Jared knew it was worth it. Tonight he would prove that theory.

*****

Billy was on the afternoon shift, cleaning floors inside the super-structure. The Slate was the biggest boat he'd been on yet. There were two more floors above deck, and it was wider.

He couldn't believe he actually made it onboard.

It was one thing to luck out and get work on the Philip, this was something else – he just wasn't sure what. Destiny? Fate? Or luck on the grandest scale? Maybe the guy last night had no idea of the crew status when he said they didn't need anyone, but that didn't make sense because the guy turned out to be the boss.

Billy finally had a name to go with the face. Jared. Turned out he was the bosun. Billy reported to him, and now was being given the gears by the guy.

"No cutting corners here native. You scrub it clean."

Billy worked the mop over the same spot, back and forth. Then he dipped the mop in the bucket, rinsed the mop, squeezed it dry and did it again. The bosun leaned against the wall and continued his verbal abuse.

"You're not one of those dumb Indians, are you? We don't got all day here."

There was no getting it right, the guy was riding him, and finding fault with everything. First, he didn't clean enough, and then he was taking too long. It was obvious that Jared didn't think much of him, or it could be the man was just a bastard with everyone.

Maybe he hated natives, some people did. The difference was enough, it's all they needed to start creating walls and finding fault.

The more he thought about it, the more it made sense. This Jared guy was in a position of trust. Billy knew the bosun was go between for crew and officers. He would know the in's and outs of the crew movements, shifts and officers involved.

It looked like the guy ran the crew with a tight grip. Billy kept his head down and his eyes open. In one way it was good that Jared was interested in him, it was a chance to build his cover, show he wasn't a threat.

On the other hand, he was going to have to be careful. This asshole was serious material and Billy realized he didn't want to get caught off guard. At this point all he could do was take the verbal crap and work hard.

Looking over his shoulder he could see the bosun still glaring at him.

*****

Hans drank straight from the bottle, no shot glasses required any more. He was angry. It was the last stage of this cycle. He knew another cycle would begin. But he found it hard to look at the bed now. The lower his degradation went, the more the guilt would build.

She was tied up, legs pulled up by her head. She'd been that way since he left for dinner. He was angry at how he felt, at what he'd done. Angry at what he was going to do.

Questions surfaced, and he wondered about them. Why did he go so far? What made him do it? It was the native that brought it on, wasn't it? After all, it was what she wanted wasn't it? Or was it deserved?

With the freighter headed north on the return leg, it brought everything to an end, and that pissed him off the most.

Hans ran a hand over his mouth. He looked down at it, wet with slobber. He knew how obsessed he was with the girl, all of them. That he didn't care about how he lost control with them was the problem.

The text tone echoing in the small room made him jump. It would be Jared answering his earlier message. The message he'd sent made it clear that it was time. Hans checked the screen.

Okay – tonight / tomorrow.

Hans felt relief, hated what was coming, but knew it was the only way. It meant he was down to one last party, maybe two if he was lucky. Everything made him angry, no matter how he looked at it.

Reaching for the bottle, Hans lifted it slowly to his mouth. He didn't want to rush any part of this last party. No one else was drinking, but that didn't matter, he didn't need company.

He'd been thinking about the girl tied up on the bed for a few hours now, and he wasn't going to wait anymore.

REJEAN GIGUERE

CHAPTER 19

S.S. Slate

Streaks of wind-blown cloud careened across the sky, grey against black on the moonless night. Waves lifted the ship high in the air, metal groaned as it twisted under load, then sinking downwards the vessel rode out the rolling swell. Rain pelted the deck, sheets of water blowing sideways made the superstructure barely visible.

The figure struggled along a drenched gangway, wrestling with a dark object. There might have been screams and howls in the air, but no one heard anything over the roaring storm. Midway along the deserted walkway the figure stopped, grabbing hold with one hand, his other arm struck downwards once, and then twice. Bending over, he lifted the weight onto his shoulder. Now he made progress, using his free hand to hold the railing, he walked around the massive corner of the structure, following along a small ledge at the back of the ship.

The storm rocked the boat violently, his arm wrenched in its socket as he damn near went over the railing.

He couldn't turn back. He couldn't put this off any longer, they would be docking in three days and he might not get another chance.

Once he was around the corner, facing the boat's churning wake, he flipped the bundle on his shoulder up into the air, thrusting with his arms to push the weight away as it fell.

The figure leaned against the railing, watching the bundle until he lost sight of it in the darkness. Then a small splash as it hit the water. Fascinated, as always, he gripped the railing, watching for any sign of movement. Trying to keep his eyes on the spot where it landed was impossible as the boat pitched and rolled with another set of waves.

It was over in seconds. There were no more screams lost to the wind.

Jared pulled his collar up around his neck. As the storm built the temperature had dropped throughout the day. Returning two-handed along the walkway, he remembered hearing Hans explain it the first time.

"No. No way. "The Captain had been adamant.

Jared had wanted to sell the girls down south.

"No witnesses Jared." The captain had shaken his head.

His original plan hadn't involved killing anyone. He would always blame the captain for making it happen.

"I seen it before. The only way you make sure it doesn't come back to haunt you is to take care of it."

Jared never did find out about the other situations that the man spoke about, but the plan had changed from that point on. If a squaw saw the captain's face, she had to go.

It had forced Jared to give the boss his own women, and it meant he had made a few trips to the back of the freighter. Just wrinkles in a plan that he worked around. But it had changed how he looked at the old man as well. Jared had no fear of the guy, but knew now there was a dark side to him, and wouldn't forget it.

Finally, with his deed done, it was time. He was alone without the crew helping him. He never let anyone know about what went on at the back of the freighter. Some things you were smart enough to keep to yourself.

It had been a long day waiting to be with her. His heart started to pound as he thought of asking her the question. He chuckled at the way she got his blood moving, the walk to the back of the freighter had been nothing compared with this.

Preoccupied, he headed down the stairway to the storage rooms. Tonight could change everything.

Standing above her, the lights out, he could see her slight form curled up under the blanket. Quickly, Jared undressed and got in under the blanket with her. The immediate warm that he felt gave him hope. Wrapped his arms around her, he pulled her close.

She seemed stiff, she didn't move limply as she had the last number of days. Instead, he folded around her and adjusted. There was no hurry. Closing his eyes, he allowed himself to relax.

Jared tried not to get excited, but couldn't stop himself. Soon he was pressing hard against her. When he started to roll her over, her curled body came as one. When he tried to push her legs down and straighten them out, she resisted. Her arms were wrapped around her legs, she wasn't letting go.

Anger pounded behind his right eye, his nostrils flared open and his teeth clenched together. Instinct almost made him hit her, then he forced some self-control. This was where he always made his mistake. Warning himself, he tried to keep the violence out of it.

Jared held her tight again, moving his head closer to hers. His mouth came to rest against her ear. He spoke to her gently, wanting her to understand. He was giving everything he had. Would she see he was sincere?

"I thought you were different from the first time I saw you." Jared pulled her tighter, engulfing her small body with his.

"I noticed how you gave yourself to me. I liked it." He was committed at this point. He was opening himself up for rejection, something he hated. She'd better understand.

"I was thinking about something I wanted to ask you." He found himself hesitating, knowing this was the moment. "Would you like to live with me?"

He held his breath waiting for her response. After a moment he opened his eyes. Hers were still closed, she didn't seem to be listening.

"You could move in with me. I have a place." He tried not to, but his voice rose as he made his case.

He waited a long time, giving her plenty of chance to say something. Anger swelled at the rejection, and once more he fought down the lump choking his throat. It really was a feat, because not very often was the tap turned off once it started to flow. However, this time he was able to stop the anger, and Jared again made excuses for her silence.

She was just shocked by the question, just needed time to think about if before she agreed. He would let her absorb the idea, figuring it would be all good once she had time. How could she not want it? They seemed to work so well together.

He found a reason to smile as he let her roll back onto her side. He'd delivered the message, she could think on it. Jared covered them up with the blanket as he curled up around her, he wasn't going anywhere.

He didn't care what the crew thought, but with his increasing absences they had to know, tonight he was staying with her as long as he could. Another hour or two at the very least.

*****

Billy almost screamed out loud, but stopped himself, it was too late. He'd watched the figure come around the corner along the walkway below. Billy leaned over the railing protecting the observation deck behind the bridge.

He'd asked the second in command if he could see the bridge. Walking the command centre watching the radar and navigation screens, it was everything to hold down his stomach in the storm. He didn't think it was a likely place, but he had to eliminate it as somewhere a captive could be held.

Too late to get the girl in Chicago, now he was just hitching a ride back to Thunder Bay to start over. When he'd noticed the observation deck off the back of the bridge, he asked to go out there, mostly out of curiosity, but also because he thought his dinner was about to make a return visit.

"Be damned careful out there, you don't want to go over."

Straining, Billy forced himself to hold on to the pitching ship for a few minutes and was ready to go back in when the figure came around the corner down below. It took a second to notice he was carrying something.

The hairs stood up on the back of his neck, he knew what it looked like. The guy heaved the bundle up and into the air so suddenly Billy hadn't been ready. The scream hung in his open mouth as he watched the bundle flying awkwardly through the air.

Billy strained, forced himself to follow the arc of the flying bundle, watching the splash as it hit the water. A wave rolled, then another, the ship tossed and he lost track of the spot. He'd tried to hold on as long as he could, watching the last moments. Staring up at the sky, he swore, "Fuck." Then again, harder, "FUCK."

He'd said he would do better with the next girl he found, and instead he'd done nothing. If he thought the girl in Chicago was going to be hard to accept, this one would haunt him the rest of his life. There was still a chance for the girl in Chicago, but this one was gone forever.

But it wasn't time for grieving. Looking down, he watched the man round the corner on his way back around the side of the freighter. The undercover cop tore himself away from the railing, realizing he'd been gripping it with all his strength.

Billy thanked the second officer on the way past, and once he was off the bridge sprinted down the stairs. Two, then four at a time, he was way behind. He went down the four flights in quick-time and caught himself against the doorframe to the deck. A quick look around ensured no one was watching, he leaned his head out to try and see the opposite corner of the structure where the guy should emerge if he hadn't already.

It was luck that there was a light near that corner, but not a surprise when he saw who it was who appeared with his face exposed. The bosun, Jared.

You just killed someone you bastard.

Somewhere in his heart Billy felt a scale tip over. He spent years trying to get away from the reserves, years trying to get a white man's job. He knew inside he'd been trying to get away from everything native.

Now he was pissed at the white man, pissed at anyone hurting natives. This case was pulling him back to his people. Standing in the doorway, for the first time he wanted to save every single one of his kind. It had taken this long to see it, but running away from it hadn't solved anything. Besides, someone had to fight for the people. If it wasn't him, then who was it?

Billy scrambled across the deck as Jared stepped through the door on the other side of the freighter. He got there just in time to see a shadow moving away on the floor below where the storage rooms were, and his senses kicked into overdrive.

The guy wasn't going to his sleeping quarters at this time of night? Where was he going? Billy heard a steel door open and close. He wondered how much of this emotional rollercoaster he could take.

Slipping down the stairs to get a closer look, he knew he'd just watched someone being killed. But this behaviour made him ask if there might be more still alive.

He couldn't do anything at the moment, but there was no way anyone was getting away. He'd seen enough for the night, and other than waiting to see when Jared left, there wasn't much he could do.

Billy knew what was next though – getting into that room. He was so sure of it he got out his phone and sent out a warning text.

One overboard. Gone. One or more alive.

*****

Shanya felt the warmth of day leave her, but it didn't matter, weather had no effect now. She heard the eagle calling out, squawking at her, but it was too far away.

There was a beat now that thumped against her like a heart the size of a house. She kept sinking lower and lower into the ground. Like Nanabozho who shrank to the size of a snake to enter the skull of a dead moose to eat at the meat inside, Shanya shrank smaller and smaller.

She was a wolf, then a rabbit. She ran along the ground as a mouse and then slithered as a worm. When she burrowed into the earth the worm became a centipede, and then something smaller she didn't understand.

The beating heart was constant, it was all that she focused on. There was comfort in the rhythm, it resonated through her body, surrounding like a cocoon.

Words tried to invade the beat, her spirit stumbled at the disturbance. Words, "Us, Together," invaded her bubble and she welcomed the thoughts, mouthing her answer, "Yes mother earth, we are together."

She went deeper into the earth finding refuge, the heartbeat of the ground engulfing her. Shanya was gone, she was no more.

CHAPTER 20

S.S. Slate

"Come on redskin, one, two, three, four. Get that drink down and pour some more."

Jared had the men packed into the small worker's lounge, drinking hard. He liked it when everyone went along with his mood. He didn't like feeling he was different than the rest of them, except when he wanted their attention.

Jared wasn't acknowledging her refusal to answer his question. It was just an adjustment period for her. He bet his next visit would confirm it. She would let him know when she was ready. In the back of his mind was the fact that they were nearing the top of Michigan, if they weren't already in the channel.

Whether it was his mood, and the others felt it, or it was the size of the native, the crew stood around the small table with Jared opposite the rookie. It had started out as innocent as usual, the crew amped up, ready for some entertainment.

The initiation ritual had taken a turn after about six or seven shots when the Indian spoke out. Billy'd accepted the ritual, no fuss. After looking around at the other guys, he'd seemed to realize it was something everyone must go through.

Jared had never had anyone back down, no one liked being called a pussy. How long they lasted was another thing. One time a young kid had puked on the table after his fifth shot. The crew had laughed for an hour.

This time the ritual took on a life of its own when the crew heard the native's challenge.

"What's wrong Jared? You can't keep up? All words no action."

Jared wasn't gonna back down in front of his crew. He poured them both a shot and the two stared eye-to-eye as they raised the liquor.

"Again." The sharp knock of the shot glasses hitting the table echoed in the small room.

Maybe that was when the others shifted slightly away from the table. To them it was becoming a two-man race, and they stood back to watch. His anger consumed the shots, fed on them, fueled his desire to beat the Indian. He couldn't believe the nerve of this guy. *No one challenged the bosun.*

What kept catching him off guard was the intensity of the native's stare. Billy never looked at the shot glass, never took his hand off it. His arm went up and down like a machine. No hesitation, down the hatch in one go.

Worst as he stared back, was the way that the Indian's eyes bore into his. The confrontation was there, the anger simmering. Jared recognized it anywhere, he'd seen it many times.

Suddenly, it hit him. The situation was escalating. He flexed his fists. Any time he'd ever been looked at like that in the past, there had been violence soon after. If he knew more about the redskin he'd have already made a move by now. In jail that look would have sent him across the table, getting in the first strike.

Jared poured them another shot. He opened his mouth to say something and the Indian beat him to it. The nerve of the guy was heightened by the murmurs of the crew standing around. They couldn't believe it either.

"I know Jared. One, Two, three, four, can't you handle any more?"

The questions were building now. The Indian's cockiness pointed to a level of confidence he could back up. One thing Jared had learned was to make sure he'd sized things up correctly before making a move. And he was going to make one here, that was sure. This redskin would pay for putting him on the spot in front of the boys. It would be a lesson for them, as well as the native.

Jared emptied the glass in one go. He watched the Indian match him and set his glass down, ready for another. He was starting to wonder if he could out-drink the cocky fucker. It obviously wasn't going to be easy.

As the bosun looked around at the crew, some of them started to file out of the lounge. The tension in the room was rising, they obviously felt it as much as he did. But he couldn't focus on them right now, turning back to face the native. Where was he from? The Indian must have done time. Where? What was the best way to deal with him?

Jared grabbed the bottle by the neck. It was beginning to look like he might not want the crew to watch the end of this duel. His glare was working as a couple more left the room. When they cleared the room he could get down to business.

*****

Billy was forcing his anger down. The challenge to drink, a stupid rookie initiation ritual had been exactly what he needed. He couldn't get the picture of the body hitting water out of his mind.

As he grew up he'd heard stories of how the natives dealt with white men who abused their women. The rusty lid from an old scup can sure cut off the balls in a hurry.

When he realized everyone was going to stand around and watch, Billy knew this was serious. If he drank until he passed out he had no idea what would happen. As mad as he was himself, he wanted to see how far he could push the bosun.

He'd challenged the man in front of everyone, so Jared couldn't back down. As the two of them drank, Billy started to like the odds better. He might not outdrink the guy, but either way the guy would be too drunk to do anything. As Jared kept pouring shots Billy wondered how far he would go. The undercover cop knew he was catching a buzz, it wouldn't be too much longer before the booze began taking its toll on him.

Billy was losing his cool, taking chances that he didn't want to, but he knew there was immediate danger to himself and any other native on the freighter. He wanted to shake this tree as soon and as hard as he could.

The laughter that had started the proceedings became hushed whispers as the two of them faced each other across the small table, drinking shot after shot. It was obvious Jared was getting uncomfortable, he kept looking at the crew and they kept trickling out the door.

The two of them were locked together now. He wondered if the bosun knew he was already in a fight? Was he using the time to figure out his opponent like Billy was? Was he picturing the final stages? Visualizing the punches he would throw? Billy was, even if it wasn't in line with his training.

He stared hard at the man's rough face, oily complexion and pasty skin. The guy was constantly squinting his eyes and clenching his teeth. It looked like he was ready to go off at any second – either that, or trying hard to fart.

Billy smiled inside, that was his training coming back, a joke to break the tension, even if it was in his head. It also brought him back to events in front of him. He had to stop the drinking. There weren't a lot of options, but it might keep Jared off balance another few hours.

Billy was sure the bosun was an ex-con. That could be used to his advantage while they talked. "One more for the night? You done with this bullshit ritual?"

He was giving the guy a chance to back out. It would tell him a lot. It also alluded that Billy wasn't a newbie on the straight and narrow. It made it seem like the drinking game was nothing.

He hadn't taken his gaze from Jared's face for more than a second since he'd been forced to sit in the chair. Now he saw the confusion, the calculation, and the eyes so narrow they were almost closed.

Billy had read the urge to hurt earlier, now it looked like someone unsure of their position. He wondered what the guy would do if he was challenged. He looked confused enough to come out swinging.

"Sure, one more."

Billy felt relief spread through his system. He didn't change his expression, but he was glad it was over. He lifted the glass, knowing it was far from over – but this battle was won. "Cheers."

The words said for the girl that went overboard, not to the asshole he was sitting with.

*****

Hans busied himself cleaning the corner table. He was sanitizing the room, cleaning it from one end to the other. It was something he had to do. The beds had been stripped and cleaned, the floors washed and washed again. There was no part of the cabin that he didn't get to.

He needed to feel clean, to feel the responsible captain he was. The shipshape room represented him erasing the memories. It always hit him at this point when he thought about returning everything to normal. What was out of order in the first place?

With the room clean he could sit back and relax. Everything was gone. There was no chance, no way in heaven that he could be attached to her. No way except through the bosun, Jared.

Of course the man couldn't say anything, but if he did…. Hans always came to this conclusion. He could do something to Jared, it was the best way to eliminate the threat but if he'd done that years ago, how many girls would he have missed out on.

No – he rationalized – Jared was good to have around. He was the bringer of gifts, ones that made the captain's life so much better. It was only a day since the bosun had taken her out of the cabin. Hans felt guilty all night and day, but as the next night came around and he finished cleaning the room, he knew it wasn't the end.

He tried not to, forcing the thought away because it was too soon, but he already wondered what was waiting back in Thunder Bay. Hans knew it wasn't the end, just a prelude to another beginning.

*****

Thunder Bay

Inspector Kelly waited for them to bring in the girl. He was invested in the case and wouldn't let any sign go unturned. As he thought of the missing native girl he couldn't help think of Billy. The rookie was getting somewhere.

Kelly had been given a mandate to investigate the disturbing trend of increasing numbers of missing Aboriginal women and find out what the hell was happening. He'd followed the missing women's stories closer over the last few years and knew in his gut there was a pattern. It was always reserve girls coming into the big city who disappeared.

It would be too hard to take them on the reserves, but here in the city no one saw anything. The Inspector couldn't focus on every possible way for women to disappear and had tried to narrow the search. Two years ago a girl jumped off a freighter in port and the first stories came to light.

Having a native to send undercover wasn't necessary, except to Kelly. Having lived in the north his whole life he had an idea of their culture. The Inspector figured that if any natives were found on the freighters, Billy would have better luck communicating, getting one of them to listen and cooperate.

The knock at the door broke his train of thought. "Come in."

A young native girl was brought in and made to sit in front of him. A typical rebellious teen from her clothing and piercings. On the surface he had no problem with it. It was her answers that mattered.

She had already been questioned by a detective a week earlier, and Kelly wanted to get his own feel for what she had said. This recent disappearance had all the signs of an abduction, it fit the pattern perfectly.

"So your name is Erin?"

The girl shrugged her shoulders. He'd seen it before. Natives didn't think they were really part of the normal process and were suspicious of the police. They also talked to each other and knew what worked, or didn't, when dealing with the authorities. He wasn't going to waste his time.

"I understand you live beside each other. I can't believe you don't care she's missing."

He saw the lips pinch together as her eyes closed briefly. So she was bothered, but putting on the brave face. She wouldn't talk to cops. Well he didn't have time to coddle her emotions.

"You sit there playing tough girl while your friend gets sold to the sex trade?"

Erin opened her mouth to protest and he never gave her a chance, "Not what I'd call a friend."

It was in her indecision that he saw the first crack. She was starting to realize where Shanya might be. He saw the fear there behind the façade.

"Who did she leave with?" He hoped to catch her off guard.

Again, the hesitation. He was sure she was holding out.

He'd learned to let the natives stew with bad news. He never got anywhere with them on the first pass. It was a pride thing, say nothing. But as they thought about what was coming next, as the potential for jail became reality, some of them would break down and give in. This is what he wanted from Erin.

Standing, he leaned over the desk. "If I find out you're lying, you will go to jail Erin. You think about that, and what is happening to your friend Shanya as we speak."

She was still holding on to the tough exterior, but he noticed her hands trembling in her lap.

"Now get out of here. You're as useless to me as you were to Shanya."

*****

S.S. Slate

Drunk from the shots, frustrated and angry, Jared stumbled down the stairs to the storage rooms. He swung the door open, bouncing it off the wall with a sound as violent as a shotgun blast, then slammed it shut behind him.

Where the hell is she?

The darkness was an obstacle after the booze and he bumped a few crates while finding her. His clothes came off awkwardly and he climbed in behind her, pulling the blanket over both of them.

Her heat soothed his nerves and he felt the anger subside as his arms went around her and he pulled himself close. With his eyes closed, he let her body settle his. She had that ability, and he couldn't believe how much he liked it.

"Do you have an answer for me?" He whispered into her ear.

She might have forgot the question, and he didn't want any confusion.

"Do you want to live with me?" His lips pressed against the small ear, harder this time.

He sensed a breaking point and tried to avoid it. "Tell me you want to." His arms squeezed her now, harder than he realized.

She didn't answer. Was she ignoring him? This was important. Why didn't she answer?

"You goddamn bitch." Jared lost it. He smacked her hard on the back of the head. Then he rolled her over.

As before, she came over curled in a ball, so he punched her thigh. She didn't lower her legs and he snapped.

Rising up on his knees, he punched down at her, legs, stomach, shoulder. He aimed for the hands holding her legs and she let go. Jared crawled between her thighs and laid on top of her.

His rage was taking over as he pinned her arms out to the side. He was livid by the time he took her, and he screamed at her.

"You had your chance bitch. You had your fucking chance."

*****

The earth was both hot and cold, a sensation that was completely unknown. Moisture and mineral mixed into different substances. Was there consciousness? Was there knowledge?

Whatever imaginary part of her that still existed sensed the earth begin to rumble, earthquakes and volcanoes came to mind. There was pressure as the earth moved around her, the pain was instantaneous, but there was nothing that could be done.

The pain was here, then there, yet nowhere. The microbe shrank to a cell, the cell shrank to a neutron. Then there was nothing.

CHAPTER 21

S.S. Slate

The effects of the booze weren't deterring Billy from his mission, but he wasn't operating at one hundred percent either. From his position inside the garbage room he could keep an eye on the other door down the hall. He would hear the large steel door when it opened anyways.

The undercover rookie was getting good at slinking around, at least for a six-footer. Of course, it had been ten days of experience, and surveillance was easy at this time of night. Everyone with a brain, was sleeping, in preparation for the next day's work.

Listening hard, he didn't hear anything for a long time. Then just as he was beginning to have visions of settling down and leaning his head back against the wall, the door swung open and the bosun emerged, locking it behind him. Jared stumbled along the corridor, one hand on the wall to keep himself stable, talking to himself as he headed for the stairs. It looked like he was pissed about something.

Jared was a bastard, no doubt about it. The way he treated people wasn't right, but then he treated everyone that way. The more people Billy met in the white man's world, the more he realized there were all kinds. He wondered how many natives ventured off the reserve and met a Jared. It didn't do much to encourage them getting off again.

Ten minutes went by, then another twenty. Was a half-hour enough time to wait? Billy sat it out another fifteen to be sure, then he exited his hiding spot, stretching his back to ease out the kinks.

Fighting the effects of the booze, he ventured into the hall, quietly working his way over to the door where he stood and stared. What now? Getting down low, bending at the knees he leaned against the door. What he wanted was some kind of contact.

Tap-tap, tap-tap, tap-tap, Tap. He knocked against the door. Again, tap-tap, tap-tap, tap-tap, Tap,. He nodded his head in time with the beat.

Every couple of minutes Billy turned his head to keep an eye on the hallway. There was only one way in, but if someone did come down the stairs, there was nowhere for Billy to hide. Sooner or later he would be answering to why he was there.

Tap-tap, tap-tap, tap-tap, Tap.

With every minute that passed the odds of someone coming by went up. All his training said you didn't stay exposed like this, but this might be the only chance he got.

Jared wasn't coming back, and Billy was already here. As much as he'd like to think he could get here anytime he wanted, he also knew everything could change at any moment. It was an all-in gamble, maybe not the best way to proceed if you had control of a situation, but here he didn't.

Ten minutes turned into a half-hour. Billy reached over his shoulder and pulled at the damp shirt sticking to his back. He knew why he was sweating, the building suspense mixed with doubt was starting to create an edge. In the back of his mind he was sure someone would be coming around at any second, he ought to leave. Was there really someone on the other side of the door? Could his guess have been wrong? If there wasn't, he ought to go.

Everything was saying to get up and go, but he leaned his head against the door and continued.

Tap-tap, tap-tap, tap-tap, tap. "Ee ah, ee ah, ee ah hay," he hummed the words to the Spirit Song under his breath.

What was that? Billy snapped to attention. Was it a noise? He must have become tired going through the motions of knocking. He was sure he just heard something. Was it a response?

Placing an ear against the steel, his eyes closed in concentration. His hand came up slowly and deliberately he hit the door.

Tap-tap, tap-tap, tap-tap, Tap. His breathing ceased, he wanted to be that still.

BANG!.

He heard that. And it was all he needed. There wasn't a second to waste in getting out of there, but he reached into his wallet and pulled out something he'd brought for this exact purpose.

He'd thought hard about how to identify himself to anyone he found. Obviously voice would be best, but he'd known it might not be possible, or advisable depending on the situation, this was one of them. He'd have to yell to be heard through the door.

It was bent in two at the mid-point, where it had been folded into his inner jacket pocket.

"A feather my son." His mother had handed him the eagle feather as he packed his bag. "It will help you find what you are looking for."

Billy tucked the feather under the doorway, holding it a second, rolling it in his fingers, moving it to attract the attention of whoever was on the other side. Then he let it go, looked both ways, and got to his feet.

He knew she wouldn't hear it, but he said it anyways, "It's almost over."

*****

She that was no more listened to the earth, the roots that grew through the soil, seeking their way between the rock and clay, shifting and moving the ground. Liquid ran through fissures opening channels for new life. The noise all around so strange, yet so powerful.

Then to her confusion she heard something new. It was difficult to locate, it seemed to come from somewhere else, somewhere she wasn't.

Of course it didn't matter, it was too late.

Again, something that seemed out of place, but still unclear, floated around her. Why did she care? It became impossible to ignore as it continued, almost repetitively.

Without control she was coming together, like a new blade of grass breaking the surface of the earth, she flowed towards the sound, she heard it clearly now.

206

Tap-tap, tap-tap, tap-tap, Tap.

Everything about the sound was abnormal. It didn't fit. Yet it pulled her towards the surface until she opened her eyes. It hurt, and she blinked slowly to work moisture into her eyelids. How long had they been closed?

Now that she was there in the dark room the noise rang out, loud then soft. Someone was tapping on the door. Who was it? Why were they doing it? Why had she come back?

Tap-tap, tap-tap, tap-tap, Tap. *Ee ah, ee ah, ee ah hay* came to mind. Was it the spirit song?

She wanted to move, but felt paralyzed. She hadn't been herself in a while, and slowly memories were rolling back. They handcuffed her with fear.

Think woman. She rallied herself. She needed to get her wits about her, find her strength. If she was coming back to this reality it was because she needed to. Shanya forced herself up on wobbly legs and stumbled over to the door, dropping to her knees. She tumbled forward slightly, ending up lying on the floor beside the entrance.

Whoever it was didn't seem to be stopping. The beat kept chipping away at the fear in her until she knew she was ready. As the next set of taps hit the door, she reached up and thumped the wall with her fist.

She hardly heard it herself. She felt her own weakness as her hand barely impacted the wall. Determined now, the next time the taps sounded out she tried again.

The tapping stopped. Had whoever it was heard her? Her stomach clenched. Was it a mistake to respond? The breath she'd been holding exploded out of her lungs when the tapping started again.

Tap-tap, tap-tap, tap-tap, Tap.

Bang. She hit out as hard as she could, hoping this time it was enough. She didn't have the strength to do it again.

As the silence built she was sure she'd been heard. So what now?

The sound near the floor scared her at first. She watched something being pushed under the door, twirling. When it stopped, her returning memory said it was a feather.

The bent feather dropped to the floor, and she leaned over on all fours to look at it.

It was hard to suppress the sudden hope she felt shivering up her spine even as doubt rattled her. Tentatively, she reached down and lifted the gift.

Carefully, she straightened the feather out, smoothing it, making it look whole again. An image of her at home came, but Jared's face flooded in just as quickly. She told herself that she was putting a lot of trust in a feather, it was opening her up to being hurt again.

Still, she pictured an eagle flying high above and it seemed so familiar. She couldn't place the bird, it was from somewhere else and she wanted to remember. She just couldn't understand why, but looking down at the feather it was a sign. The tears dropping on the hands folded in her lap she took also as a sign, a sign of being alive.

*****

Derek Jacobs stared out from the condo tower that looked over the bay. It was something he would never tire of. You could see for miles on a good day.

He ought to be moving to a bigger city. Maybe he'd go south someday. He'd rather stare out at fancy yachts, mega boats, and luxury living instead of the run-down factories, grain elevators and the lake freighters he was watching right now.

Derek chuckled to himself. *Easy there man, one step at a time.* He had Thunder Bay locked down solid, product moved and he took a cut on all the action. The girls loaded onto ships worked like clockwork.

His cell number passed between like-minded people, and he'd added a few more freighters just this past spring. Really, he should be thinking about where the next step would take him. Hitting the big city would put him in a place where he could funnel more and more into the pipeline. Product, or girls, he didn't care – just as long as his empire grew.

Derek heard the woman moving around in the bed and it distracted him. Looking at her, he couldn't help but smile. He'd seen the uncertainty in her face when they met in the underground parking lot. She hadn't believed he lived there.

He'd talked her up while they waited for the elevator, then left her with an open invitation for a drink sometime. She'd declined that night, but he knew she was interested. Derek felt he was good looking enough once they got pass their fear.

The second time they met he talked about his view up near the top of the building that she ought to see, and the vintage bottle of wine he had stashed away. This time she said she would stop by sometime, and made sure he knew she was a lawyer. He counted on her being a professional, it was the reason he'd approached her in the first place.

Derek pulled the sheet off of her as he sat on the edge of the bed. Her long legs and dark skin were inviting again this morning. Just seeing her body was enough, his business plans would have to wait.

The vibrating cellphone was a sudden irritation, and Derek got up off the bed quickly, walking towards the large windows to gain some privacy. He read the screen as he lifted the phone to his ear. "Yeah?"

"Hey bro, you know who this is?

The question stopped Derek in mid-step. A bell went off somewhere in his head. That was a weird question. He knew who it was and had to figure they were trying to be discreet.

"Yeah." What else could he say?

"The boys have been around. They been talking to everyone who was at the last party." There was a break while Derek waited, "Thought you'd want to know."

That wasn't good news. No, it was bad all around. *Why?* He didn't need to even think about it, he knew the answer already. He'd had a few nightmares in the last ten days, now he knew they were a premonition.

He'd wondered about her just as much when he was awake, and knew she wasn't the normal kind he took, too clean, maybe too smart, too something – but he wasn't sure what. Either way, he knew they were asking questions because of her. There was no doubt in his mind. None at all.

"Fuck." He looked at the freighters stacked up waiting their turn in harbor. They didn't make him smile like they normally did, and something surged through his head. One thought that led to a feeling.

A bad feeling.

CHAPTER 22

S.S. Slate

The light the beast had left burning in the room was a blessing and curse at the same time. It wasn't as bad with light, the dark had made her scared to move. However, Shanya had to look at herself now and it was shocking.

Numbly, she took time to clean herself and find her clothes, pulling on her jeans, the shirt with a tear at the shoulder and the single sock she had been able to locate.

Leaning up against a crate, she stared at the door. Had it really happened? She held the feather tightly between her fingers. Without it, she would have doubted.

With everything that had happened lately she couldn't rely on her memory to tell her the whole truth. It was like she only had pieces. Images of being small as a bug, walking between the blades of grass, skipped behind her eyes. That didn't make sense, did it? Softly, she ran the feather through her fingers.

It still didn't explain anything, but did serve a purpose. Shanya was thinking harder than ever of getting out of her situation. But a spiral of images kept jumping from her subconscious and she couldn't keep them straight. One image, where she felt herself burrowing into the ground, made her think of a worm.

She rubbed her arm, just above the elbow. There were new bruises, she didn't know where they came from. Or perhaps better said, she knew where they came from, but didn't remember getting them. What had happened to her over the last days? And how many days had it been?

And where was the beast? When had he come by last? Shanya thanked the spirits that it was daytime. He wouldn't visit when the sun was up would he? Shanya knew her last attempt at dealing with the man hadn't been very successful. What would she do when he came this time?

She didn't welcome the legend that floated up to the surface of her thoughts. Her mother's stories felt like a thing of the past now. Still, she let it play out in her head, searching for anything she could use.

The feathered grebe decided not to fly south for the winter, to stay and help a few friends who were injured. Both the whooping crane and mallard duck had broken their wings and would be stuck in the snowy land until spring came.

At first he fed his friends with mice and squirrels, and when winter came with fish he caught by diving through a hole in the ice. This angered the Spirit of Winter and he froze the hole while the grebe was still underwater. The bird swam under the ice near to the shore where the reeds and bulrushes were. He used his beak to pull one down under the ice, and escaped through the hole.

Once home he realized someone was peeking in his wigwam. He lit a large fire but it was still cold inside the wigwam because the Spirit of Winter was outside his door. The grebe took a handkerchief and pretended it was hot. "Gee, but it's hot in here." The Spirit of Winter thought the fire was hot enough to melt him, and he ran away.

Later that winter the grebe had a feast and invited the Spirit of Winter who arrived like a blizzard, with icicles hanging from his nose and face. Grebe built the fire hotter and hotter, getting the wigwam very hot. The icicles were melting off the Spirit of Winters face, but he liked the bowl of wild rice too much to leave.

Finally, the grebe said, "Whew, it's very warm in here, it must be spring already."

The Spirit of Winter got scared and ran out of the wigwam to his home in the north, the snow melting behind him.

The grebe had made the spring come early.

Shanya thought about it. The power of nature was undone by the intelligence of a bird. It was a remarkable feat. Not anyone would believe it was possible. Right then she had a single moment of clarity as it dawned on Shanya that it hadn't mattered whether the Spirit of Winter believed he was smart, just as long as the grebe believed in himself.

The feather in her hand allowed her to believe a little more. Her conviction was building with her strength. Taking a deep breath, she slowly let it out. A calm came over her, and it felt like being reborn. Her hand raised the feather beside her ear as her fingers rolled it back and forth, making it twirl around one way and then the other.

With her eyes closed, she could hear the feather's soothing whoosh-whoosh, but what she saw in her head was her parents' home. It seemed far away, off in the distance at the far end of her vision, but she knew it was home.

*****

All day Jared ran the crew ragged. If his mood was foul, then everyone else would suffer too. He'd been up most of the night and now he growled as he yelled at them all. None of them were smart enough, fast enough, or anywhere near pleasing him enough this afternoon.

He'd let himself get soft for the fucking squaw, and now he was stuck with her. He knew he should have dropped her off in Chicago. It was the way it was supposed to be done. *Follow the plan idiot.* Why had he let her get to him?

He'd tried to understand women when he was younger and given up. He liked the fun and the sex, but couldn't figure out the long-term thing. Every damned time he ended up pissed-off, just like he was now. Goddamn native. Jared spit off the side of the freighter trying to get the taste of disappointment out of his mouth.

Feeling like an idiot annoyed him, and embarrassed him even more. His own ego was bruised, and Jared realized he was the one who had brought it on. Showing signs of weakness was never a good thing, a lesson he'd learned early.

He shook his head. The first cell he was placed in had a tough guy who was already living there. As he stood there in the doorway, the fresh meat clutching everything he owned in the world the guy had asked a few questions that seemed irrelevant, and then a few more that were personal. When Jared had answered them honestly, the guy had taken him for a pushover.

He'd learned later that you didn't answer to anyone you didn't know, to do so was showing you weren't tough enough to say fuck-off. The guy had rolled out of the lower bunk and started to undo his pants.

The dude was a lot bigger standing up, and Jared suddenly realized what was going on. His survival instincts kicked in as the guy pointed to the floor, "Get on your knees boy."

Jared had lunged forward, catching him with his hands holding his fly open and hit him hard in the side of the head. It stunned the guy and he stumbled sideways against the bunks. It was just long enough for Jared to hit him again. This time the guy went over, folding into the lower bunk where Jared used his fists to beat him to a pulp. It turned a seven-month sentence into eleven.

Now here he was, shamed by some young bitch, and he couldn't let it go. Well, he had to now, and that posed another question. Where?

They were in the channels now, on their way to the locks into Superior.

"Get your ass moving you fucking prick." He ripped a Chinese deckhand up and down.

Later that night when he'd have a decent chance it would be too late. He needed big water. Well really he didn't, but he preferred it. He could dump her here, but the channels had constant traffic, changing currents, and the shallows along the sides made it unpredictable. He ran the risk she would wash ashore or be seen floating around by some other boat.

On the big water there was little chance of that. Bodies sank so far down that they never came back up. That meant he'd have to wait until they were through the locks, which pissed him off. Right now he hated her so much he wanted to throw her over the side in broad daylight. What a regret she was already.

After pacing around the ship, he kept ending up back at the same place. Watching the rookie, Billy. Anger flowed a little more, just bubbling over the top of the lid, as Jared watched him work.

This is what had him really pissed off. Jared had never backed down before and he knew in his gut he had given in the previous night. The question was why? At that point he'd been still hoping for the girl to answer his question – that was one reason.

The other reason was Billy himself. Jared knew that once you went through hell you were stronger for it and could use the experience. He'd met some crazy natives in the pen. And heard some of their stories. He knew that Billy could have seen a lot, and done a lot for that matter. He was sure most reserves had their share of violence and opportunity for those who wanted to go the criminal route. All the illegal cigarettes, the banned booze and drug sales promoted it.

When the Indian had challenged him to drink as an equal, it had ruined Jared's plan. He never got the chance to beat him into the ground once he passed out.

"Redskin, you got to be the worst fucking crewman I've ever had."

Billy didn't even look his way.

"You clean like a woman. You not have any muscle on those toothpick arms?"

One way or another, the guy was going to pay. He'd show the dickhead who had the balls. If Jared thought about someone long enough he could always build up the desire to hurt. Confidence was something you nurtured and grew. And so was hate.

"Seriously boy. You don't start working for real, I'm going to kick your ass."

Jared watched the asshole from his vantage point. The injun's eyes focused on his work, ignoring the bosun.

"We'll see how fucking tough you are."

*****

Hung-over, Billy struggled with the ship's movement. He knew now that he would never have a good set of sea legs. His stomach turned and turned again. With so much to think about, he kept his hands busy on the broom, anything to avoid being reminded of his churning stomach.

There was a native girl on the other side of the door. He never saw her, but heard her, and it energized him. She needed help from someone, anyone, and he would do. Who was she? Was there more than one inside there?

Billy realized that was important. He'd already started to formulate escape routes and more than one girl would change things. It was something he had to clarify.

Too many things weren't adding up, how did he stumble on this so fast? Pure luck? Nothing made sense from that perspective, but on the water where he was it was simple. She was there, he was here, and this was his chance.

Which brought him to his second problem. Jared. He went over it again and again, and couldn't figure out why the guy had backed down the night before. It was obvious he was a hardass. He'd taken control of the freighter, and in his position as bosun had the weight to enforce it.

Billy had expected a fight to break out right at the drinking table, but instead the two of them stared at each other and Jared had backed down. Now today, it was obvious something had changed again.

Jared ripped him a new asshole every time he came around, and that seemed often. There was no letup in the constant stream of abuse. The first few times Billy looked over his shoulder to check the bosun's facial expressions. There it was, the menace of a criminal he expected. Jared was angry, and Billy knew he'd better keep his head down going forward.

As the sun went down he tried to walk around, hoping to keep an eye on the storage area, but it was obvious Jared would be drinking with the crew for a while. Billy wondered how long he'd have to wait. Walking around a corner he stumbled into two guys who looked like they'd been waiting for him. He walked right into the smaller one.

"Hey, watch where you're going boy." The older muscled man wasn't smiling.

"Sorry about that. Didn't know you where there." Billy didn't think it was a big deal, but from the looks on their faces apparently it was.

"You talkin' back injun?" The guy stepped forward, his companion crowding in on Billy's left.

It hit him at that moment, they'd been sent to rough him up. Jared still had no balls, but he did have a crew. Billy wanted to strike out first, get an advantage, but that was only useful if his goal was to win. Right now his brain was telling him to lose the fight, let them kick his ass.

Jared would get the news, and think he'd been put in his place. They wouldn't think he was that tough, and it might buy him some space. At the least it would gain him an advantage in the next fight, he wouldn't hold back a second time, when they'd be expecting a pansy.

He decided to force the situation, knowing he felt better in the lead. "Fuck off if you want to be an asshole."

He saw the punch coming as the guy on the left's fist came out of nowhere. Forcing himself not to respond, he took the hit to the head, getting knocked over for his trouble.

Punches and kicks rained down as Billy tried to get back to his feet. Faking a beating was one thing, getting hurt was another. He never saw the punch that knocked him out, just the sight of the steel deck before be blanked out and his face hit the floor.

*****

Lake Michigan

The figure worked by the night-light. Something he did often, and like usual he stopped to rub his eyes. It was time to think about retirement, but he put off the thought like he usual did.

The action was definitely heating up. There had been in constant contact with shore as the events seemed to be coming quicker by the day. Heading for Thunder Bay, they had stowaways to deliver.

Peering at the small screen, reading the email in front of him. He carefully reread the response he was about to send, making sure it was right. Confident as usual, he hit the send button.

Following. Will be next in line at the locks.

*****

Thunder Bay

Derek pulled the S.U.V. out of the underground parking, slowly edging the front out onto the street. He was always careful to take the time he needed to look around the area. He made it his business to know what cars parked where, which ones were day shift or afternoon.

It was always in the details he told himself, especially when the heat was on. Nothing stood out today, which was all right by him. It was looking every day that allowed him to ensure nothing seemed off.

He had business to take care of, heat or not. Today he was moving money. The normal system of picking it up at the party house was out of the question. He'd have one of the guys meet him somewhere. Derek would call him at the last minute when he was sure everything was clear.

What was always a routine job, with manageable risks, could explode into periods of intense pressure and fear whenever the cops were involved. The usual worry of bad drug deals and rip-offs were replaced with visions of going to jail. He knew that would be a whole new kettle of tea.

Derek tapped the wooden dash of the Range Rover. Jail was somewhere he had no intention of ending up. These periods were another level of cloak and dagger that he got through, but every time he wondered if it was his last.

It should be. The sooner he took the plan to Toronto the better. He had the people in place now, they moved the product and he knew the girls would be no difference to them. Money spoke volumes in their world.

His phone went off, he glanced at the number, "What's up?"

This was concerning, the plan they'd agreed on was Derek would make the call.

"The cops were around again." The caller realized Derek wasn't going to answer. "It's the third time in two days. I'll be late getting downtown, leaving now."

Now the call made a little more sense, he was letting Derek know he was running late. The warning was worrying. They really wanted to find him. At least he knew he could count on his guys. None of them would speak to the cops, he was sure of that.

Suddenly, Derek slammed on the brakes, there were too many things going on in his head, he almost went through a red light.

Damn it man. Get ahold of yourself.

CHAPTER 23

S.S. Slate

The workers lounge was loud, Jared was drinking harder than usual and the crew was doing its best to keep up. He wondered if anyone had any resentment that he still had a piece downstairs and they were going without until he restocked.

He supposed that was just one more reason he should have dropped her off with the other one down south. It would have been a lot easier than what was coming, and it was bothering him. He'd justified all the other girls, that was Hans' doing. It was never for him, and that made it easier. This one was going over the side directly at his choosing, and it wasn't sitting well.

It went against the code he lived by, you didn't hurt women. Slapping them around was one thing. This would be a lot different.

He poured another shot and slapped the glass back down on the table to fill again.

They'd be in the locks tomorrow, tomorrow night she was gone. Jared washed the thought down with another whiskey. It didn't seem the booze was helping his mood like it usually did, but he knew that a few more might tip the balance and poured another one.

Once in a while he answered a question or two from the boys, but otherwise they drank and yelled over the music while he sat there stewing in his own mess. He sure wasn't going to make this mistake again. Squaws were for fun. Period. Nothing more.

Jared wondered if it was just the time he lived in. Shit, he was sure the cavemen didn't get into this crap with women. Did they even talk to the broads back then? Or did a man just take what he wanted?

What about the Romans and those orgies he'd heard about? He learned from the smart guys in the pen, white-collar crime guys with all the irrelevant crap they knew. Why couldn't he be living in those times? It would have been easier.

Thinking about women had his thoughts wandering. He ought to have her one more time. Do it like it was supposed to be from the beginning. No falling for her, or thinking she's special. Just some plain-old fun as he took her one last time.

Jared leaned back and grinned. He was building himself back up, getting cocky again, and it felt good. Tomorrow he told himself, before he took her to the back of the freighter. Tonight was all about the booze and drinking with the crew. He poured another shot, he wasn't really participating in the festivities, but he wasn't ready to admit he was drowning his sorrows either.

Jared wasn't sure what time it was when he'd finally had enough. As he carefully pushed himself to his feet he didn't notice that most of the crew were gone, it took all his wits to keep moving in a straight line as he headed towards the door. Everything was a moving blur.

*****

Billy laid up in his bunk nursing sore ribs. It really wasn't much more than aches and pains, but he would have a helluva shiner. There was already a bump growing on the side of his face under his left eye.

He'd woken up lying on the corridor's steel floor. It shocked him initially, the rookie cop knew they could have picked him up and thrown him overboard. He thanked his luck that the bosun wasn't that smart, and didn't see the level of threat he was.

Slowly, he remembered the two assholes pounding on him, and not much else after that. Thinking about the decision to let them win made him shake his head. "Nice move smartass."

As he lay there, Billy kept track of people coming back from the lounge. When he was sure his group of bunks were filled, and he heard the steady buzz of snores, he knew it was time.

Getting up and out of the bunk wasn't as easy as it used to be. He almost grunted at the pain where he'd been kicked just below the ribs, that was going to hurt for days. He'd felt it after some particularly violent hockey games, too many slashes on the hip and too many hits from behind slamming him into the boards.

Standing outside the bunk he stretched, loosening up his shoulders, rolling his neck around for the same reason. Then quietly he slipped away from the bunks.

On the way down the hall a quick peak into the lounge confirmed no one was there. Billy took his time, he couldn't afford another fight. There wasn't enough energy left to take a swing at anybody as he worked his way towards the staircase down into the storage area.

Taking fifteen minutes to check out the doorway to the stairwell before approaching required a level of patience he was having a hard time finding. Any position he crouched in hurt like hell within seconds, and it seemed the more he tried to focus, the more the swollen eye filled with water, blurring his vision.

Finally sure he was alone, he moved through the doorway and down the stairs, pausing again at the bottom to listen. Jared could be around and there was no way of being sure. At least not yet.

He felt his heart beating harder against his ribs, the adrenaline was flowing freely, reducing the aches and pains. Billy turned his head to the left, and then the right. He needed to keep his wits about him, be alert and rely on his street-smarts to kick in if there was a threat. Right now he wanted to focus on that steel door.

Some day he might become better at waiting it out, spending all day watching through a photo lens, or lounging on long stakeouts. But here it was people on one side of the door, him on the other. He wanted to break the door down right now, but knew he had to stick to a plan to make it work, he'd probably only get the one chance.

They were close to the Sault Ste. Marie locks, the freighter was almost back from its two-week run on the lakes. The crew had told him they made the trip every couple weeks like clockwork.

Billy knew the locks were too crowded, no undercover wanted to come out from his case on the front pages of a newspaper, it ended a career quickly and the uniform job came next. Yet he knew it was the best place.

The more he thought about it the more he realized it would have to be as soon as they left the locks. He could start once they were out of sight of the lights and the crew headed back to their bunks for the rest of the night.

His eyes checked left and right again, still no one to bother him. Billy got down on his knees outside the door, somehow that way it just felt like he was hidden a little in the barely lit hallway.

He couldn't waste time though. Success depended on not getting caught, especially this night when he was already done in. Billy raised his fist up with his knuckles facing the door. He rapped against the door three times, much harder than the night before. He couldn't wait the hour or two it had taken last time.

No sound came back his way, so he did it again, this time listening hard for any response. Still nothing, and he felt a slight surge of anger. *We don't have all night girl.*

He tried to convey his urgency by speeding up the rate of rapping against the door, three hits coming quick in succession. He only waited a moment before doing it again, then again.

BANG! He heard the response and felt his pulse jump. Okay, he had her attention. What next?

Knowing he needed answers, there was only one way to get them. Billy spread himself out on the floor, his face down at the crack under the door. Reaching into his pocket, he pulled out the small piece of paper and stuck it through the opening. Holding the end with his fingers, he waited for her to take it.

The paper was pulled from his grasp, disappearing under the door. Now all he could do was wait.

*****

The later it got, the harder time Shanya was having keeping it together. She almost wished the lights were off now. She didn't want to see the beast when he came, it was better if she was hiding in the dark. She hated this part of being back, alive, in the room.

What if it was the other person who came? Hope put spring in her step and she was up pacing around the room like the first night. She had allowed this new person to occupy her thoughts all day, and she really wanted to know who it was. Did they represent an opportunity to escape, or was it someone playing games with her?

When it came time to sit down, she couldn't make herself sit in any of the spots she usually rested. She wanted to do something different, but didn't know what. Actually, she knew. She went over by the door and slid down the wall beside it.

Shanya wanted the person to come by so badly that she would wait here, ready. She wondered why they had kept on knocking the night before, when she took so long to answer. All day she realized she was thankful for that person's effort, grateful that they had the patience to wait for her. She wasn't making the same mistake this time.

An hour went by, then two. When Shanya thought she heard something she stiffened up, then leaned forward, watching for shadows in the hall under the door.

She heard noise again, and then the shadow blocked the light. Bent over at the knees, watching, she waited. Started to tremble, fear took over again as Jared's face appeared in her head.

Shanya wanted to close her eyes to the future, but forced them to stay open. When it appeared that someone had dropped down to the ground on the other side, she exhaled in relief. It had to be the same person. Her hand raised to cover her mouth.

The first taps against the door were much louder than the last time, which was confusing. Was it the same person? Why so loud?

When the taps started to come faster, she kicked herself. She'd said she wouldn't make him wait this time. The next set of raps against the door encouraged her, and she hit the door with her palm.

It sounded loud to her, she feared too loud, and suddenly she worried it would bring attention. The rapping stopped and her stomach twisted. What would happen next? Seeing the shadow move under the door, she kept her eyes fixed on the movement.

At first she couldn't move when the piece of paper slid under. What was this? Some trick? When it was obvious she was supposed to take it, she quickly reached out and pulled. With the paper in her hand she still stared at the crack expecting something more to happen. When nothing did, she looked at the paper.

On the ground to talk.

Shanya gasped. She hesitated only a moment before putting her face sideways to the ground.

It shocked her to see one brown eye and part of a face. The skin around the eye looked swollen and purple. It scared her again.

Too many emotions, too many thoughts. She couldn't get her head straight and the first words he said didn't help.

"*Aaniin nishiime*. Hello sister, how many of you are there?"

Her brain was trying to catch up, but her spirit was soaring. Somewhere in her head she was missing the most important thing that was going on, not recognizing the obvious.

She blinked, and reread the piece of paper in her hand. The note was written in Ojibwe, and the words she just heard were her own. Shanya looked at the swollen eye under the door with a newfound interest. Who was he, and why was he out there?

As she summoned the courage to answer his question, she wondered if he could see her as clearly as she could see him. Did he see her tears hitting the floor?

CHAPTER 24

Nervous energy kept Shanya from sitting still. Time wasn't moving fast enough. She fidgeted, changing positions repeatedly. There wouldn't be any more tears, she'd cried the well dry during the night.

One of her own. She couldn't believe it. It made her feel bad for doubting the legends, or the way of her people. She tried to tell herself it was justified, she was under so much duress that she lost her way.

How could he show up right when she desperately needed someone? How did he find her?

She had always planned to become educated in helping others, dedicating herself to natives in need, perhaps focusing on shaping and encouraging the children. Now it was her being helped. Actually, she was being saved and all he'd said was to be tough, ready and willing.

She didn't even care if the beast came now. She'd endure it, knowing there was a new light at the end of the tunnel. So many disjointed questions popped up one after another, she couldn't keep up. Where was she? How many days had passed? When was he coming for her? What were they going to do?

The excitement had her legs dancing again, and she pushed to her feet trying to walk off the nervousness. As she paced from one side of the small room to the other the anger she had bottled up tried to surface again. She wouldn't acknowledge it, but she wondered how long it would stay with her. Maybe forever she reasoned.

Revenge wasn't a good portrait of one's self, but she couldn't help it. Somewhere deep inside she really needed the beast to pay. Instead of fighting it, Shanya welcomed the legend that came to her.

It was known that many years ago the Buffalo never had a hump. The big animal spent its summers running hard across the prairies just for the fun of it. Foxes ran in front to warn the smaller animals the Buffalo was coming.

The Buffalo trampled and scattered the small bird nests that littered the ground, and they cried out their protest, which was completely ignored by the big animal. When Nanabozho heard why the birds were crying, he ran ahead of the Buffalo and Foxes to stop them.

Angry, Nanabozho hit the Buffalo on the shoulders with a stick, causing it to hump up its shoulders and hang its head to avoid another blow.

Nanabozho lectured the Buffalo. "You should be ashamed. You will always have a hump on your shoulder, and will always carry your head low because of your shame."

The foxes dug holes in the ground to hide from Nanabozho, so he warned them, "And you Foxes, you will always live in the ground as punishment for hurting the birds."

Justice had a way of sorting itself out she thought. She wanted Nanabozho to take care of the beast, to teach him a lesson. The more she thought about it, came the realization that it wasn't about the revenge. It was more about making sure it didn't happen again, so that no other woman would have to suffer like she did. The sickness needed to stop.

Shanya relived the conversation with the Anishinaabe, he'd wanted to know how many there were in the room. She'd said just one. He'd been silent a few moments after that answer, but eventually had kept on asking questions. Could she walk? Was she healthy?

They seemed strange to her, why did it matter? Just get her out of there. What was the difficulty? But all she could focus on were his last words – we will go tomorrow night.

She couldn't sit still. It was midday, with hours to go until the night set in. She had no idea what the brother meant by going tonight, but she would be ready. Thinking of escape made her get up and run around the room for fifteen minutes to get her legs working again, certain they'd become weak. Everything ached as she worked the muscles loose.

A new life was just around the corner, she could feel it. There wouldn't be parties or strange people in her life ever again. The image of her parent's house came again, she could see it closer now, the fences were almost visible across the far end of the clearing, and she could just spot some of the trees in the garden. Was that her mother's cooking she smelled in the air?

Shanya stopped walking and blinked, she was staring at the door again. It was the hundredth time that day. She was going crazy with anticipation when she ought to be relaxing and conserving energy.

Forcing herself to sit, she couldn't stop herself from staring at the door. She'd deal with whoever came through it, begging in her heart for it not to be the beast.

The only thing she had to hold on to was the name he'd given to her. She said it over and over.

"Please hurry Billy."

*****

Hans guided the freighter towards the locks, they'd lost too much time during the night because of traffic. They'd started to queue up for the locks the previous evening, only to be put back by issues on the shore. The only thing they could tell him it was something about a malfunctioning gate.

In the dark, he aimed the ship between the concrete walls of the first lock. He had a lot of things on his mind as usual. Fear of returning to the crime scene was a small part of it, but so was the level of degradation he'd lowered himself to. Lastly, he thought of Jared and the other girls.

Hans knew they kept one down there for themselves, it was the only reason he got one of his own. They had to keep him happy and on their side to be able to enjoy the catch themselves. He always worried at this point about Jared. He wasn't sure how smart the guy was. A successful criminal yes, but how intelligent? Hans shrugged his shoulders.

He pulled his phone from his pocket and clicked off a message. He knew it was late to ask the question, there was no turning away from the lock now. It would look worse than driving up to the border and then turning your vehicle around.

After one last look at the question he'd prepared, Hans hit the send button.

*****

Jared was topside with the crew, everyone was on deck as they went through the locks, if you weren't working – you were watching. He'd initially been upset with the delay they had in getting into one of the parallel lanes of waiting ships. As time went by he realized they were getting closer to the morning. To do his deed he needed the darkness of the night, it was the only thing on his mind.

He'd slapped a few beers back before they started to move, something he didn't usually do. He was still on edge when his phone buzzed. He read the message from Hans, frowning at the words.

Everything clean for the locks?

Jared knew what the captain meant, and it wasn't about how neatly folded the linens were. Hans was referring to any other women that had been on board, wanting assurance they were all gone, that no threat remained.

They weren't completely gone, but there sure wasn't any threat. She was just a squaw no more, no less. Jared's thumbs attacked the open face of the phone.

Everything clean captain, no problem.

This run seemed harder than the others, and he had to admit that part of it was his own fault. The sooner he fixed the problem, the sooner he could get back on track. Forget happy endings, life wasn't like that, and he promised himself to never think that way again.

The freighter slipped under the overhead bridge that crossed the south end of the locks. His men were stationed at bow and stern, while others stood along both the port and starboard sides.

The locks were just another routine to this crew and the freighter moved gracefully through the Saint Mary River. Jared watched the land go by, every foot they passed was a step closer to Lake Superior.

When he was sure they were going to make it through without issue, he let himself think of her. He was looking forward to their last visit. It was more about him claiming his manhood back than the sex, but then he knew he'd enjoy that as well.

All he really wanted was a couple shots of good liquor, and a couple hours with her. But he knew he should take his time, make everything seem normal with the boys first, he didn't want any of them noticing anything out of the ordinary. It was about being smart when you were doing wrong.

The bosun stuck around on deck until he was able to watch the locks slipping away. It was late in the morning, yet some of the crew were already in the lounge. Jared joined them for a shot. It was best to have a few and keep things normal.

The first mate passed him the bottle. "Cheers!"

Jared looked into his empty glass for a moment before muttering under his breath, "Cheers squaw, your time has come."

*****

Billy was hiding behind the forward pulley housing, watching the shore getting smaller as the crew heading off deck towards their quarters. Specifically, he watched as Jared stepped through the bulkhead door into the superstructure.

236

Then the undercover was running, he hit the doorway in time to see which way the last crewman went, glimpsing them filing through the lounge door. So he'd have some time, hopefully the amount of time he needed. After the long night waiting to get through the locks, and with the light about to come up outside, he expected more than a few of them would be sleeping shortly.

It was about helping his own now. Briefly his mind paused, realizing it was the first time in his life. The pang of guilt hit him hard. Looking back, he couldn't see where he had helped the native cause. Why had it escaped him all those years? Why was it now that he was out in the wider world that he realized he could have done more, that everyone should do more.

Enough dammit.

With no time to spare, Billy looked left and right, then ran for the storage areas. This was now a gamble, he figured if he ran into anyone he was done. He slid up to the door and fumbled for the lock picks he'd learned to use in training, feeling the first beads of sweat forming on his forehead.

Having looked at the mechanism both other times he'd been here, it was a simple system, and there shouldn't be a problem. But all that did was put more pressure on him.

Using the one pick to stabilize the lock and force it slightly to one side, he kept pressure on it while he used a second tool to roll the tumblers in place and then force the door lock to open.

The clicking noise sounded ear-splitting to Billy, no one should hear it at this time of night because no one should be around, still he hurried as he jerked the door open.

Where was she?

*****

Shanya heard the running steps outside in the hallway, her every sense was locked on the door as someone seemed to struggle with the lock. Was that a good sign? Was it Billy?

Maybe the beast was drunk and fumbling with the keys. Her heart started to pound as she inched along the wall, easing closer to the door. She couldn't stay back even with the fear gripping her. She needed it to be her rescuer. Anything else and she might break inside.

Stopping, closing her eyes, she forced herself to focus. *Think!* She needed a plan, quickly.

If it was the beast, she could run out through the door before he could close it. It didn't really matter which way she went, as long as she kept away from him. She decided she'd turn right. Right through the door, and right down the hall – then run. Hard.

The lock noise stopped, and the door squealed slightly as it was flung open.

Shanya stood there staring at his profile as he scanned the room. Tall, his head shaved, there was no mistaking his heritage. And she never felt happier to see a Native in all her life. His hands stretched out for hers and she jumped forward.

With no idea what was coming next, she felt herself pulled from the room.

*****

The captain swore at the men through his microphone, "Move it men, move it."

The S.S. Slate was disappearing quickly. His men were hanging off the front of the ship with binoculars, two stationed on the walkway on top of the superstructure looked through their high-powered scopes.

He wasn't happy with their progress through the locks and worried they would lose sight of the freighter ahead. That wouldn't be acceptable. His call to the dock, explaining his needs had speeded up the process, and the S.S. Forester's screws were churning water before the final set of steel gates were fully open, chasing the newer freighter ahead.

"Anyone still have on eyes on it?"

"Yessir, I got'em." Randall had been stationed on top of the superstructure because he had the best set of eyes on the boat.

Flynn knew he wouldn't lose them now that he was cranking out the horsepower. The old girl might look like a rust bucket, but the engine room held the best marine engines available. They were in the fight now.

Leaning closer to the window, staring hard ahead, eyes straining to see through the dark, impatiently, he waited for the day to come, the light to appear. Beside him the wheelman could see the intensity on the captain's face but he never heard the words he mouthed.

"Hold on kid. We're almost there."

*****

Jared was ready. He'd spent some time with the crew, most were gone to their racks, already passed out. He told the rest it would be light soon, they ought to call it a night. Once he left the lounge, he rushed down the hallway.

A few glances told him everyone was in bed, the way was clear. He didn't notice anything unusual as he clomped down the stairs, but as he turned towards the storage room he almost had a heart attack, followed by confusion, and a sudden pang of fear.

The oversized steel door was hanging wide open, light from the room spilling out into the hall.

What the fuck?

Jared started running, grabbing the doorframe and skidding around the corner into the room. He didn't need to look, the feeling in the pit of his stomach told him she was gone.

Kicking at the closest box, he lashed out, his fist connected with the door, slamming it back against the wall, the boom of steel against steel echoing down the corridor. Everything was getting out of control and he couldn't handle it. He wanted to think, but his anger won out.

For some reason he didn't understand, he screamed out in anger and desperation.

Jared screamed once more, getting it out of his system, then preservation kicked in, and the main question hit.

Where in the fuck is she?

CHAPTER 25

S.S. Slate

Shanya gasped for air. This is what a spooked deer felt like. She wanted to keep running now that they were out of the room. The fresh air in the hallway fueled her energy as she sprinted frantically to keep up with her rescuer.

Billy pulled her along, even as she tried to match his long strides. Upstairs, around a corner, down a hall – finally they stopped after stepping into a tiny room at the end of a corridor.

She could tell he was worried as he constantly looked back over his shoulder. Now he listened intently while they leaned against the wall catching their breaths. Shanya tried to understand who he was, but his appearance didn't give anything away. He could just be a labourer on the ship for all she knew.

When he reached forward and put his hands on her upper arms and squeezed them together, he had her attention. Shanya answered yes to all his questions. Each question ramped her intensity up just a little farther.

There was something unsaid in the conversation, and she wasn't seeing it. The magnitude of the escape was overwhelming her thoughts. Everything he asked was pointed towards escaping and there was only one answer to that. Yes.

"Okay Shanya, we're going now."

The words galvanized her. This was the moment she'd given up on ever happening. She looked him in the eyes, wanting to remember his face, no matter what happened.

She ruthlessly crushed the small bubble of fear lurking inside, there was commitment now. Nothing that happened next could be worse than what had happened in the cage. His words snapped her focus back to the little room.

"No time to talk on the deck. No indecision, no hesitation. Do as I say."

Shanya nodded, her throat was dry, unable to speak even if she tried. Billy turned and eased them out into the hallway. Cracking the door to the deck, he made sure there was no one on the other side before pushing on the heavy door. Wind blew through the opening, buffeting them and whistling down the hallway. Then Billy stepped out into the darkness, pulling her with him.

*****

There was no time to be gentle. Billy pulled her hard as he ran down the hallway. He had to admit he was impressed with her effort to keep up. She clearly was a runner.

"You really want out of here?" He turned back to her as he kept his feet moving.

"Yes."

Knowing, the small equipment room would be empty, he yanked open the door and swung her through it. Swiftly he closed the door, leaving it open an inch so he could hear anything moving out on the walkway.

"You're not hurt, everything is okay?" He needed her healthy, the plan depended on it. Time was pressing, every minute mattered.

"Yes." She nodded vigorously.

"Okay, this will get crazy before it's over, but it's the only solution I could put together this fast." It raised the question of moving too fast. But at this point it didn't matter, he was doing what he thought was right. A quick vision of the two girls he'd missed helping came to mind and solidified his motive.

In his head he was tracking time, marking off another minute passed. Billy had to let her get her breath, keeping in mind what she'd been through.

On the other hand, their lives were more at risk with each tick of the clock. It was starting to ring louder in his ears. TICK, TICK. He didn't need the reminders and was ready to go, was she?

Squeezing her arms he checked how stable she seemed. She balanced with her feet and hips to correct for his motions, and he decided she was okay.

"Okay Shanya, we're going now." He watched for hesitation, thought he saw something, but it was gone in a blink and she said yes. "No more talking now, just do as I say. Okay?"

He waited for her to nod again. "No hesitation now."

It was important she agreed.

She was going to be shocked at what he wanted her to do, and he needed her to follow without question, there was no time for them to argue on deck. They couldn't afford to be seen, and that mattered at all cost.

Billy reached down and grabbed her hand. Slowly he pushed the door open and pulled her into the night. With a hard grip on her arm he ran towards the rear of the freighter.

He'd gone over it more than a few times, but this sure wasn't covered in the training he'd had in Regina. The concept was simple, but on a freighter this big – who knew what would happen.

With no one to ask for advice, he had to come to his own conclusions about the best way to do this. The final decision had been made when he remembered what he saw Jared do the other night. The walkway around the back of the freighter was the place. Laughing to himself, he relieved his own anxiety.

Before rounding the rear of the structure, he reached inside a small door and pulled out the two lifejackets. Billy didn't give her an opportunity to complain, even as her mouth opened wide in understanding. He put the jacket on her, slipping it over her head and lifting her arms up as needed.

With her jacket secured, he put on his own. Off the back of the boat he could still see the city lights in the distance. He wondered how far it was back to Sault Saint Marie. Perhaps heading directly towards shore to the left was a better idea. It was another thing he had to make a quick decision on, but not until he was in the water.

Again, Billy pulled her as they took off running around the corner towards the back of the superstructure. There was no thinking about what they were going to do, or he'd talk himself out of it. This was about saving her, and that gave him the strength to do what came next.

Billy stopped and turned to face her. Shanya's face was calmer than he expected. Her eyes darted left and right as she avoided looking down.

"We can swim Shanya, we will make it." He held her chin so she had to look directly at him. "Now you need to get up on the railing so you can jump. Don't worry, I'm right behind you."

Again, he didn't wait for her to do it herself. He picked her small body up and lifted. He saw her feet moving up each rung and her courage amazed him.

As she steadied herself on the last rung he pushed her hard, as far away from the freighter as he could. It would be rough water in the turbulence behind the freighter. Billy was hoping that it would settle quickly and then they could make some progress towards land.

The undercover cop climbed up the three rungs of the railing and jumped, using every ounce of strength in his legs to launch himself off the back of the freighter. A Toronto job, a vision of shuffling papers, flashed in his head. No chance, Billy grinned as he plunged through the air. His heart was in his throat as the seconds went by and he realized hitting the water was going to hurt like hell.

As the boat's wake rushed to meet him he took a breath, and held it in as he hit the churning water. Plunging deep into the lake Billy let his downward momentum loose it's speed, waiting until he felt himself start to rise before giving a couple strong kicks.

His head burst through the surface and he gulped for air as he bobbed up and down with the waves.

"Shanya!"

*****

The last step was the hardest, and there was doubt, but his conviction, his belief, was overwhelming her. Then the push made all doubts irrelevant. She now knew why the birds didn't fly at night – you couldn't see where you wanted to land. Then the moonlight flashed on the waves just before she hit, and Shanya held her breath.

She slammed into the surface like she was falling onto concrete. Her arm jerking sideways felt like it was coming right out of the socket, but she didn't care. *She was free!*

What was seconds seemed like hours as she flailed under water. The sudden calm that came over her was outside of her control. There was a sense of peace that spread through her at the same time as the cold water made her feel more alive than ever.

Relaxed, Shanya let her body go and it floated towards the surface where suddenly she was bobbing back and forth, staring at the lights of the departing freighter. That had been the only goal that mattered, nothing else did. She wondered where land was and using her one good arm tried to move in a circle searching every direction, but inside she really didn't care. *She was free.*

On some level she was with nature now, for her there was no better way to go. She marveled briefly at how small she felt in the water, how insignificant she was. The lumpy lifejacket held her on the surface, face up, staring at the sky. That was okay. It was reassuring to know that it didn't matter what she did, she wouldn't sink. It took her a second to wonder where Billy was. Did he jump?

"Shanya!"

She didn't answer out of a sudden fear, was it Nanabozho talking to her? Or Wemicus, the trickster spirit?

"Shanya!"

She saw him now, fighting his lifejacket as he clumsily worked his way through the choppy waves. She smiled. Billy wasn't leaving, he'd jumped in with her.

With her right arm up in the air as high as she could get it, she screamed out, "Over here!"

"Over here!"

*****

S.S. Forester

"Man overboard! Man overboard! Two. Two people in the water!"

The words exploded out of the intercom forcing Flynn to ask for clarification. "Where?"

"Off the Slate."

The captain knew it was one of his guys scoping the freighter ahead. His training took over as he stepped up to the large windows. "Mark that freighter." He wanted the co-ordinates locked down.

"Marking sir."

"Half-speed ahead." Flynn's eyes were focused into the darkness.

"Half-speed ahead." The confirmation of an order followed.

"I want calculations. Wind, drift, current – where will they be?" He paused a second. "Sound the alarm. I want all eyes on deck, get the zodiac ready."

Most of the crew was already in a heightened state of alert, they knew their year of hard work on the water was coming to fruition. The second-in-command barked orders as the ship came alive with activity.

Flynn sorted through a flurry of thoughts. There was a slight wind and a low swell, but he thanked their luck that it wasn't a bad night.

Who was it? Were they alive or weighted-down and gone? He wouldn't let his hopes go in either direction. Not yet.

Could they find them in the darkness? And that begged the question; what time was it, and how much longer before it would get light?

His thoughts were interrupted by the Chief Mate.

"Sir. Five hundred meters from expected location."

Another decision to make, were they far enough away from the S.S. Slate? Was anyone watching?

"Take the ship two hundred yards past the location, and cast spotlights back towards Sault Ste. Marie." He figured it would make the searchlights harder to see from the departing Slate.

He wrestled with his own decision as time went by. He hoped the extra few minutes weren't critical. Flynn was sure it was important to keep it a secret if he found them.

Staring out the window, he watched his men filing out of the doors onto the deck, spreading out to line the rails on either side. This team needed something just like this to dig their teeth into, endless drills never produced the adrenaline of real-life situations.

He chuckled as he shook his head, it had only been a few weeks and the kid had done something. Shit, he had probably busted the thing wide open. Flynn didn't know how he'd done it, he wasn't sure yet, but he damn well was going to find out. For some reason he just knew who was in the water.

A muscle under his right eye twitched repeatedly as he stared out across the dark lake.

"Hold on kid "

*****

S.S. Slate

Jared charged into the lounge, veins bulging in his neck, his reddened face dripping sweat. He was near to losing it, trying desperately to keep his shit together.

The initial shock at seeing the open door had locked up his mind for a moment, then the consequences hit home, causing him to explode. He checked the storage area, before realizing the freighter was too big to search alone, at least not without his boys.

There was fear on the men's faces, which was good. They needed to be scared. He was.

Catching the eye of two of his main guys, he nodded for the door. He didn't wait for them to respond, heading to the hallway.

His patience was tested when a minute seemed to go by. He was about to storm back in when the door opened and the two men appeared.

"What's up boss?"

He wasn't wasting their time with small talk, he had none, just anger. He wanted her bad.

"You get the others. That fucking squaw is loose on the freighter."

He knew the real problem would be if she came in contact with Hans. That would piss the old man off to no end. It might even jeopardize everything Jared had built. Squinting his eyes so tightly he couldn't see, his teeth were clenched together so hard they wouldn't grind back and forth.

"You find that bitch – no matter what."

CHAPTER 26

S.S. Forester

Everything happened so fast, she was still trying to sort out the events that had her lying on a stretcher. Initially the tubes running into her arm caused a little concern, but she was assured it was just to rehydrate her lost fluids.

She tried to look at the doctor sitting over near the door without him thinking she was staring. Shanya didn't know who he was, but it was clear she was safe here.

And when she closed her eyes she was back in the water.

Billy had almost drowned them both by trying to help. She'd finally convinced him to leave her alone, that she was all right. For a while they had bobbed up and down beside each other, looking into each other's eyes.

Shanya didn't know if making it to land was realistic, but she was off the freighter and had never felt so free. She wanted to thank him, but he spoke first.

"Use your legs, let's move towards those lights." Billy pointed to some pinpricks in the distance. "That looks like the closest shore over there."

Doubting their chances, she nodded anyways. The water was cold, too cold on some level, but the rocking motion was comforting. There was no shame in dying here, and even though she kicked with her feet and paddled with her good hand following Billy through the waves, she knew she wouldn't make it.

He kept looking back, making sure she was still moving, but her legs were slowing down and it was getting harder to keep up. The lower half of her body was feeling numb and Shanya wondered if her legs were actually doing much down there in the dark water.

Shanya refocused back on the clean white room. The man was still watching over her and her head felt heavy. Was she on medication? As she watched, everything in the room blurred and tilted sideways before finally righting itself and stopping in its proper place. It was an interesting effect.

Someone poked their head in the room, "Is she ready to go?

"Another five minutes."

What were they talking about? Where was she going? It was hard to sort everything out when she wasn't even sure where she was.

She remembered Billy yelling at her. "Come here, come here." Shanya thought his face looked scared as he swam back in her direction.

"There's another ship coming." He pointed towards the south.

The sight of lights moving towards them terrified her. She held on to the rope on Billy's life jacket, unsure what to do. His obvious uncertainty was unnerving.

She paddled as hard as she could with her one good arm. There was no way to warn the oncoming ship, the two of them were going to be run over and pushed under the water. After escaping from the beast, it just wasn't right. *She didn't deserve it.*

When it seemed the freighter was slowly heading past them deeper into Lake Superior, she became afraid they weren't going to be rescued. Shanya started to scream while struggling with the water splashing into her mouth.

Billy joined her shouting, and they made a racket yelling into the darkness. Still the freighter sailed past. Just as the bobbing humans were ready to give up hope, they watched the ship turn sideways and large spotlights lit up the water.

The lights were so powerful Shanya lost sight of the ship behind the glare and turned her focus to the place where the lights hit the water. Her excitement grew as the patch of light sweeping across the lake came closer.

A hundred yards away the light searched the waves, fifty yards, thirty, then just twenty yards away. Suddenly, the light washed over her face and Shanya stared up into the beam. Her body could only take so much relief in one day. If Billy hadn't been there, she didn't think she'd have been able to stay afloat. The only thing that was keeping her above water now was the life jacket and his firm grip.

Commotion made Shanya open her eyes. A man was standing beside her, three others behind him. The panic attack started, sweating, her breathing came fast and furious. What did these people want? Who were they?

Shanya burst into tears, she was safe now and everything that happened to her was started to catch up. The enormous weight of pain she had been hiding hit home with a vengeance. She started to shake violently.

"She's going into shock!" The words hung in the air, but she had no idea where they came from.

"Okay men, let's go. The chopper's here."

Someone began pushing the bed she was lying on. Where was she going now?

On some level she was cognizant of being lifted, and then the coolness of the fresh air outside the building washed across her face. The sounds of the helicopter should have been hard to miss, but Shanya didn't hear anything at all.

The eagle flew long slow circles as it rode the currents above. She could see herself flying beside him, tilting her wings as she came back around for another pass.

"I'm coming," she spoke to the blue canvas spotted with clouds that spread out in her mind.

*****

Billy was sure he could make the shore, but Shanya was lagging behind and she was in trouble. He could never have imagined this scenario, getting her off the ship and then losing her in the water.

The freighter bearing down on them initially scared the shit out of him. When he'd heard the engines power down a few hundred yards out and watched the freighter slide by to the south, he was sure they were safe. What he couldn't figure out was why was the freighter slowing down. Had the Slate noticed they were gone? Was there an S.O.S. already out for them?

As long as it wasn't the Slate coming back for them, he didn't care who these guys were. As large spotlights flashed on when the freighter swung sideways, Billy felt they really had a chance.

He hadn't recognized anyone on the small craft that collected them from the water. As he came up the ladder something seemed familiar. First the rusted blue of the exterior, then the name of the freighter became visible, Forester. He'd have loved to see what his face looked like when he'd climbed onto the deck.

There was no time to think about the coincidence as he ran smack into Captain Flynn waiting at the top of the stairs. Billy couldn't put into words how happy he was to see the old geezer, whatever the reason.

Three crewmen ran forward with blankets, wrapping up Shanya before picking her off the ground and carrying her away. Just the care they took showed Billy there was nothing to worry about.

He was left facing the captain. Relief flooded his system, having won this one he let his guard down, there wasn't much energy left.

"Great work Blackwood." The captain beamed.

What did he know? There was that funny feeling again.

"I don't know how you did it, but that was good work."

Nothing was making sense again. Who was this guy and why did it seem he knew what was happening?

Everything leading to this moment had strangeness written all over it. Billy had always had an itchy feeling, but had never figured it out. Now bells were ringing. What was he missing?

So preoccupied with the mystery, he didn't see the hand stuck out in his direction. Finally, Billy looked down and lifted his own hand, still unsure why he was doing it.

"Captain Samuel Flynn. RCMP Marine Detachment. Welcome aboard."

All the tumblers fell into place. Billy didn't know if he should shake the hand or salute. He starting putting things together. This man pushing his buttons, the fight he'd had – it had all been training. They'd done it all on purpose.

He looked Flynn in the face and smiled, "You bastard." Somehow getting on those ships so easily made more sense.

The captain laughed all the way across the deck, his arm wrapped around Billy's shoulders, leading him into the interior.

Billy took one last glance at the lake just as the first light broke through the darkness.

*****

Jared was in another foul mood this morning. They had searched for the girl for two hours before he let the boys get some sleep. Daylight had been so close and they had shifts to work.

He rescheduled a few of his guys off work detail. They searched, but he still wasn't any closer to figuring out where in the hell she was. He left the crew alone, didn't take it out on them, leaving them work away at their responsibilities. They knew what they were expected to do.

Instead, he roamed the ship himself, trying to sort things out. At one point he saw Hans at the other end of a hallway, and Jared stepped through a door and ran up a flight of stairs.

He was keeping it together, but he had no intention of dealing with the boss until he had taken care of the problem.

It wasn't just about who had keys to the room. He was working through all the possible scenarios in his head. Those locks were too damned easy to pick. So who had those kind of skills? He had put a tough crew together, and it could be a number of them.

Everything Jared had been thinking that morning went out the window with one conversation.

"Boss! Boss!" The deckhand was panting as he skidded to a stop.

"What's up Jack?"

"That Indian – Billy. No one's seen him today."

The news was like a brick to the gut.

"When does he work?"

"He's supposed to go on this afternoon, but he isn't anywhere around."

He waved his man away and started to walk again. The native was new, Jared didn't have much on him except a gut feeling. It seemed to make sense, a native helping a native, but where were they? He sure couldn't let them come dancing out of hiding once they made port.

Jesus! It was driving him nuts. When he found them it was going to be a fucking horror story, beating the bastard till he was dead. Maybe even the same for her, before dumping them both over the side.

Jared stopped dead in his tracks. *They didn't jump did they?*

Now his mind sped up. There was no way they'd survive, was there? *No way.* It was suicide. If the cold didn't get them quickly, the currents would take them.

Unfortunately, that thought bothered him, which way were the currents flowing in this area? Thinking back he remembered the locks at the Soo, suddenly afraid that they jumped off there. It would be easy, but the crew had been on deck the whole time. Someone would have seen them.

If they were crazy enough to jump after that, then they'd have to live with it. The joke hit him and he smiled, fat chance on living. It was a long-shot, you'd have to be crazy. Insane, considering it was Superior. Jared pictured the native's cold stare during his initiation.

The worst thing was, he wished it was that last scenario. It would be easier to live with than finding the two of them stowed away somewhere on the Slate. No, the more he thought about it, he really wanted to find them. He hadn't wanted to hurt someone this bad in a long time.

He kept seeing Billy sitting across from him, drinking shots like they were water. The redskin's challenge still irked him, along with the fact that he hadn't gotten a chance to really put the bastard in his place. He kept thinking the native was somehow more than he looked. Did it matter now?

Probably not.

Maybe the asshole had done him a favor, saved him from having to do it himself. If Billy had talked the bitch into jumping, then he was the one killing her. Every time he thought about it, the more he wished it was true.

The longer they went without finding them on the freighter the more he could believe it.

258

The slight jump in his step was brought back to earth at the next thought.

Jared shivered as he wondered how cold it was in Superior this time of year. Then he stopped his teeth from grinding.

"Fucking cold, I hope."

*****

Flynn let the crew say their piece as they surrounded the rookie cop. Billy was catching up quickly as they sat in the galley in front of a drink. They'd offered warm liquid, anything he wanted, but the kid had asked for a beer. Flynn thought he might want a shot after jumping into Superior himself.

The more he thought about it the more he was sure the kid had what it took. He'd watched as Billy had spotted the shiner on the guy he'd laid out at the card game back in the beginning.

Billy apologized more than once while everyone laughed.

"Hey, sorry about that shiner you got there."

"Don't worry son, we do worse in training."

Finally the captain had moved the crew out except for a few senior members, and got to work.

"Okay Billy, we need to go over a few things." He let the lad refocus and get his bearings.

"You need to describe the set-up of that freighter. What's the layout? Who's involved?"

There was a reason you debriefed someone as soon as possible. In Billy's case it made perfect sense. Everything was fresh to work with. At this point he would remember clothing brands, exotic colors, and overheard conversations. Weeks from now, after exposure to other sights, places and people, he would only remember basic shapes and colors and maybe words of what had been said.

"Tell me about the captain."

Flynn kept at the list of questions, some over and over, ensuring detail by repetition. Suddenly there was knock on the door.

"Come in."

"The chopper's here sir, and the girl's ready to go."

"Okay, we'll be there."

He made sure his senior officers were happy with the intel. Then had them leave. He wanted a moment alone with the young rookie.

"I already told you it was a good job you've done on this case." He paused, he wanted the kid to appreciate the next words.

"We have Chakwania, the girl you missed in Chicago. We took the plates from the van and had Chicago PD pull them over. She's already back in Thunder Bay."

The grin said the kid was glad to hear it. It was something Flynn had guessed would be bothering him. There was no need to mention that Ronnie had travelled with her, the two young men had never met.

"I wish you luck son. But now you need to get on this chopper to Sault Saint Marie. Let's go."

Flynn followed the kid out onto the deck where the girl had already been loaded and he watched Billy climb into the front. He reached up and held his hat in place as the rotor blades sped up, causing a windstorm before lifting off the freighter.

The captain stood for minutes watching the object get smaller and smaller as it disappeared on the horizon.

CHAPTER 27

S.S. Slate

Duluth, Minnesota, the last stop of the run. Jared and the crew off-loaded their cargo quickly. The ship wasn't staying in port and there wouldn't be any time on shore, everyone just wanted to get the work over with. One more run, another two weeks and they would all get a few days off while the freighter had scheduled service.

It wasn't much to look forward to, but spring, summer and fall were complete write-offs if you worked the freighters. Then the winter came and you had months to unwind. This run was no different than any other to the captain and crew, it was him alone who had let things get off the rails, now it was Jared who was struggling with the events.

Twenty-four hours had passed. There had been traffic on the radios, but no mention of survivors and no coast guard vessels with sirens blaring. Those two obviously got what they deserved for screwing around with him in the first place. In his head their fate was a done deal, the consequences slipping off his shoulders once and for all.

It would take a little bit longer to really forget them, but he knew in a week this whole episode would be old news pushed to the back of his head. That brought him to the next course of action. Judging by the text the bosun received while pouring his morning coffee, Hans' thoughts were obviously already on the next trip.

Will there be supplies for the next run?

Really, it wasn't in doubt. Any process had occasional issues and hick-ups along the way. Depending on the breach, you ignored the concern, changed the process to avoid the concern, or shut it off completely.

At this point there didn't seem to be anything to worry about. Jared thought briefly about the native girl. Jesus, she had been sweet. He wasn't kidding himself, there obviously would be more supplies.

Fishing the phone from his pocket, he found the saved number. Waiting for an answer, he looked back at Duluth's disappearing docks. The S.S. Slate was heading out to open water.

"Hey! Well if it isn't the Clipper. What's up?"

Jared noticed the upbeat tone in Derek's voice, and decided to match it. "Hey there. What's it like on dry land you dog?"

"Better than where you are buddy. You can count on it."

Jared couldn't argue with him. Every time he ran into Derek the guy seemed to have the world by the tail. With nice clothes and fancy vehicles, Jared knew the native had some profitable system set up for sure.

"Listen, we just left Duluth. I should be tied to the dock in a few days. You got something for me?"

There seemed to be a hesitation. Jared almost spoke again before Derek finally responded.

"Sure. What do you want? Any issues with the last run?"

The second question was asked so casually that it seemed to almost slip by. Jared wasn't a newbie, he knew how to read the signs, and this one caught his attention. Derek had never asked about his runs before, nor had Jared expected him to. Professionals never asked questions. Well – not unless there was a problem.

Did Derek know something? How could he? What else was going on?

The fact was he did have some problems this time round, and it was the only run he'd ever had issues with. So when it happens to also be the run that Derek has questions about, it wasn't sitting well.

Now it was Jared who hesitated as the phone call filled with silence. He realized he might be paranoid, but the question had been so out of place.

"Everything cool here, I need three again. How about with you?" He listened intently, waiting for the answer. For some reason Jared felt what came next was important.

"Three it is. No sweat, everything's okay 'round here."

Did he sense a change of tone in the last sentence? Was the upbeat missing? Was the conversation forced in some way? Because it just seemed like it wasn't normal.

"I'll call when we get in the harbour. See you then." Jared put his worry aside. Derek had nothing to do with his problems. He wouldn't know anything. Damn it, over-thinking again, and that was as bad as not thinking in the first place.

Derek's answer put him at ease, if only a little bit. "I'll be waiting."

Jared tapped the text message icon, and replied to the captain.

*****

Hans had his head on straight again. The punishment he always put himself through lasted for days. Every fiber of his being knew what he had done was wrong. Worse, he reveled in it and lowered himself to please his needs.

Those needs were changing as time went on, each run brought him lower, and he abused them more. Was it his fault that he was in the position where he could do as he pleased? What option did he have but to take advantage of a situation that presented itself?

Really, it was like experimentation. He incrementally ratcheted up the degradation, becoming mesmerized by the outcomes. He knew it wasn't always for the pleasure anymore either, it was just the checking off of a tick-box on an endless list of debaucheries.

Duluth was behind them now, and Thunder Bay ahead. He felt the onrush of new worry as the cycle was about to begin again. He'd sent a message to Jared and was now pacing the bridge, while he waited impatiently to hear back.

Unable to wait and see what happened, he needed to know there was another one coming. It had been days, and his mind was starting to think about it more and more.

He didn't worry about what the girls would think or feel, they were just squaws. Nobody ever missed them anyways.

Hans didn't care that he saw the natives on some different level that other women, it made it easier to separate their feelings from his plans.

The buzz of a text made him jump for the phone. His anticipation sky high.

Fresh supplies in Thunder.

Staring out the large window on the bridge, the captain smiled ear-to-ear, anyone watching saw a crooked sneer.

*****

Inspector Kelly waited for them to bring Erin into his office a second time. So much had changed in a few days. The case had gone from concept to functional, and now there was fact following reality. Unfortunately, it was building an ugly picture.

He didn't understand what made people behave so badly, he supposed at the end of the day no one did. There were just those that woke up each day ready to prey on the less fortunate and anyone they could take advantage of. One small part of society was just completely degenerate and morally corrupt.

Kelly knew the battle was never-ending, there would always be another racket to investigate. This one, missing native women, hit close to home. Most of the missing came from northern parts of the country, that's where most of the reserves were.

The door opened and Erin slunk in. The toughness wasn't as pronounced as it was before. The inspector wondered how her parents took having investigators visiting their house, alleging that Erin was with Shanya when she went missing. How had that made things in the home?

He waited until the officer left and the two of them were alone. She stewed in silence as he let the pressure in the room build. He had all the advantages now, with more information than needed. Her unwillingness to talk didn't mean anything. Her information was no longer of use, except in one area.

"Well Erin, I won't waste your time." Kelly waited for her eyes to rise from the floor.

"One of the three girls taken from your party is dead. That's for sure."

"It wasn't my party."

Kelly cut her off, "We already have the witnesses Erin. Everyone says Shanya came to the party with you. They told us that she was really shy and never went out to parties. So it was your party."

Her body language said she was involved, her shoulders slumped, her hands fell to her lap as her eyes went back to the floor. Kelly had her where he wanted her.

"This is your last chance to get it right Erin. It's not your fault unless you get in the way of the investigation." He watched her thinking about his words. "I need to know about Derek. What happened at the party?"

Bingo. Her eyes shot open. There was the realization that the police knew as much as she did. She had nowhere left to run or hide. He watched her take a breath and force it down.

"He put something in her drink." She spoke muffled words to the desktop.

"Who did?" The inspector wanted facts.

"Derek did."

"Is that what happened to the other girls?"

"I don't know, I only seen Shanya's bottle."

He was pretty sure she was telling the truth. It fixed the final piece of the puzzle in place. *How were they were getting the girls to cooperate?* They weren't given a choice.

Kelly sat alone in his office. The female officer had removed Erin when he'd finished questioning her. That girl didn't know how close she came to going to jail for her part in this. His mind was already moved forward, needing to decide what to do with the case.

He had the opportunity to keep it quiet, send in the next undercover, or even put Billy out there again and find the next ship. On another level, this story needed to be public. He'd spent lot of time researching native issues when the upper echelon came down on him, reminding him to be sure he wasn't wasting his time.

If the facts that were already available didn't cause the government to change its approach to the native's plight, maybe this would. After taking their land, to segregating them on reserves, or forcing them into residential schools, it had been one mishandled blunder followed by another, decade after decade.

This story, he wanted to see go nationwide. Aboriginal girls were being systematically taken from the Thunder Bay region by freighter in the grasp of criminal individuals and sexual predators.

A new window needed to be opened on the subject, and he was confident he could do it. But that was a secondary issue, the primary issue was the S.S. Slate. The inspector leaned his chair back as he put his feet on the desk. How was it all going to play out? He put his effort into figuring out how he was going to maintain complete control over the operation.

Another knock on the door broke his concentration. "Blackwell's flight has landed. He's ready to see you sir."

Kelly smiled. Just a rookie thirteen days ago, the kid had done good. Better than expected. The inspector looked forward to seeing the new experience on the young man's face.

"Great, send him in."

CHAPTER 28

Sault Ste. Marie

Waking in the dark brought back flashes of Shanya's captivity on the ship. Stubbornly, she forced her pounding heart to slow as she listened to the unfamiliar noises, realizing they were different from the squeals and rumbles of the steel freighter.

As the fear subsided she examined the tubes in her arm. She was firmly tucked into a white bed. The bone-numbing cold of the lake had faded, and she thought she might actually be warming up. *Where was Billy?* Then she slept again.

The next time her eyes opened there was light slanting through a wide window. Her mother stood nearby, her father hung back, as if unsure how close to get. Shanya's eyes blurred with tears, blinking she tried to clear the liquid.

The guilt she felt pressed down on her. Ashamed, she tried to find the words to explain it to her mother. She knew what she had done could only have brought them a difficult time.

"I'm so sorry."

Her mother leaned down and hugged her "Shhhh." Her mother squeezed her tighter as she put her mouth to Shanya's ear.

"It's okay baby." Her mother paused. "The same kind of thing happened to me when I was young. It's the reason why we live so far away from everyone. I wanted to protect you. It's me that is sorry."

Shanya never felt so happy to be with her mother. She felt her mother's tears hitting the side of her cheek.

When she felt her father lean over the bed to wrap his arms around them both, Shanya closed her eyes.

She could see the arch over the gate, her hand ran along the top of the rough fence. It was just a matter of walking the last few steps, she was home.

*****

S.S. Forester

Flynn rode the bridge, his legs spread, his fists leaning on the window ledge. Timing was important as he guided the freighter into Thunder Bay's harbour, not an easy task as he slipped past the other freighters stacked up waiting their turn.

The Coast Guard had quietly notified each of the other vessels, warning them to expect the S.S. Forester to pass them, to make room, and keep it off the airwaves. The Coast Guard would be monitoring.

Flynn knew he probably wasn't needed at this stage, but then again people could try anything, and he was going to make sure escape by water wasn't an option.

Slow and steady was the trick in port, don't get out of control. Flynn reached for the intercom.

"Five minute warning." His men were geared up and ready to go, waiting inside the structure hidden from view.

The captain spoke over his shoulder to the steersman, "Ease it up slowly, stop bridge to bridge."

The Forester rounded the last corner and aimed towards the Slate tied to the dock a hundred yards ahead.

Flynn picked up the cell phone sitting on the console in front of him. The call was already open.

"Flynn here, two minutes." He was coordinating with the ground team.

"Kelly. We see you."

Interesting, the boss wanted in on this one. That meant it was going to be a big show. Didn't matter at the moment. He had more important things to worry about. Was this going to turn into a shootout? Anything was possible.

The Forester slowed the closer it got to the Slate, the big rusty vessel was hardly moving as the bow slipped past the stern of the other freighter. Then it was a third of the way up the other ship's side, half way.

"Put them together." Flynn radioed the tugboat hiding in their shadow near the bow on the off side, its crew waiting for the command to push the big freighter sideways.

The two freighters came together slowly until steel ground against steel, the tug's engine's growling as the Forester slid squealing and screeching the last thirty yards to stop side-by-side with the Slate. With the two ships nearly identical in height, Flynn had his face hard against the glass staring across at the other bridge.

There was another man staring back in disbelief. Was that their captain? He sure hoped so. He could see the fear mixed with anger on the man's face.

Flynn raised his intercom's microphone with one hand and the cell phone with the other. Talking into both at the same time, he calmly started the raid.

"Take that ship."

*****

S.S. Slate

Hans was preoccupied with his internal fantasies. He wondered if they would always be like that? The question intrigued the hell out of him. They were all different it some way, there was always something new to look forward to.

He really didn't need to be here watching the loading process, Jared always had everything under control. The bosun was a right hand in more ways than one.

"Captain! That freighter's too close!" The helmsman was looking out the bridge's rear window.

Hans turned to see the approaching freighter. *Jesus, what the hell were those idiots doing?* There was nothing to do. He was tied to the dock.

He looked closely at the oncoming ship, something wasn't right, the approaching freighter was hardly moving, almost at docking speed.

It looked like they were going to slip past so close he could spit and hit the other ship. Hans didn't take long to get angry, the weather-beaten skin of his forehead wrinkled up as his lips puffed out. He couldn't believe the nerve of this asshole. *Was he drunk?*

The freighter slid halfway past before veering suddenly towards the Slate. "Bastard!" He swore out loud when the two freighters came together, grinding against each other until they were stopped side-by-side.

An accident in port? What the fuck was going on? Someone was going to lose their licence for this, and he didn't want any part of it. The fucking paperwork alone was going to be brutal. Hans stared across at the other bridge, and to his surprise there was someone staring back.

The intensity on the other man's face caught him off guard. In this sort of circumstance he expected confusion or apology, not the stone-cold glare that beamed back his way. That was when Hans realized the other captain had done this on purpose, pinning their freighter against the Slate for some reason.

Watching the other captain barking orders into both a phone and a microphone, his stomach clenched. Suddenly, the doors on the other freighter burst open, slamming back against the outside walls as men with guns charged out towards his boat. He was in trouble.

The only course of action that came to mind was to back the freighter away from the dock and escape. The exact thing he couldn't do, now that the lunatic blocked his way.

As men swarmed over the ship's railing he heard heavy booted feet pounding up the stairwell as they came for him. He backed against the window as four men in tactical gear burst through the door, guns leveled his way.

"Police! Hands in the air. Don't move."

Hans did as he was told. There was no way to fight this many people. Grabbed and forcibly turned around, his body was slammed against the window.

With his face pinned sideways against the glass, his hands were jerked together behind his back as he felt handcuffs closing hard against his wrists. Just before he was pulled away from the window, Hans looked over at the captain on the other freighter.

The other man stared back with a lopsided grin.

Hans was led down the stairs onto the deck where he saw the police cars and swat truck parked on the dock, lights flashing. Everything was cordoned off.

The first of the officers coming up the gangway hit the deck and spread out in every direction. Hans turned to look up at the Slate's superstructure one last time. He knew he wasn't coming back. Men were running away from the police as if there was somewhere to go. Others just put their hands up and waited.

Hans didn't give a shit about the crew. He had his own skin to worry about. And where the fuck was Jared? This was his fault.

Then an image of his wife getting the news hit him, and his whole body shuddered.

*****

Jared watched the loading process with little interest, he had a few people stopping by with supplies later, including Derek. This stuff right now was routine work, and the crew took care of it.

The shouts as the other freighter bore down on them took his complete attention. He'd never seen two of the steel-hulls hit each other before.

When the freighters came together the ship rocked and Jared bent his knees for balance, his ears were assaulted by the screeching, grinding noise at deck level. As if hypnotized, he watched the two ships slowly line up against each other until they were side-by-side.

When men burst out of the other freighter's side door and swarmed over the railing, rushing towards the bridge he thought of running. This was bad news.

More piercing noises from behind drew him to turn towards the dock as cop cars and a swat truck formed a semi-circle around the freighter. Heavily armed men ran towards the lowered gangway.

It didn't help that he had good instincts, not when he was cornered. He couldn't run. *Could he hide?* His eyes slid from side-to-side. Slowly he took a step back, he felt light on his feet. Like a cat cornered with nowhere to go, he searched for his escape route. At the doorway into the super structure he looked back. Was anyone following? He threw his cell phone as hard as he could over the side figuring that was his only connection to Derek and the squaws.

Most of the crew stood around with their hands above their heads. They'd never done time. If they had, they'd be running. Someone was coming his way. He looked closer, focusing on the face.

As he ran down the steps he wondered where he was going. Thinking of the engine room, he didn't know it well. Other than the lounge and quarters he didn't really know where to hide. With all the cops around it was too hard to get into the loaded bays where he could burrow into the grain or amongst the steel beams.

Jared kept his feet moving, he heard the main door open behind him, then slam closed as he hit the end of the hall, racing down the next set of stairs. At the next floor he kept going, down another flight, the sounds of someone chasing him echoing in the tight enclosure, clanging boots on the metal grating.

Sprinting down another hallway, he stood looking down the hall to the storage rooms. He knew this place. Jared took the stairs in two steps, landing heavily before sprinting for any one of the doors.

It occurred to him as he entered the room that this was one of the places he'd kept the natives in. It was just one of the doors left open to load supplies. The bosun sprinted into the room and found boxes stacked near a crate. Quickly, he organized the boxes on top of the crate and crouched behind them.

It wasn't really a hiding place. The person following was going to find him. The bosun was a step ahead of that, and hoped he'd gone far enough into the ship to lose everyone else. This way it was just the two of them.

He couldn't believe it when he recognized the fucking redskin. That the Indian was running in his direction meant he was singled out as a target.

Jared was shaken, and pissed at the same time. If Billy was still alive it begged the question – what about the girl? That scared him even more. What was the Indian's connection to the cops? The knowledge he was going back to prison hurt so bad he wanted to take out his revenge in advance. And that fucker was the one who caused the problem.

If he finished him quick, then maybe Jared could still find a better hiding spot and get off the ship during the night. Down here he could take his revenge slowly, there would be plenty of time.

Remembering the fights he'd had in the pen, he focused on the ones he wished had gone on longer. Behind bars it was necessary to do as much damage as you could, as fast as you could, you never knew how long you had before it was broken up.

Jared flexed his shoulder muscles and rolled his neck loose. Shaking his arms, he flexed his hands open and closed to get the blood flowing. He might be going down, but he sure as hell wasn't going without a fight.

"Come on you fucker, let's get this over with."

*****

Billy shoved the door open. His feet were moving before the car skidded to a full stop. Fighting with the brass to get in on the raid was a given, he'd started this case, and wanted to finish it. It forced the inspector to keep the press out of the loop, at least until the raid was over and he was gone. Billy felt the inspector owed him the right to be there, and had said as much.

They'd waited for the Forester to block the Slate before rushing the dock from behind the huge grain elevators. Billy ran up the gangway and turned towards the stunned crew, hardly glancing at the captain who was being led away in cuffs. He was too busy searching faces as he ran.

Spotting the runners he scanned their backs as they sprinted in the other direction, scattering to the far corners of the ship. He finally caught a glimpse of Jared at an open door and veered that way. Billy followed the bosun through the door, down a hallway, down the stairwell, then into another hallway. He couldn't believe the direction Jared was headed.

Everything in his head was telling Billy to slow down, to not charge into an ambush. He paused only a moment before descending the stairs to the storage rooms. One door was hanging wide open, the same one Shanya had been in. Was it coincidence or justice?

Carefully, Billy eased up, needing to get his wits about him before he waded in to the room. Taking a deep breath, he moved forward, quickly stepping to the right, away from the door. His eyes adjusted before scanning the room from where he stood. There was nothing to see.

Billy was ready, he knew what was coming. There was no doubt in his mind that Jared would fight. Slowly, he ventured further into the room, one step at a time. Every few feet he scanned around, looking for anything that stood out.

There it was. He wondered if Shanya had used the small window to give her light. The daylight streaming through the little round window cast a shadow from behind Jared's position.

Billy could see the dark outline on the floor running out from behind the pile of boxes. It was all the advantage he needed. Taking three running steps to gain as much momentum as possible, putting his shoulder down, he leaned forward as he hit the boxes in a half-decent football tackle.

The cardboard slammed backwards, knocking Jared off his balance. Billy kept pushing forward and slamming Jared onto his back, the momentum carrying him until he fell on top of the bosun, one of the boxes sandwiched between them.

Deliberately, Billy kept the box there. With Jared pinned, he threw punches into the man's ribs and head area. He wanted to hit him as many times as he could before anyone found them and pulled him off.

This wasn't how he was trained, but people weren't supposed to target your people for such abuse. This guy was a full-on criminal. Billy had confirmed it in briefings with the inspector, therefore the bosun knew what he was doing and had to know what was coming.

Jared finally pushed the box away, and Billy scrambled to get in its place. Jared rammed his knees upward and Billy ignored the move, slamming his elbow down into Jared's face, trying to do it again and again.

Jared managed to thrust upwards with his hips, dislodging Billy to the side. As the bosun tried to capitalize and roll to his knees, the young officer swung his long leg, adding momentum to it as if kicking a soccer ball. He felt his victim's head absorb the blow before ricocheting away from his foot, taking the body with it. Jared collapsed on the cold floor.

Billy levered himself to his feet, then stared down at the bosun. Was the bastard dead? He got down on one knee and slapped Jared in the face. No response. He ran his fingers under the man's chin. *Good, a pulse.*

With nothing to do but try and wake him up, he slapped him again and again until the bastard opened his eyes. When Billy was sure he had the bosun's attention, he leaned over and whispered his message.

"What I'm saying is for Shanya. Your ugly face will be plastered all over the news soon. You should think about the Indians in jail knowing what you did. They are natives, and proud of it."

Billy wanted to hit the asshole again but the SWAT team burst through the door, one of them a little steamed – he'd been supposed to keep the rookie out of the action.

"Jesus Christ! That's enough Blackwood, we got it from here."

Once back on deck, he stood and took a long breath. Billy'd be told soon enough how he'd done on the case.

He felt good about it. Wasn't saving one girl better than none?

*****

Southern Ontario, Highway 69 South

The signs were easy to follow, and it wasn't the first time he'd made this trip. William Rivers drove a simple dark green Honda Civic. He was making good time on his way to Toronto.

The fifteen-hour drive from Thunder Bay usually took a full day, but he was on the last stretch. Almost in Parry Sound, four hours from the big smoke. He kept going over the details in his head.

Everything was based on the preparations he'd made early in the game. The name Derek wasn't his, but he'd adapted to it in the beginning and given it to anyone who asked.

The Land Rover was burned, his name wasn't attached to the condo, and his name wasn't on the party house. Everyone at the party house, and that he did his business with, knew him as Derek. Right from the start he'd been thinking of the next step, and sometimes you have to know when to close up shop and start over again.

The guys at the house might keep their shit together and not say a word. They had nothing to do with the girls, so as long as they weren't carrying when they were taken down, they should be able to stay in the clear. But they'd probably sing like a bunch of pussies. Really, he didn't care, there was no way they could affect his plans.

Having everything set so you could just step out was the strategic part. William knew he had it almost right. Only one thing bothered him, a detail he had no control over.

He tapped the steering wheel with his finger, tapping harder with each mile. It was going to drive him crazy knowing Jared – the Clipper – had his number in his phone. Even if it was for Derek, who didn't exist, it was the last string floating in the air.

EPILOGUE

Thunder Bay

After two weeks off to unwind, Billy again sat across from the inspector and Kelly was still smiling.

While he was off, Billy had time to digest the events of the prior two weeks. Everything had happened so fast there hadn't been enough time to breathe. The police work was everything he'd imagined. Those two weeks were the most exciting weeks he'd had in his life, the scariest too.

"Well Mr. Blackwell." The inspector corrected himself, "Mr. Simon. What did you think of your first case?"

Was it really a case? It seemed like a quick series of events to him, but Billy was still working out what he'd accomplished, and time would help him settle that.

"Just glad to help, sir."

Kelly's red face seemed to flush brighter, the collar of the shirt still too tight.

"Just help? You did a good job of bringing this to the public eye Billy. Hopefully this time the exposure will change the urgency this gets treated with. Maybe with today's social networks this will be too much to ignore."

Hearing a man who genuinely cared about his people was positive, he hadn't seen it much growing up. He had to imagine there were others who thought the same. Maybe with time and with this kind of people pushing the matter, with broader exposure, the fight would be worth it.

"I hope so inspector. I really do."

It was hard to think of the future with the present so fresh in his mind. The captain and bosun from the Slate would be going away for a long time. Ronnie would be one of the star witness. Some of the crew would get off with shorter sentences. Chicago PD had a crew locked up and waiting for trial down there, and that was about it. Was it enough?

"Did we do enough?" Billy wanted to know.

Kelly's lips puckered as he thought for a second. The older man rubbed his chin as he prepared his reply.

"Every case is different. You never know where it goes, or how it ends. In a short period of time we uncovered a pipeline, exposed a disgusting trend, saved two girls and prevented who knows how many more from being snatched. For today that has to be enough." The inspector tapped his pen on the desk, "And we could look at it from every angle and decide to do something different here or there, but I think we lucked out and did okay. Real good in fact."

Billy was still thinking about the one who got away, Derek or whatever his name really was. A native for sure, obviously intelligent or experienced, either way it looked like he was long gone. Having seen a picture of the guy, shown by investigators in Thunder Bay, he'd never forget the face ingrained in his memory. Just maybe, some day.

The next words made Billy pay attention.

"I guess this brings us to the most important issue here today." The inspector opened a file folder and picked up the top sheet of paper.

Billy had wondered what this meeting was about. The debriefings and wrap-ups had already taken place. The reports had been written. The case was out of his hands now. What more could he bring to the table?

"How did you like the undercover work Billy?"

Realizing he should have expected the question, he was a rookie after all, his answer came easy, "It was okay sir. I feel good."

"And what about the subject of the missing native women."

There was the guilt again. Just a few weeks ago Billy had wanted to get away from everything Indian. Now he'd saved his own kind. More so, he'd seen what kind of abuses his people were enduring up close. His heart swelled, it was a worthy cause.

"It's important sir. Important to me." The words sounded like a commitment, and it felt good.

"Well tell me Mr. Simon, have you ever done any long-haul trucking?"

Billy thought about the endless miles of roadway along the TransCanada highway. Only the people in southern Ontario thought the country was populated, everyone in the north knew there was nothing but endless miles of spruce and moose.

Suddenly, all Billy could see was endless miles of wilderness and too many places to be rid of a body.

*****

Two years later
Lac des Mille Reserve

It was a trip he'd wanted to make often in the last two years. His work kept him away and again another case was heating up. Still a break had presented itself, Billy was smiling and a little anxious as he parked outside the community centre.

The little bit of research he had to do to get his timing right wasn't a bother. Hanging back, he watched the crowd gather before the course was to begin. The children's class was about Aboriginal Culture and history. Many of the children and their parents were dressed in traditional clothing.

As the crowd flowed into the classroom, Billy again hung out in the back. He tried to stay unnoticed, standing behind a few of the taller parents near the back wall. But, like the others in the room, he couldn't help but be swept up.

There was a brilliance about her that stood out. There was no misunderstanding, the young woman was native to the core. Her dress was embroidered with colourful beads and jingling bells, her braids were wrapped in matching ribbons.

Billy had known she was special the second he'd opened that steel door. Even in the stark conditions of the storage room, many days into her horror and abuse, she had shone like a light, her spirit radiating from her soul. He's known the second he saw her that he'd been doing the right thing.

Now he watched as Shanya talked to the children like they were her own. He smiled for her. She talked of the legends that had always been told by the elders.

"The legends and tales are our history. They guide us and remind us."

Billy could see the kids hanging on her every word.

"But it us who make the future. Remember the deer that walked a strange trail? He knew others had been there before him, because there was a small track to follow that weaved through the forest. But one day the deer decided to venture off the trail into unknown territory and soon found himself walking among tall buildings which he knew nothing about."

No one said a word, the children sat on the floor with their legs crossed, leaning forward as everyone waited for Shanya to continue.

"When the deer noticed another of its kind mixed in with a new type of animal, he went over to ask a question. Why are you here fellow deer? The other deer replied that for him it was better than to only live in the forest, that there was benefit to walking in two worlds."

Now the kids gulped and looked at each other. Billy was curious where this story was going.

Shanya explained, "The young deer asked if it was dangerous. Of course, said the older deer, you need to learn new ways, and understand enough to fit in. But at night I jump back over the fence and return to the forest."

Billy nodded, she was saying that natives needed to learn how the white world worked, to be able to walk in both worlds. He understood the words. The children needed to understand all of society, not just an aboriginal one.

After the class, he watched her talking to the parents, seeing the exact moment she noticed his face. Her eyes exploded with light as they opened wide. Her hand came to her mouth and tears flowed. She seemed to stagger a second before rushing across the room to jump into his arms.

Billy felt strange to have her holding on tight, her head buried in his chest, as the other parents raised their eyebrows in question. Shanya shuddered in his arms, and he held her up when she went limp.

Finally, she put strength to her feet and stood on her own. She pushed back to an arms-length and looked up at him. "Thank you for coming Billy. I've waited every day to see you."

"I know Shanya, I wanted to see you too." He didn't want an awkward moment, so he spoke again. "What you are doing with the kids is great, there will always be obstacles, racists, and challenges to overcome. But we cannot stay rooted in the past, or focused on old transgressions. It starts with looking in the mirror and not accepting what we see there. We need to take control of our community's future creating personal growth and learning opportunities, creating environments conducive to evolving with society instead of outside of it.

She wasn't really listening, there was a mist in her eyes as he searched her face. Then she startled again, letting out a small squeal. Heading to the door, Shanya stuck her head into the hall and called out for someone.

"Chakwania, come here."

A young woman entered, confusion on her face. Shanya put her arm around her, dragging her towards Billy.

"Chakwania, this is Billy. He's the one who saved us." She pulled him by the hand towards the shocked girl standing there perplexed. The girl smiled as she looked him in the face, a single tear running down her cheek.

Billy stepped forward and hugged her hard, this is the one he thought he'd lost. It felt so good to know she was here. Good to know that the two women had each other.

He was glad he'd come, knowing it was the right thing to do. Billy'd always look out for Shanya, they'd always have a bond.

The End

If you enjoyed this book, please take a moment to leave a review at <u>Goodreads</u> and help spread the word.

REJEAN GIGUERE

About the Author

Rejean Giguere is an avid outdoorsman, adventurer, photographer and artist. He enjoys fishing, hockey, golf, tennis, skiing and snowmobiling, his V-Max motorcycle and vintage Corvette.

He grew up in Canada and Europe, and enjoyed a business career in Toronto and Ottawa.

Visit his website at www.rejeangiguere.com

REJEAN GIGUERE